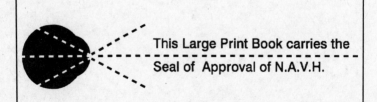

This Large Print Book carries the
Seal of Approval of N.A.V.H.

THE DETECTIVE

THE DETECTIVE

JAMES PATRICK HUNT

THORNDIKE PRESS

A part of Gale, Cengage Learning

GALE
CENGAGE Learning·

Farmington Hills, Mich • San Francisco • New York • Waterville, Maine
Meriden, Conn • Mason, Ohio • Chicago

GALE
CENGAGE Learning®

LIBRARY OF CONGRESS CATALOGING-IN-PUBLICATION DATA

Hunt, James Patrick, 1964–
  The detective / by James Patrick Hunt. — Large print edition.
    pages ; cm. — (Thorndike Press large print mystery)
    ISBN 978-1-4104-7013-3 (hardcover) — ISBN 1-4104-7013-X (hardcover)
    1. Murder—Investigation—Fiction. I. Title.
  PS3608.U577D48 2014b
  813'.6—dc23
                                                  2014007021

Published in 2014 by arrangement with James Patrick Hunt

THE DETECTIVE

CHAPTER ONE

Chicago, 1979

A brown, unmarked 1974 Plymouth Fury whisked through the wet street and came to a stop above the subway depot and a detective from the Grand Central division stepped out. The detective was working the four to midnight shift and he was about twenty-five minutes from end of watch when the night patrol lieutenant alerted him to the Northwest CTA stop. Five dead bodies on the platform.

The detective, whose name was David Beckman, thought it had to be a mistake. Five witnesses, maybe. But five victims? All deceased? Not on a long winter night like this.

It was February and the city crews had still not gotten all the trains running since the January blizzard, the worst blizzard Chicago had suffered since 1967. People were relieved to have any public transportation at all. Relieved for what they had, but still angry at what they perceived as City Hall's incompetence at handling the storm and its aftermath. Cars still stuck in snowdrifts, uncollected garbage piling up. Recent news reports said that the Lakeshore Racquet Club was destroyed and would have to be rebuilt. It was near the beginning of 1979, but to many Chicagoans it was the beginning of Year 3 A.D. — After Daley.

Beckman was dressed for the cold. Long johns under his gray slacks, t-shirt under his oxford shirt and tie, a red crewneck sweater over that, a gray tweed jacket, and galoshes over his shoes.

Beckman saw Halloran and Keough pull up as he got to the subway entrance. He waited for them to join him before he took off his wool hat and descended the first set of stairs.

Halloran and Keough were longtime veterans of the homicide squad. Beckman had only been with the squad for three months. Beckman was thirty-three years old and he didn't want to make any enemies anytime soon by preceding senior men down steps. He knew how over-assured young cops were treated on performance evals. Not that Beckman felt young. He hadn't felt young since the war. But what

8

he thought or felt didn't much matter now.

On the way down the steps, Halloran turned and acknowledged him and said, "Thought you'd be heading home now." There was a slight smile on Halloran's face when he said it. Beckman had seen the smile before. He still didn't like it, but he wouldn't let the Bill Hallorans of this world know it.

"Slow night," Beckman said.

"It was," Keough said.

Halloran said, "You could be at the precinct writing reports. Be warm at least. Or on your way back to your apartment."

Beckman didn't answer him. They passed some uniformed patrol officers and then they came to the patrol sergeant. The patrol sergeant was a man named Nicks who Beckman had worked with when he was in uniform. Nicks gestured to two witnesses who stood with a couple of other officers. The witnesses were two women in their twenties who worked as cocktail waitresses at a nearby bar. Sergeant Nicks said they were walking down the stairs when they saw the body of a young woman at the bottom. At first they thought she was sleeping. Then they saw the blood.

They screamed and ran back up to the street. It took them almost fifteen minutes to hail a cab and tell the cabbie what they saw. When the police arrived they found four more bodies on the platform. Then another train arrived and they had to keep passengers from getting off.

Keough said, "Have you notified transit authority?"

The sergeant said he didn't think so.

As the senior detective present, Keough had supervisory authority. He said, "Well you need to do that right away. We can't secure the scene with trains dumping people here every fifteen minutes."

The sergeant delegated that task to a patrolman. After he did that, Keough asked him to put an officer at the entrance to the subway to prevent the media people from coming down.

Beckman said, "Has the medical examiner arrived yet?"

"No," Nicks said.

"Any suspects?"

"None at this time."

Beckman looked at the older detectives and Halloran said, "Let's go."

This was Beckman's fourth homicide investigation. As he walked down the corridor he thought back to the procedure he had learned even before becoming a detective. Preserve life, arrest the suspect, protect

10

the scene.

He had to remember all that when they reached the bottom of the stairs and saw the five dead bodies.

"Jesus," Halloran said. "It's a fucking massacre."

CHAPTER TWO

The chief of detectives arrived in a shiny new black Chevy Caprice. He had to park a block away because by the time he got there the streets were filled with emergency vehicles of all kinds. Snow and mud covered the tops of his wing-tipped shoes as he walked to the subway depot and he cursed himself for not wearing boots. The chief of detectives was a dandy dresser who favored gray and black suits and starched shirts with his initials embroidered on the cuffs.

The chief of detectives, whose name was Jim Stumbaugh, did not sign the chronological log sheet before entering the crime scene. He ducked under the yellow tape and walked to the command post. There, he saw people crying and wailing. They were being held back by uniformed officers and Stumbaugh knew they were relatives of the deceased. Several people, not just one or two.

Stumbaugh said, "Shit."

Stumbaugh had been with the Chicago Police Department for twenty-four years. He had once worked a three-car accident in which four people were killed, two of them teenagers. It had been left to him to inform one set of parents that their son was dead. It was not something you got used to.

Stumbaugh lit his tenth cigar of the day. A uniformed patrol officer said, "Excuse me, sir? You're not allowed to smoke at the crime scene."

Stumbaugh turned to regard the young patrolman.

The patrolman said, "Oh. Sorry, Chief."

Stumbaugh asked, "Is Lieutenant Gregory here?"

"Yes, sir. I believe I saw him downstairs, sir."

Stumbaugh found Lieutenant Hollis Gregory at the bottom of the steps talking with detectives under his command. Among them were detectives Keough, Halloran, and Beckman. Detective Sergeant Regan was there too.

Detective Sergeant Tom Regan was the one Lieutenant Gregory seemed to be focusing on. Regan was in his late forties, older than the other detectives and older than Lieutenant Gregory by three years.

Regan had a lot of hair for a man his age and he was built like a bear. Regan chewed gum when he was thinking and when he wasn't. His colleagues would look to him after they made comments to see if he approved or if what they had said was stupid. Though it was hard to tell what Regan was thinking most of the time. Regan worked days and Beckman had had little contact with him.

Lieutenant Gregory said, "Hello, Jim."

"Greg," Stumbaugh said. "What do we got here?"

"Five dead bodies. Shot to death. Photographers have finished. Forensics is almost done."

"Good," Stumbaugh said, not thinking much. He was not insensitive to the grieving of the living, but he had long since grown used to the sight of dead bodies. He was a homicide detective and to him dead bodies were a problem to be solved.

Stumbaugh stayed with them when they examined the bodies. Four of them had identification on their persons. They were:

Helen Futterer, twenty-six, white female, Chicago. A registered nurse at St. Mary's Hospital. Shot in the face and chest.

Catherine-Anne Corbett, twenty-four, white female, Chicago. A nurse's assistant also

14

employed at St. Mary's Hospital. Shot twice in the chest and once in the abdomen.

Lionel Pearce, thirty-seven, black male, Chicago. A cook at a North Side restaurant, apparently on his way home from work. He wore a stained chef's smock beneath his hooded winter coat. Shot three times.

Nathan Wald, forty-six, white male, Skokie, Illinois. Shot twice in the back and once in the head at close range. In his coat pocket there was a switchblade.

The fifth victim was for now listed as a John Doe. He was a white male who looked to be in his late fifties.

Stumbaugh stopped at the body of Nathan Wald and checked the driver's license himself.

"Oh, hell," Stumbaugh said. "Not this guy."

It was Detective Halloran who said, "What about him?"

And Lieutenant Gregory said, "Nathan Wald is — was — the leader of the Jewish Defense Alliance."

Keough said, "He was on *Donahue* just last week. Donahue called him a fascist."

Detective Halloran looked at Beckman then. Beckman looked back at him for just a moment but didn't say anything.

15

Keough said to no one in particular, "This is all we fucking need."

CHAPTER THREE

The sun was coming up when Beckman returned to his apartment. He parked the take-home Plymouth and walked a block back to the entrance and picked his newspaper up off the front step. There would be no mention of the massacre today. Beckman flipped the paper open as he walked up a flight of stairs. The front page was still on the snowstorm. The mayor had offered his latest semi-apology for the city's inaction, assuring Chicago that he was doing all he could. Another story said that Jane Byrne was ahead in the polls and at this rate could be elected Chicago's first female mayor. The election would be held in about two weeks.

It was cold in Beckman's apartment. He had left the thermostat at sixty-five degrees, but it felt colder than that. He checked the dial and the temperature read sixty-one. Beckman sighed and turned it up to seventy.

It was a one-bedroom apartment that had

the typical, lonely look of a woman having left it behind. One couch and a folding chair. A small black-and-white Philco television on a stand. White squares on the walls where pictures had once hung. On the floor, a Luxman receiver with a Technics turntable on top of it, Koss speakers on the sides, albums stacked against the wall. In the bedroom, box springs and a mattress on the floor. A small kitchen with beer in the fridge and leftover Chinese food. Near the fridge there was a Formica table with two chairs that didn't match it.

Beckman put his .38 snubnose Chief's Special on the nightstand next to his bed. He turned on the lamp to give the bedroom some light. Then he hung his jacket in the closet and walked back out to the living room. He checked the messages on his answering machine. The first one was from his mother, reminding him of Albert's birthday later in the week. The second call was from a woman he had met at a bar but not taken home. Beckman had a vague memory of her. It had been dark when he talked with her. She had told him how much she loved Jewish men but not like that little one who was in *The Goodbye Girl* 'cause he was just obnoxious. She asked Beckman if John Belushi was Jewish too and Beckman

18

said he wasn't sure but kind of doubted it. Somewhere in there Beckman had lost the urge and had gone home.

Later he felt guilty because he had told the woman about Elyse and the pending divorce. The woman said, "awww" and then "well, it'll be her loss, huh?" and Beckman felt he shouldn't have been talking about Elyse at a bar. Maybe because he still loved her or maybe because they had known each other since they were kids or maybe because the woman was talking about Elyse and didn't know her.

"Didn't work out, huh?"

Beckman had shrugged then. He had already said too much. And if he said more he wouldn't like himself very much, running down his ex-wife to a stranger. His wife had left him because, she said, she got tired of waiting. Waiting for him to finish law school, waiting for him to quit being a cop, waiting for him to get off his ass and make some more money. It was an old story: she had liked him at first because he wasn't, as she said, "typical." But then they got married and she resented him for not being typical. The people she had grown up with were now business owners, doctors, and lawyers. When he told her he was planning to leave narcotics to become a homicide

19

detective, he thought she would be happy. He was wrong.

She said, "De*tect*ive? You act like that's some sort of step up. It's a step *down,* for Christ's sake."

"It's highly coveted."

"Yeah, if you're Irish, maybe."

"For any cop."

"You're not supposed to be a cop, David." She called him David when she was mad at him. Not Deke. "It's something you're supposed to be doing while you get your law degree. But I don't think you've been straight with me. I think you like it there."

He didn't argue with her there. And a few weeks later she left.

Now he missed her. Even though he knew the split up was inevitable, he still missed her. They had been a couple in high school, had laughed together and shared a lot. They knew each other's families. In a way, they were like cousins. When he went to Vietnam, he told her not to wait for him and she didn't answer him. But he wrote to her anyway and she to him and when he came back, she was there for him.

And yet . . . not really there. He didn't like to talk about the war much, not even with other veterans, and he didn't talk about it with her. Like many vets, he had come away with the conviction that the war was stupid, wasteful, and immoral. Certainly, it had left him with a deep distrust of authority. But, also like many vets, he had little more than dismissive contempt for the anti-war protestors who, he believed, didn't know what they were talking about and used protest as a means of accessing pussy and drugs. He felt little sympathy for the protestors the Chicago police roughed up in '68. He did not want the war to define him. And one day, he overheard Elyse tell a friend that he had been in Vietnam, but that was because he wanted to be a senator someday and he knew it would be good for his political future. Beckman had never told Elyse any such thing. He wondered then if she was ashamed of him for going to Vietnam or, worse, if she was just plain embarrassed because people might think he had been there because he was poor or stupid or both. He wondered how well he really knew her and she him.

He wasn't poor and never had been. What he had been was a middle-class kid who was drafted and didn't try to get out of it. His father had fought in the Second World War, a corporal at the Battle of the Bulge. And for reasons of his own, Beckman didn't want his father to outshine him in that

21

regard. So he accepted his number and fought at Ia Drang.

The old man was dead now, killed by a negligent truck driver. Beckman's mother had since remarried and seemed happier with her second husband. Now she was Mrs. Albert Pintoff living in Lake Forest.

Shit. Albert's birthday was coming up. Which meant Time with the Family. Marty and his wife, Natalie, and their three kids. None of them yet knew that Elyse had moved out. He could hear his mother now, saying, "I *told* you." He wondered what lie he could come up with when they asked where she was.

CHAPTER FOUR

When Regan got home from the subway station, his wife was cooking breakfast for the children. The smell of bacon permeated their small kitchen. His two teenage boys sat on opposite sides of the small kitchen table.

Mrs. Regan, whose first name was Kate, said, "Working all night again?"

"Yeah," Regan said. He wouldn't tell her what it was about. He rarely discussed his work with his wife or his children. His wife would likely find out about the murders on the evening news. But even then she wouldn't ask him about it. Her life was the church, her children, and her husband. There were four children, two left at home, the other two old enough now to be out of the home.

Mrs. Regan said, "You want some breakfast?"

Regan shook his head. "Not hungry."

"Sean called last night."

"Oh. How is he?"

"Good. They promoted him to produce manager."

"Ah. And the baby?"

"She's doing fine. Be her second birthday next week."

"Already?"

"Yeah."

One of the boys checked his watch, then stood up to leave. The other boy followed him. Regan felt a pang then which he didn't try to analyze. He had wanted to sit with them for a while. He said, "What's the hurry?"

His older boy said, "We gotta catch the bus."

The other said, "They're actually running on time now. See ya, Dad."

Regan heard the front door open and close. He remained standing in the kitchen with his overcoat on. His wife sat at the table and picked up a piece of bacon that had been left untouched. She looked up at him briefly and said, "You sure you don't want anything?"

Regan sighed. "I'm going to sleep for a couple of hours."

Regan lived in a two-story house in Bridgeport, about ten blocks from where Richard Daley grew up. There were three bedrooms on the second floor and one bathroom. A few years back, they had a second bathroom installed in the basement. Regan shared a bedroom with his wife, but not a bed. They had bought twin beds before their fourth child was born. It was Regan's idea. He was often insomniac and he didn't like to wake his wife when he got out of bed to go downstairs. Sometimes when he went downstairs, his boys would be watching television in the living room. So Regan would go into the kitchen and read *National Geographic.* When it was warm enough, he would go out to the back porch.

The beds had matching covers. Between the two beds, a crucifix hung on the wall. A copy of *The Thorn Birds* lay next to his wife's bed.

Regan undressed and put on his pajamas. He pulled the shades down, set the alarm on his clock radio, climbed in bed and went to sleep.

The alarm woke him at ten-thirty a.m. He showered, shaved, and dressed. He stood in the upstairs hallway and listened. He was alone in the house. He went into each of the boy's rooms. In one of them, he found a

Hustler magazine under the pillow. He blew anger out his nostrils and took the magazine downstairs with him. He put the magazine into the kitchen trash receptacle with the other garbage. Then he pulled the trash bag out, tied it at the top, and carried it out to the back-alley can. He would speak to the boy about it tonight after dinner. He would not tell the boy's mother.

He thought back to when he was the boy's age. Sixteen and one of four children of a man who worked at the Union Stockyards. His older brother had been killed at Okinawa before that. His sister became a nun. Regan had worked since he was twelve. When he was twenty-one, he had taken the policeman's exam and had been accepted into the academy. The day he was commissioned was one of the happiest of his parents' lives. Whenever he was promoted, his mother told everyone on her block, and she kept clippings of all the newspaper articles about the important cases he had solved.

Back in the kitchen, Regan thought of his mother and smut magazines and the changes of life. Christ Almighty, if Ma had known what her grandson kept under his pillow. What kind of world were they living in now where a teenage boy could walk into a convenience store and buy garbage like that? But Regan knew that his anger had as much to do with his sons' indifference to their grandmother as it did with any magazine. He had told them once how they didn't have air conditioning when he was a boy and how on those interminably hot summer days his mother would work all day to take care of them and then lie in her bed at night with a cold washcloth on her head just to be able to sleep for a little while. They barely gave him a nod when he talked about such things and went back to watching *Three's Company* or some other trash show. They didn't appreciate her, they didn't appreciate their uncle who had died for his country, and maybe they didn't much appreciate him either. To his mother, he was a hero. To his sons, he was a bore and a stiff. To them, law and order were terms of derision. They did not see beauty in order. They had grown up during Watergate and now were vegetating in a country run by mediocrities like Jimmy Carter, an era of dimmed sensibilities and lowered expectations. Regan wished they'd get off their asses and believe in *something*.

Regan drove his blue, unmarked '78 Nova to the station. He sat at his desk in the homicide squad room. He reviewed his report from the previous night. Then he called ballistics. They told him they had not concluded their report yet. He had just hung up when a detective came up to his desk and told him the lieutenant wanted to see him in his office.

Regan had no problem with Lieutenant Hollis Gregory. Greg was a couple of years younger than him but he had done his time. Greg was a clever politician and made the right friends, wore the right clothes. Regan would not be surprised if Greg became deputy commissioner someday and would not begrudge him if he did. Mainly, this was because Greg usually left him alone to work his cases.

Regan walked into Greg's office and saw Greg sitting behind his desk. Greg wore a gray three-piece suit and a red silk tie.

"Hello, Tom."

"Greg."

Regan saw Chief of Detectives Jim Stumbaugh then, standing on the other side of the office, in a place where the blinds hid him. Stumbaugh was in a dark suit and his usual starched shirt. Stumbaugh said hello to him too. Then Greg asked Regan to close the door.

Stumbaugh said, "How are you, Tom?"

"Good."

"Get much sleep?"

"A couple of hours. I just got off the phone with ballistics. They're not finished yet."

Stumbaugh asked, "What do you expect from them?"

"Well," Regan said, "I don't want to jump to conclusions. But from the positions of the bodies, I'd say it was one shooter. And the patterns don't indicate the use of a machine gun."

"Right. And there are no suspects at this time?"

"No."

"And no known witnesses at this time?"

"No, sir."

Stumbaugh took his time lighting a cigar. As he was puffing it to life, he said, "How's your partner? Is he getting better?"

"Andy's good," Regan said. "They removed a lung. But his other one's still good. Doctors say he should be able to return to work in a couple of months."

Lieutenant Greg said, "Is that what he wants?"

Regan paused a moment. Andy Renfro was his friend as well as his partner. Some part of Regan thought Greg was intruding on something.

"What do you mean?" Regan asked.

Greg said, "Does Andy *want* to return to work? Has he told you that?"

"He hasn't said he doesn't want to. Why? Does he not have a place here anymore?"

Greg said, "No one's saying that, Tom. But the man has been diagnosed with lung cancer. He's eligible for a disability pension. God knows he's earned it."

Regan said, "He's only forty-three. He's got another three years before he gets his twenty. He's a good detective."

Stumbaugh said, "We know that. That's not the point anyway."

Regan raised a hand, conceding things for now.

Stumbaugh said, "But you are without a partner for the time being."

"That's right," Regan said.

"Yeah," Stumbaugh said, "that's right. Listen, Tom. Greg and I, we agree, we know we're going to need you on this subway thing. You're one of the best we have. I'd say the best but I don't want you to get too carried away with yourself. The commissioner wants as many detectives assigned to this thing as possible."

"Okay," Regan said, waiting to see what was coming.

Stumbaugh, a smart detective himself, saw that Regan was waiting. He said, "What do you know about Detective Beckman?"

Regan looked briefly at Lieutenant Greg, then back at Stumbaugh. He shrugged and said, "I don't really know him. He's on nights, pretty new. Seems like a nice guy."

Stumbaugh said, "Well, we want you to work with him on this."

After a moment, Regan said to Stumbaugh, "Is this your idea?"

Stumbaugh frowned. "What are you suggesting?"

Regan said, "I'm not suggesting anything. It's just that I think Beckman's pretty green and this is a mass murder we're talking about, not a run of the mill saloon killing."

Stumbaugh said, "I know every homicide detective in this city. No one gets here without my okay. Beckman was with narcotics for four years. He did good work there. His reputation is solid."

"I'm sure it is. But this isn't narcotics. Look, Chief, I mean no disrespect here. But I don't think this is the sort of case to train someone on. I'm not going to have time for that."

Greg said, "You're not going to be training him. He'll be assisting you."

Stumbaugh said, "Do you have a problem with him?"

"I told you," Regan said. "I don't know

31

him. I just think this is the wrong case to be
. . . playing politics with."

Stumbaugh said, "What's that supposed
to mean?"

Regan didn't answer him. A few moments
passed. Then Stumbaugh picked up his coat
and hung it over his arm. He said, "It's
already been decided, Tom. It's an order."

Stumbaugh closed the door on his way
out.

Regan looked at Lieutenant Gregory.

Greg said, "It's not my call."

Regan said, "A Jewish activist is murdered.
So we have to have a Jewish detective working the case? Really?"

"Look," Greg said, "It probably wasn't
the chief's call either. In case you haven't
noticed, a couple of weeks ago we happened
to have the worst blizzard Chicago's seen in
twenty-two years. People still can't get their
cars out of the snow and only half of the
city's trains are running. I'm just a police
officer and people have been giving *me* shit
for it. The election's in less than two weeks.
Before the snowstorm, *before,* the mayor
was virtually guaranteed to be re-elected..
Now it looks like a *woman* is gonna beat
him. Why? Because the people think the
mayor didn't do enough to clear three feet
of snow off the city of Chicago. Like it's

something that can be done overnight. Trains aren't running and they're blaming him for it."

Regan remembered the Mike Royko column he read last week. The man said city crews didn't have a clue about dealing with snow because their skills revolved around cranking out votes.

"Politics," Regan said.

"Yeah, you're goddamn right it's politics. This is *Chicago,* Tom. Bad things happen and somebody's gotta take the blame for it. I don't make the rules, I just live by them."

"If the mayor thinks putting an inexperienced Jewish cop on a homicide case is going to get him the Jewish vote, he's . . . it's crazy."

"Well, Beckman's the only one this division has. Besides, you heard what the chief said. Beckman's a good cop."

Regan said, "The chief doesn't know Beckman any better than I do."

Lieutenant Gregory looked down at his desk. It was the closest thing to an assent Regan was going to get out of him. At that moment, Regan almost felt sorry for the lieutenant. An ambitious man wanting to rise in the department while maintaining the respect of the men under his command.

"Well," Greg said, "in any event, the

decision's already been made. David Beckman is now your partner and you are to treat him accordingly."

CHAPTER FIVE

Beckman was asleep when the telephone rang. He rolled over and answered it. It was Lieutenant Gregory.

Greg said, "Chief Stumbaugh will be conducting a briefing on the subway murder at three o'clock. We need you there."

"Yes, sir."

"Something else," Greg said. "We're moving you to day shift, effective immediately."

"Oh . . . great."

"You'll be partnering with Sergeant Regan on this one."

Beckman hesitated. He barely knew Regan. He almost asked if Regan had asked for him, but then decided not to. He said, "Okay. Listen, Lieutenant —"

"I'll see you at three," Greg said, and hung up.

Beckman got out of bed. He wore gray sweats, a t-shirt, and athletic socks. He undressed, showered, and shaved. He had gotten used to seeing his face bare in the mirror. He wore a beard when he worked undercover in narcotics. Beard, hair long enough to wear in a ponytail, leather jacket and boots. The Serpico years. He didn't miss them. Elyse had thought it was cute at first, married to a man who was effectively a spy. But she soon grew tired of it like everything else. He grew tired of it too. Acting a part then, later, starting to become the part and feeling seedy doing it. There was a reason the department didn't want men in narcotics and vice too long.

Driving to the Northwest station, Beckman thought of the lieutenant's call. He was confused at first, but now he was excited. He was going to be working a high-profile murder. It sparked life in him. A feeling of hope that he couldn't dare share with Elyse or anyone in his family. Since he had become a homicide detective, he had worked a handful of cases, all of them run of the mill killings. Husband beating his wife to death, bar fight that led to a lethal stabbing, a gangster killing a member of a rival gang who trespassed his neighborhood. Open and shut cases. But this was something more. A challenge. A chance to use his head.

There were ten detectives at the briefing,

not including Chief Stumbaugh. The department's public relations officer was there too, though it still wasn't clear if he would be giving the press statement later or if Stumbaugh would. Stumbaugh was good in front of the camera.

Lights were dimmed and photos of the victims put on a projector screen. Stumbaugh went through the photos and identified the victims. The two young women, the black cook, the John Doe, and the Jewish activist. Chief Stumbaugh noted that one of the young females had attempted to crawl away before the final shot. Some of the detectives shifted in their seats.

Chief Stumbaugh said, "We've received the report from ballistics. Eleven slugs, total, fired into the victims. But there were twelve fired shell casings. Which means he missed once, but only once. Nine millimeter bullets. We believe the weapon was a Browning semiautomatic pistol. In case some of you don't know, that gun has a fifteen-round clip."

Stumbaugh placed a sketch on the overhead projector. Measurements, X's, and dotted lines.

Stumbaugh said, "We believe the shooter was standing here. At first. Nathan Wald was here. Which places the killer . . . here. Then the John Doe, here. Then the cook. Then the two young ladies who worked at the hospital. We've determined that the girls were coming down the steps to get on the train and that's where they ran into the shooter. Here."

Detective Keough raised his hand.

"Yes."

Keough said, "So is it fair to say that Wald was the target and the other people were just witnesses the killer wanted to eliminate?"

Stumbaugh said, "We don't know that yet."

"But they were in the wrong place at the wrong time."

"We don't know that yet. There are five victims here, not one."

Keough said, "So then it's just a massacre?"

"It's the murder of five people," Stumbaugh said. "I want all of you to resist using the word 'massacre,' particularly in front of the press. We don't want to sensationalize this thing."

Sergeant Regan appeared to rub his forehead.

Stumbaugh said, "Certainly, it appears that Wald was the first one shot. But that finding is not conclusive."

38

Another detective asked, "What's the estimated time of death?"

"We think between eleven-ten and eleven-fifteen."

"Was Wald getting off the train or waiting for one?"

"We don't know that yet."

"What about the others?"

"The cook was waiting to get on a train. The two women were coming down the steps to catch a train. We don't know yet about the John Doe."

Beckman raised his hand.

"Yes."

"Have the people on the train, the train that stopped at that stop, have they been questioned yet?"

"No."

"Do you want us to find them?"

Stumbaugh looked at the young detective. "Of course I do."

Keough looked over at Detective Halloran and smirked.

Stumbaugh said, "Mr. Wald had a switch-blade knife in his pocket. There was no evidence he had taken it out. This was the only weapon we found on any of the victims."

A detective asked, "Have the next of kin been notified?"

"Yes. All except the John Doe." Stumbaugh sipped coffee from a cup. Then he said, "At this time, we don't know what the motive for this was. I welcome any reasonable theories. The most obvious theory is that Nathan Wald was the target of this shooting. As you know, Nathan Wald was a controversial figure. He was a suspect in the bombing of the Soviet cultural building in Washington. The NYPD also believes he was involved in the bombing of the Lebanese Consulate in New York. Here in Chicago, he and his gang clashed with members of the American Nazi Party at one of their rallies a few months ago. I'm sure you all saw that on the news. There was a lot of bloodshed that day, but fortunately no one was killed. Then."

Someone murmured, "Commies and Nazis." No one laughed.

Stumbaugh said, "We'll investigate *every* lead. Not just the ones related to Wald."

Stumbaugh assigned detectives to investigative canvasses and concluded the briefing.

Beckman made his way to Regan.

"Sergeant?"

"Yeah."

"David Beckman. The lieutenant said I was supposed to partner with you on this."

Regan gave him a look that was neither friendly nor unfriendly.

"Did he," Regan said.

Beckman had been about to offer his hand to shake. Now he decided not to.

"That's not a problem, is it?"

Regan shook his head. He didn't make eye contact.

Beckman said, "Well, I'm glad to be working with you. I hear you're one of the best."

Regan didn't seem to hear him. Regan walked to his desk at the homicide squad room. He gestured to the empty desk across from his and said, "I guess that's yours now."

"Oh," Beckman said. "Well, I'll have to move my stuff."

Regan looked at his notebook. He sat down and picked up the telephone.

"Yes, Sergeant Regan here. I'm a detective with the Chicago Police Department. I wanted to know when the funeral is scheduled . . . No, I'm a detective assigned to the investigation . . . No, the body is at the coroner's . . . I have no control over that . . . All right, I'll call back later."

Regan hung up the phone.

Standing behind his new desk, Beckman said, "You want to go to the funeral?"

Regan looked up, as if noticing that Beckman was still there.

"Yeah."

"How come?"

Regan looked at him, expressionless. Then he said, "You always send someone to the funeral to see if the murderer shows up."

Beckman stopped himself from asking why. He said, "But how would you know if they do?"

"You ask a family member to point out anyone there they don't know."

"Oh," Beckman said, and regretted it.

Regan opened his desk drawer and rummaged around in it. Beckman sat down. Regan took a pen out of his desk drawer, shut it, then stood up.

Regan said, "Let's go."

"Where are we going?"

"To see Wald's wife."

Chapter Six

They took Regan's vehicle. Regan drove.

Regan didn't say anything at first. Didn't ask Beckman where he was from or when he joined the PD or what he had been doing before he got on at homicide. Beckman figured he already knew or didn't care. It didn't take long to figure out that it wasn't Regan's idea to work with him.

Beckman said, "I hear your partner had some health problems."

"That's right."

"Is he doing okay?"

Regan nodded.

They came to an intersection. Regan slowed the car, pumped the brakes, released, then pumped again. The Nova slowed safely to a stop.

Beckman sighed and said, "Look, do you have some sort of problem working with me?"

Regan slowly shook his head. He kept his

eyes on the road.

Beckman sighed again and looked out the window. It was another gray and white winter day in Chicago.

Beckman said, "Well, it wasn't my idea either."

Regan said nothing. Expressionless again. Beckman told himself to forget it and to concentrate on the work.

Beckman said, "Back there, the chief talked about Nathan Wald's enemies. The Soviet Union and the American Nazi Party. But he left something out."

Regan said, "What's that?"

"The Arabs. Wald advocated the expulsion of all the Arabs from Israel. He wanted all of them 'transferred out.' Kicked out."

Regan did not turn to look at him. His eyes remained on the road.

Then Regan said, "Really?"

"Yeah," Beckman said. "That was well known."

"I didn't know it."

"Well . . ."

Regan said, "Let me ask you something: why didn't you say anything about this during the briefing?"

Beckman was silent for a moment. Then he said, "Well, I thought, I thought that was well known. Wald admitted it in an interview

44

he did with *Playboy Magazine.*"

"Did he now? Well, not all of us look at *Playboy*s. Is that the real reason you didn't bring it up at the briefing?"

Beckman felt his face burning. He knew that Regan knew the real reason he'd kept his mouth shut. He didn't want to draw attention to himself at the briefing. Didn't want to draw attention to the fact that he was a Jew. Regan was a sharp detective, all right. But they were off to a shitty start.

There were a group of young men standing in front of Nathan Wald's house in Skokie. Some of them wore beards. They were dressed in army fatigues and scarlet berets. All of them held clubs. Another young man on a porch held a rifle.

Regan parked the Chevy Nova across the street. He cut the ignition and said, "Those aren't Nazis, are they?" He didn't seem scared.

Beckman said, "No. They're the Jewish Defense Alliance."

"Hmmm. Know any of them?"

"Now why would I know any of them?"

"Just asking."

"I don't know them," Beckman said and got out of the car.

Regan crossed the street with him.

45

Nathan Wald had lived in a modest two-story house. It was not unlike the house Beckman had grown up in.

Beckman counted six young men on the sidewalk, not counting the man on the porch with the rifle. A man of about thirty stepped forward.

"What do you want?"

Regan showed the man his badge and said, "I'm Detective Sergeant Regan, Chicago homicide. This is Detective Beckman. We're here to talk to Mrs. Wald."

One of the toughs in the line said, "Where were you *before*?"

Regan ignored that and said to the man in front of him, "Who are you?"

"Mickey Shaivetz. Sergeant at arms."

Regan seemed to smile. A display of insolence at the young man.

Regan said, "Of what?"

"The Alliance."

Mickey Shaivetz was older than the young men behind him. He stood the same height as Regan, but Regan was broader in the chest and shoulders. A bear next to a wolf. Maybe a coyote.

Regan said, "Well. Sergeant. There's a law in this city against having open firearms. Your man there's got a rifle."

"We're in Skokie, not Chicago. Besides,

46

he's got a hunting license."

"What's he hunting in Skokie?"

"We have the right to defend ourselves. God knows the American police won't do it."

"Well, when the KGB shows up, let us know. Right now we're going to talk to Mrs. Wald."

"What about?"

"I'll tell her that."

"Yeah, well, she's grieving now. Come back later."

"I'm here now. I come back later, she may not be here."

"That's *your* problem."

Beckman wanted to step forward and punch Mickey Shaivetz in the mouth. Beckman had his gloves on and he knew it would feel good to do it.

But Beckman looked at Regan and Regan didn't seem at all rattled by the man. Regan looked at Shaivetz in his army fatigues and his beret as if he were a child.

"Come here," Regan said and turned and walked a short distance down the sidewalk. Shaivetz followed him.

Regan drew close to Shaivetz. In a lowered voice, he said, "Listen, Sonny. We're going to go in there whether you want us to or not. Not because we want to make you look bad in front of your boyos. But because we want to find out who killed your friend." Regan gestured to the young men with the clubs. "This way," Regan said, "you get to say it was your idea."

Shaivetz said, "I'm not afraid of you."

Regan nodded his head, but didn't say anything.

Shaivetz said, "Don't take too long."

Beckman followed Regan into the house.

Esther Wald was older than Beckman expected her to be. In her early fifties at least, with angry streaks of gray in her hair. Beckman believed she had not bathed since hearing of her husband's death, which would have been in accordance with orthodox mourning.

After the introductions, she led them into the kitchen. Right away, Beckman knew it was a Jewish home. The smell of onions and herring, noodle pudding, chopped livers in a hardboiled egg mixture. In the refrigerator, there would be a jelly glass full of rendered chicken fat.

Beckman said, "Ma'am, where are your children?"

Esther Wald said, "They're safe at a friend's."

Beckman said, "You have two, correct?"

48

"Yes. Seventeen and fifteen." She stated it as fact. She was not seeking empathy. Not her.

Regan said, "We're sorry for your loss, Mrs. Wald. And we certainly don't like bothering you at a time like this."

Esther Wald said, "Ask your questions."

Regan said, "Okay. What was your husband doing the night of the murder? I mean, where was he going?"

"Probably to meet someone."

"Do you know who?"

"No."

Regan waited for her to add something to that. She didn't.

Regan said, "You sure you don't know?"

"I told you I didn't. My husband doesn't tell me — didn't tell me his business. He said it was better that I didn't know details."

"Details of what?"

"What he was doing. I just said that."

"He didn't trust you?"

"He didn't trust the police. He didn't trust Americans. My husband's been arrested over fifty times, in Israel and in the States. Arrested by men like you. He was always worried that I would be questioned by police about his doings. So the less I knew the better."

Beckman said, "In this state, Mrs. Wald,

49

you can't be forced to testify against your husband. But that privilege died with him."

Esther Wald said, "Are you suggesting I'm keeping things from you, Detective?"

"No, ma'am," Beckman said, though he was. "We just want to find out who killed him. We hoped you might be able to help us. Is there some reason you don't?"

"No reason," she said.

Beckman said, "Perhaps just some background information then."

Esther Wald said, "All right."

Beckman said, "When did he found the Jewish Defense Alliance?"

"Nineteen sixty-eight."

"And he was born here?"

"Yes. South Chicago. He came to Skokie in '71."

Beckman said, "My understanding is, he used to be a rabbi."

"He was. His father was a rabbi and his grandfather."

"But he didn't continue in that role?"

"He found the role . . . uncongenial. But he was still a rabbi."

"Is it true he advocated expulsion of the Arabs from Israel?"

"What's wrong with that?"

"Nothing. I'm just asking if he advocated that position."

"He did. He did *not* advocate the slaughter of Arabs. He just wanted to transfer them out of Israel."

"Did he ever receive any threats because of that position?"

"Of course."

"Can you be specific? Who threatened him and why."

"I don't know of anything specific. Not from the Arabs."

Regan said, "What about the American Nazi Party?"

"What about them?"

"Threats?"

"All the time. That pig May said Nathan would be buried."

Regan said, "Vernon May, the leader of ANP?"

"Yes."

Regan said, "When did he say that?"

"At that rally they held last spring. Don't you read the papers?"

Beckman said, "You mean the rally they held on the anniversary of Israeli Independence?"

"Yes."

Beckman saw it on the news and read about it too. American Nazis carrying signs saying "Gas the Jews" and posters with swastikas on them. Nathan Wald and about

51

a hundred of his members came and rushed the Nazis. The Skokie police said it was a miracle no one was killed.

Regan said, "Do you suspect May in your husband's death?"

"Of course."

"Do you suspect anyone else?"

"It's either him or someone who works for him."

Beckman said, "Your husband had other enemies, though. Didn't he?"

"Political enemies, Detective. Not people who wanted to murder him."

Beckman said, "Is it true your husband assaulted May?"

"*Assaulted?* Is that what you call it? How about *defense?* Out of all the places in the United States, out of all the places in greater Chicago, why do you think the Nazis chose to come to Skokie? Because, per capita, it has the highest Jewish population in the country. They came to *our* place, Detective. You think we should *let* them?"

"I'll put it another way, Mrs. Wald," Beckman said. "Is it true your husband hit May? Hit him with his fist and bloodied his nose."

"Yes."

Beckman paused for a moment. Then he said, "Did your husband ever consider doing something worse to Vernon May?"

"What do you mean?"

"I think you know."

"You mean kill him?"

"Yeah."

Esther Wald said, "What the hell kind of question is that? My husband is dead."

"I think it may help us in the investigation, Mrs. Wald. If there was some sort of ongoing feud . . ."

"*Feud?* Feud! Is that what you call it? These animals come to our home and hold signs saying burn the Jews and you call it a feud?"

"Your husband has said things in public."

"What things?"

"He said, more than once, that it would be morally right to assassinate a member of the Nazi party."

"I know what he said. He said that if an American Nazi Party leader posed a clear and present danger to American Jews, then *not* to assassinate such a person would be immoral. At least get it right."

"In your husband's opinion, did Vernon May pose a clear and present danger?"

"Of course he did. But he took no steps in that . . . he did not try to kill that pig."

Esther Wald seemed to forget about the presence of Sergeant Regan at that moment.

53

She focused her gaze on the younger detective.

"Beckman," she said. "What is your first name?"

"David."

"Are *you* a Jew? You are, aren't you?"

Now both Regan and Esther Wald were looking at him.

"Yeah," Beckman said.

"I see," she said. She leaned back and showed him a rather unpleasant, satisfied smile.

Beckman sighed and then heard himself say, "What is it you see, ma'am?" He regretted saying it immediately.

"You're one of them. Another one."

"Mrs. Wald —"

"You don't want to make trouble. You want to be *liked*. Accepted. You think the way you look, maybe you can pass for a gentile. And you want to, too. Well, my husband wasn't like that. He had no time for the well behaved, gutless Jews who want to fit in. He hated pacifists and liberals. People who counsel accommodation and compromise."

"I'm not here to counsel anything, Mrs. Wald. And believe it or not, I'm really not interested in arguing with you."

"What *are* you here for?" she said. "To

appease *me?* To help the *goyim* look good?"

Regan said, "Now hold on, Mrs. Wald. We're not here to discuss politics."

"I don't want to talk anymore. I'm tired. Can you see that? I'm very, very tired."

Regan tilted his head to Beckman and picked up his hat. Beckman followed him. At the kitchen door, Beckman turned and said, "Mrs. Wald, your husband was not the only one killed that night."

CHAPTER SEVEN

Regan said, "Would you mind telling me what that was about?"

They were in the car, driving back to the station. The windshield wipers intermittently brushed off snow that blew up off the road.

Beckman said, "What do you mean?" Beckman thought he was talking about Esther Wald. Wondering why she had been so difficult.

But Regan said, "You fucked up that interview."

Beckman was genuinely surprised. "What are you talking about? I was trying to get some information out of her."

"Were you?" Regan said. "Or did you want to show her how much you knew?"

"You take *her* side?"

"Or maybe show me."

"What is this?"

Regan slowed the car to make a turn. He

56

said, "How long you been a police officer?"

"Almost eleven years. Why?"

"How long in homicide?"

"A few months. You know that."

"I also know that rookies tend to be too aggressive."

"I'm not a rookie. I've —"

"I know who you are. You were in narcotics and you were a high producer in arrests. You got respect. That's all . . . that's all great, but you're a rookie here. When you question a witness, especially a bereaved witness, you want them to trust you and see you're there to help. You try that first."

"I told her we were trying to help."

"She didn't believe you and neither did I. And now we don't have any more idea of who would want to kill Nathan Wald than we did this morning."

"Look," Beckman said, "you don't want to work with me, don't."

"I wish it were that simple," Regan said.

When they returned to the station, Regan was speaking to him again.

Regan said, "It's seven o'clock now. I'm going to go home. Tomorrow, I want you to check out the John Doe. We need to find out who he is."

Beckman said, "I thought the theory of

57

the case was that Wald was the target?"

"That's *one* theory. For all we know, it could have been Wald who was in the wrong place at the wrong time."

Beckman didn't believe that. It angered him. But part of him was relieved Regan hadn't gone to the lieutenant to ask to have him pulled off the case.

Beckman said, "You want me to do this on my own?"

"You don't need my help."

Well, Beckman thought, that's it then. Assigned to a meaningless task.

CHAPTER EIGHT

The next morning, Beckman checked with AFIS (Automated Fingerprint Identification System) to see if the John Doe was in the database. He wasn't. So Beckman went to the pathologist to look at the body.

The John Doe was in the pathologist's lab with the other decedents. Stark naked and blueing. Beckman was not shocked or horrified or even depressed. He'd seen much worse in the war. He had not been able to detach himself from war, but he was, to a degree, able to detach himself from his work. He was still a relatively young policeman and despair was not threatening to overwhelm him.

Once in the lab, he decided to look at all the bodies. He figured he was already down here. But he went to the John Doe first. The John Doe had black and gray hair and sideburns down to the bottom of his ears. Skinny legs and a potbelly. Then Beckman saw something that hadn't been in the medical examiner's report. A tattoo on the man's shoulder.

Beckman drew closer to look at it. It was a flower and sword. Beckman thought there might be a serpent in there, but there wasn't. Just the flower and the sword.

Beckman examined the other victims. The nurse, the nurse's assistant, the cook, and the Jew. That he was how he classified Wald. *Jew.* And he knew the other police officers classified Wald the same way. They would say "Jewish activist" to be diplomatic, at least around the media, though probably not around him. *You're doing it too,* Beckman thought. *Doing it to yourself.* He didn't like Mrs. Wald and she knew it. Regan had known it too and had given him heat about it. And Beckman had wanted to defend himself, wanted to tell Regan that every major Jewish organization in the country had denounced Wald. But then Regan would have thought he was being defensive or maybe just trying to show off his "Jewish insight" again. Beckman suspected that Regan would have criticized him no matter what he would have done.

There were times in his life that Deke Beckman gave sardonic thought to certain cultural expectations. Was it better to be the happy, optimistic, and, above all, nonthreatening Jew known for his "warmth"? An endearing figure who shrugs his shoulders while emitting cute, harmless wisdoms?

Obviously, Nathan Wald didn't think so. Wald told the reporter from *Playboy* that he hated *Fiddler on the Roof*. He said anyone who asked a Jew why he couldn't be more like the humble, simple people in *Fiddler on the Roof* didn't understand Judaism. To Wald, Tevye was an embarrassment. A Jewish Uncle Tom. Wald didn't like comforting people, not even his own. *Particularly* not his own. He offered up the side they didn't want to have exposed: the aggrieved, the pessimistic, the xenophobic. The Jews Leon Uris *didn't* write about. Wald warned of a second holocaust, this one in the United States. He said he believed there was a physical threat to Jews in this country. He didn't say a holocaust was *going* to happen, only that it was "quite probable." Only.

Regan had thought Beckman had some sort of problem with Wald's wife. Regan was off the mark, though not by much. Beckman didn't like Mrs. Wald, but he wasn't angry with her. He was angry at her husband. Not because he thought Wald was right, but because Wald was dead and now some people were going to believe his murder

61

somehow validated what he stood for. To thousands of impressionable young Jews, Wald was a man of vision. Beckman thought he was a hustler. Beckman had had his fill of hustlers.

Beckman had gone to Vietnam with some ideals. Love for his country, hatred for Communism, belief in duty and service. The next couple of years changed him as it had changed many soldiers. He returned with a simmering contempt for people like General Westmoreland, Robert McNamara, President Johnson and then later Nixon. People who he believed had lied to him and all the others. He regretted that he didn't know anything about the Vietnamese when he went there and didn't know anything more when he left. When he became a policeman, he soon found he had to keep his opinions about Vietnam to himself. A lot of cops were World War II and Korean War veterans and they supported the Vietnam War. It was no use trying to persuade them Vietnam was different. Trying to persuade others on the subject was wasted emotion. If Vietnam had taught him anything, it had taught him about the human capacity to construct a worldview that can blot out very dramatic and very obvious realities.

He endured mild anti-Semitism in the

Army. Nothing too awful, nothing like the sort his parents had had to endure, but there nonetheless. An officer had said to him, "What are you doing here?" Like it was a surprise to find a Jew willing to fight for his country. A vague suggestion that he might feel more at home protesting the war on an Ivy League campus.

Attitudes weren't much more enlightened at home. Television and movies throughout most of the seventies had perpetuated the stereotype of the drug-crazed, violent Vietnam veteran. Hopeless, psyched-out losers holding up banks or playing Russian roulette. Beckman never considered himself traumatized by it. Horrified to be sure, but not traumatized.

But he was different when he came back. Contrary to popular melodrama, no one had spit on him. Rather, what offended him was not hostility, but indifference. The *lack* of curiosity. People at home were concerned with who was dating who and when they were going to the beach, buying houses and cars. He had left people who were fighting, maimed, and dying. When people at home told him they were proud of him, he was embarrassed and, at times, even angered. They wanted to hear things that made them feel better about their country and themselves. They wanted to be relieved of any guilt they might feel. They soon figured out he didn't want to talk about any of it.

Beckman went back to the John Doe and re-examined the tattoo. He didn't think he'd seen the tattoo before. If a photograph had been in the file, the tattoo had not been in close focus. But there was something familiar about it . . .

The *USS Basilone.*

CHAPTER NINE

"Squid?" Regan said. "What does that mean?"

"A sailor," Beckman said. "It's an expression, slang. A sailor."

"You mean he was in the Navy?"

Beckman said, "I'm pretty sure, yeah."

"And you think this because of a tattoo?"

"Yes."

They were at their desks in the homicide squad room. Paper was curled into Beckman's typewriter. In the background telephones rang and went unanswered.

Regan said, "I looked at the body too. I didn't see a United States Navy insignia."

"There isn't one on him. The tattoo doesn't say 'USN' or show an anchor. It's a flower and a sword. I think the work was done in the Philippines. I've seen it before. Not that exact same tattoo. The one I saw had a serpent instead of a flower. But the flower is very distinctive."

"Where did you see this . . . flower?"

"On a Navy ship in Vietnam. The *USS Basilone.* A sailor I knew had a very similar tattoo on his shoulder. He told me he got it in the Philippines."

"You were in Vietnam?"

Beckman was not surprised at Regan's surprise. He had gotten used to this. *What were* you *doing there?*

"Yeah."

"Hmmm," Regan grunted. Like he was either surprised or unimpressed. Or both. Regan said, "Why would a Navy veteran not have identification on his person?"

Beckman said, "I don't think he had a home. I called the local veteran's hospital to see if they had anyone missing. They're checking into it. There are a lot of disabled veterans in the city."

"He didn't look disabled to me."

"The coroner's report said his liver was shot. Severe cirrhosis. They also said there were traces of cocaine in his bloodstream."

"So he was a boozer and a coke snorter."

"The liver damage may have been caused by hepatitis. They're not sure yet."

Regan shook his head. "I'm not buying it."

"Why not?"

"Cocaine traces? The guy was a bum. He

didn't look like a serviceman to me."

Beckman sighed and tried to repress his irritation. He said, "He didn't, huh? Did you serve?"

Regan bristled at that one. "What do you mean, serve? You mean in the Army?"

"Army, Navy, any branch."

"No. I was thirteen years old when the Second World War ended. When the Korean War started, I was drafted, but the medical review board wouldn't take me. They found an ulcer I didn't know about."

"Oh."

"Okay?" Like, *are you satisfied?*

"I was just asking."

"Sure."

"Anyway. The truth is, drug use was rampant in Vietnam. Particularly near the end."

Regan said, "Your point?"

"My point is, it's not unusual to find cocaine in a veteran's bloodstream."

"Maybe not for a Vietnam veteran. But your John Doe was in his fifties. Little old to be a Vietnam veteran."

Christ, Beckman thought. There was no talking to some people. Men like Regan had worldviews that were shaped by television shows like *Father Knows Best* and Eisenhower faux-optimism. Everything was just

67

perfect in this country until the hippies and pinkos came along around '67 and had to fuck everything up. Of course it wasn't possible for a veteran of World War II or Korea to be mixed up with drugs. They were *above* that sort of thing. Beckman thought cops, of all people, should know better.

Beckman said, "Anyway, I think we should take this to the media. See if we can get the local television news programs to show his picture and say that the police think he may have been in the Navy. Ask the viewers to call to see if they know him."

"The police? It's your theory, not ours."

Christ, Beckman thought again. "Well, that's what I'm going to write in my report."

"Write what you like."

"Tom, what are you mad at me for? You told me to look into the John Doe and I did. I didn't take this to the lieutenant, I didn't go behind your back. I brought it to you. It's a lead."

"We'll talk about it later. The lieutenant wants to see us now."

As soon as Beckman saw the guy in the gray suit, he knew he was a fed. Clean-cut, no sideburns, short hair, crisp white shirt and club tie. With his even white teeth and straight build, he looked like he could be

68

modeling slacks for Haggar. A sharp contrast to the plainclothes officers of Chicago PD who seemed to take fashion cues from the cast of *Barney Miller.* The guy was young too, about Beckman's age. Lieutenant Gregory introduced him as Ken Gravley and told them he was the Assistant Special Agent in Charge (ASAC) of the FBI Chicago field office.

Lieutenant Gregory gestured the detectives to the chairs. Agent Gravley remained standing.

Lieutenant Greg said, "Agent Gravley dropped by to help us out."

Agent Gravley said, "Thank you, Lieutenant. Let's see, which one of you gentlemen is Detective Regan?"

Regan said, "I am."

"Ah. Good. Agent Keeler — my boss — told me you had dropped by to see him this morning."

"I did," Regan said. "I waited for forty-five minutes."

"I'm sorry about that. But you should have called first to make an appointment."

"I did call. I left a message with his secretary."

"But you didn't make an appointment. Well, water under the bridge. Anyway, gentlemen, I've come to tell you that you

69

needn't worry about the FBI invoking jurisdiction on your investigation. It's your baby."

Regan said, "I wasn't worried about that. I wanted to speak to Mr. Keeler, Agent Keeler, about Nathan Wald."

"What did you want to ask?"

"What I wanted to ask is why the FBI *wasn't* investigating this."

Agent Gravley smiled. "I don't understand. Is there some question of federal jurisdiction?"

"No, sir," Regan said. "But Nathan Wald was known to have been antagonistic to the Soviet Union."

Still smiling, the agent said, "So's Ronald Reagan."

Sergeant Regan did not smile. "Ronald Reagan was not suspected of bombing the Soviet cultural building in Washington D.C. Nathan Wald was."

Beckman said, "Agent Gravely."

"Gravley."

"Gravley, pardon me. It wasn't just that. Wald had other clashes with the Soviets. In New York, he poured blood on the head of a Soviet official. And his gang — I mean, his group — was suspected of bombing the Chicago office of a Soviet airline. They were even suspected of firing gunshots into the

70

window of the Soviet mission to the United Nations. The point is, he was not exactly a mild protestor."

"Are you saying he was a terrorist?"

Beckman said, "That's not my point."

"Of course," the agent said. "Your point is, I guess, that maybe Mr. Wald was assassinated by agents of the KGB?"

Agent Gravley seemed to think the idea was silly, with his condescending smirks and pressed white shirt. *I guess.*

Regan said, "It's not exactly far-fetched, Agent Gravley."

"Well," the agent said, "it actually is. We at the Bureau are well aware of Mr. Wald's protests against the Soviet Union policy on the question of Jewish emigration. But Wald was hardly the only Jew to speak out against that policy."

Regan said, "He did more than speak out."

Agent Gravley said, "Be that as it may, Soviet spies are not in the habit of killing American citizens on American soil. In fact, there is no documentation of such a thing ever happening before."

Regan said, "Yeah, well, there's a first time for everything. Besides, my understanding is that it's the FBI's job to investigate domestic threats to national security. Is the FBI conducting an investigation?"

"On this?"

"Yes."

"No."

"Why not?"

"Because it's not a matter of national security. Mr. Wald was murdered on a subway platform along with four other people. Nothing about it suggests any sort of involvement of the Soviet Union or . . . 'espionage.' Now, it's not my case, of course, but it would seem to me your most obvious suspect is this neo-Nazi fellow. Verner . . ."

Beckman said, "Vernon May."

Regan said, "Can we at least see your file?"

"On May?"

"No. On Wald."

"What makes you think we have a file on Wald?"

Regan said, "You guys have files on everybody. And I know you have one on Nathan Wald."

Agent Gravley turned to look at Lieutenant Gregory. Perhaps he could reason with these men?

Lieutenant Greg said, "If you have one. It would be helpful."

Agent Gravley said, "I'll look into it."

Beckman stood and said to his lieutenant, "If that's all, sir."

Lieutenant Greg said, "Yes, I think so."

72

Beckman walked out the door without shaking the fed's hand.

Beckman sat at his desk and watched Lieutenant Greg shake the FBI agent's hand at the door to his office. When the agent was gone, Regan said, "That little prick. He knows more than he's letting on. You'd think *he* was working for the KGB."

"Yeah," Beckman said. "He's right though."

"About what?"

"About KGB agents not killing Americans on American soil. It's never been done."

"How do you know?"

"I've never heard of it."

"Doesn't mean it hasn't happened. Besides, Wald wasn't an American citizen."

"Actually, he was."

"What? I thought he was Israeli."

"No. He tried to become a member of the Knesset, but they barred him from holding political office. The medical examiner told me his family wants to have him buried in Jerusalem."

"So *now* they'll take him."

Beckman bristled, but didn't say anything. Regan said, "Was he a dual citizen?"

"I think so."

"I thought you knew everything about him."

"I never said I knew everything about him." Beckman looked at the report that was still in his typewriter. It still wasn't finished. He said, "You know, you might have told me you went to the FBI before this."

"Before what?"

"Before that meeting in Greg's office. I didn't know anything going in."

"You seemed to know plenty."

"I didn't know you'd gone to the FBI. If Greg or, for that matter, Agent Gravley had known you didn't share that with me, they might draw conclusions."

"Like what?"

"That you don't want my help on this thing."

"Don't want your—ah Jesus. Let me get this straight: do you really expect me to *check* with you before I go on interviews? Because I'll tell you right now, I'm not going to do that."

"I'm not going to keep things from you. I'd appreciate it if you returned the favor."

"Return the favor. Jesus, kid, you got gall. What do you think, we're contemporaries?"

"I'm only saying —"

"I've been in homicide for almost fifteen

74

years. You've been here a few weeks. So understand we're not on the same level. You're smart, all right, but you don't know everything."

"I never said —"

"Yeah, I know, you never *said* it. But it comes across, believe me. I was about your age when I got here and I was glad to get the assignment. I was *grateful*. Another difference is, I *knew* I was green. So I watched and I listened and I learned. Wouldn't kill you to do the same."

Fuck, Beckman thought. *Dumb fucking Irishman talking about his experience but probably still mad about the crack about military service. Probably go home to his dumb-ass Irish wife and ten kids and bitch over his mashed potatoes about the pushy Jew he was being forced to work with. Fuck it. Let it go. You want to work homicide, so let it go.*

Beckman said, "Look, I haven't heard anything back from the Veteran's Administration. So I figured I'd go to the homeless shelter on Western and show pictures of our John Doe. See if anyone recognizes him." Beckman paused. "Is that all right?"

"No, you'll have to do that later. We're going to see Vernon May."

75

CHAPTER TEN

The headquarters of the American Nazi Party was a two-story house in Cicero. On the porch of the house stood two men with crewcuts. They wore gray shirts with black ties and armbands. On the armband was a circle containing a bolt of lightning. They both had holstered pistols.

When Beckman saw them from the car, he thought, *losers.* But his heart rate quickened and he knew he was frightened. Perhaps from genetic memory, perhaps present impression. People had dismissed Hitler as a loser at the beginning.

Regan parked the car across the street and looked out the window.

Beckman saw the men on the porch looking back at them. Seeing two men in a plain Chevy Nova who looked like cops. Armed but not seeming particularly alarmed. Still . . .

Beckman said, "What's the matter?"

Regan said, "This could be pretty unpleasant. You want to wait in the car?"

"No, I don't. Are you asking me to?"

"No, I'm not asking. You want to come in with me, come in with me. But if you do, I think it might be a good idea if you . . ."

"Don't tell anyone I'm Jewish?"

"Something like that, yeah."

"You think these guys would try to harm or kill a cop?"

"I don't know and I don't want to find out. Mainly, I want this guy to answer questions. And he's more likely to do that if he doesn't know . . . if he doesn't know your race."

Race, Beckman thought. Jesus.

Regan said, "It's nothing personal."

Beckman laughed and shook his head. Nothing personal. Just some guys who want to exterminate him and his people. An Irish partner telling him to keep the Jew stuff to himself.

"Don't worry," Beckman said. "I'm not here to fight."

Regan held his badge and police identification out as he approached the house.

"Police officers," Regan said.

"What do you want?" It was the one with the blond crewcut who asked.

"We want to talk to Mr. May," Regan said.

77

"Is he here?"

The guards relaxed a little. Not deciding to be friendly, but not fearing attack. Now they were close and Beckman could see their faces. Ugly guys with mottled faces and scary teeth. The look of most American white supremacists.

The guards conferred with each other. One of them went into the house. The blond crewcut stayed on the porch and considered Regan and then Beckman. He gave Beckman no more attention than Regan. The other came back out and said, "You're Chicago police officers?"

Regan said, "Yeah."

"State, municipal?"

"Municipal. City of Chicago."

"You're not Zog?"

Regan said, "Zog?"

"Feds. FBI. Zog. The commander doesn't speak to federal agents."

"We're detectives with the Chicago Police Department. No feds here."

The blond nodded and said, "Okay. The commander will see you, but we'll have to confiscate your weapons."

Regan smiled and said, "Sonny, you're not confiscating anything. Now you go in there and tell your boss he can talk to us here or we can haul his little white ass down to the station."

The blond crewcut was broad in the shoulders and chest and was at least twenty years younger than Regan. He tensed up and Beckman felt his heart start racing again. Quietly, reflexively, Beckman pulled his overcoat back so that he could reach his .38 revolver. Beckman would later admit to himself that he was frightened. But he looked at Regan and was amazed. Because Regan *hadn't done anything.* He just stood there staring down the young Aryan who was younger and stronger and, worse, closer to a weapon, but it was the Aryan who was scared. The Aryan who looked at the middle-aged detective and saw something he'd probably never seen before. The cold-eyed, utter fearlessness of the Irish cop. The silent, primal message that here is a man who simply doesn't give a fuck if he lives or dies. Who is hard to kill and would easily bite off your nose and spit it out. This was no pose. Regan wasn't hiding any fear. He had no fear to hide.

Beckman felt something then that he later realized was pure envy. He was younger than Regan and probably could outbox him in a ring and certainly outrun him on a track. But Beckman didn't have the ability to *be* fearless. It wasn't in him and it never

79

would be.

In a low voice Beckman had not heard before, Regan said, "You want to say something to me?"

The blond crewcut stared back at him long enough to save face. But then he walked back into the house. He came out shortly after and made the other guard escort them inside.

Vernon May had done his best to make the living room of the house into a sort of chamber. The windows were covered with black curtains and, apart from a lamp on his desk, the room's only light came from candles. The carpet had been pulled up from the floor, but the wood underneath had not been refinished.

Vernon May sat behind a large oak desk with a green top. His desk was clean and well organized. Behind the desk hung a large black-and-white portrait of Hitler. Swastikas hung at the sides.

May was a man in his early to mid thirties. His hair was almost golden blond and his facial skin was baby smooth. He was more handsome than the detectives expected. Fit and compact and narrow in the waist. With his hair short and somewhat curly, he could pass for a Roman. He was seated in a high back chair and he made no move to get up.

Vernon May said, "Who sent you?"

Beckman said, "No one sent us, Mr. May. We're detectives, not envoys."

"You're civil service. You are the status quo. In service to a nation that has allowed itself to become corrupt and sick."

Regan said, "Right. Well, we just want to ask a few questions."

May said, "I know why you're here." May gestured to the chairs in front of his desk. The detectives sat down.

May said, "Rabbi Wald is dead, yes?"

"Yes," Regan said.

"Does the City of Chicago wish to avenge him?"

Regan said, "We're not in the vengeance business, Mr. May."

"Who are you?"

"Detective Sergeant Regan. This is Detective Beckman. And yes, we are here to investigate the subway murders."

"And because the professional Jew Wald was shot, I am a suspect. Yes?"

Regan said, "What do you mean when you say 'professional Jew'?"

"That's what Nathan Wald was. A full-time Jew. That's what he was selling."

Regan said, "And what about you, Commander? What are you selling?"

"The truth. I'm a man who believes in his country, his people, and the supremacy of the white race. Nathan Wald was not so different from me."

"In what respect?" Regan said.

"He too opposed racial integration and intermarriage. I share his contempt for the Arab sand niggers."

Regan said, "Are you glad he's dead?"

"Of course. But I didn't kill him. Sergeant Regan, you haven't read me my rights."

"I haven't arrested you."

"Are you questioning me?"

"Sure."

"I have the right to remain silent."

"You certainly do." Regan talked out the rest of his rights, making it sound like a conversation. Regan ended by saying, "I mean, you understand all that, don't you?"

May nodded.

And Regan said, "You say you didn't kill him; can you account for your whereabouts that night?"

"Indeed, I can. I was at a meeting in Kenosha. I did not return to Cicero until the next morning. At least two dozen witnesses will attest to that."

"Two dozen witnesses," Regan said. "Members of your outfit?"

"We have people everywhere."

"Well," Regan said, "last time I saw you guys march on the news, I counted about twelve guys."

"We don't all operate out in the open, Sergeant. But believe me, our numbers are legion."

"Over twenty?"

"Much more."

"More than fifty?"

"Absolutely."

"So can you account for all the members of your legion that night?"

Vernon May smiled. "That was a nice trick, Sergeant. No, I can't account for all of them. But my men were with me."

"But not all of them."

"I didn't send anyone after Wald."

"You say you have alibis. Can you name them?"

"I don't have to. Under the First Amendment, we have the right to peaceably assemble."

"First Amendment doesn't say anything about protecting the identities of your socalled alibis. You don't give me names, addresses, and numbers, I'm going to presume you're lying."

Vernon said, "Herndon."

"Yes, Commander."

83

"Give the sergeant a copy of our roster of our meeting in Kenosha."

"Yes, sir."

Regan said, "We have witnesses who say Nathan Wald punched you in the face. How did you feel about that?" Regan smiled.

"He struck me while I was being held. That's how they fight, you know. Never directly. They get other people to do it for them."

"He didn't get someone else to do it, he did it himself," Regan said. "Come on, Vernon. You telling me you were going to take that?"

May said, "I'm not a fool, Sergeant. You're not going to trick me into admitting something I didn't do."

Regan said, "You say you're glad Wald is dead. Because of who he is or what he is?"

"What he is," May said. "Sergeant, you misapprehend me. My principal message is the separation of the races, not massacre."

"You're not planning another Holocaust?"

"Another? I'm still waiting for proof of the first."

Regan said, "You don't believe there was a Holocaust?"

"Not for one minute," May said. "Oh, a few thousand died to be sure. But six million? Not remotely possible. There were well over a million innocent and good Germans killed by Allied bombs dropped on Dresden. *Those* were the corpses filmed for the Jewish propaganda. It's all a hoax. Do you believe it, Sergeant Regan?"

"Sure."

Vernon May turned to look at Beckman. "How about you, Detective?"

Beckman looked back at May's clear blue eyes. "Sure."

May studied Beckman for a few moments. Beckman stared back at him impassively.

Regan said, "But you said you were glad Wald was dead."

May returned his attention to Regan. "Yes," he said.

"Why?"

"Because he was a traitor."

"Because he was a Jew?"

"No," May said. "If Jews are loyal Americans, everything will be all right. If they are traitors, they shall be executed."

Beckman said, "They're not *all* traitors?"

"No. Just about eighty percent."

Regan said, "So you want eighty percent of them executed?"

"I didn't say that. I said the traitors *should* be executed."

"You said 'shall,' not 'should.' There's a difference."

85

"You misunderstood me."

Regan said, "No, I understood you just fine. I don't think you killed Wald, Vernon, because I don't think you have the guts. That's why you had someone do it for you. We'll find whoever it was and then we'll bring you down. It's just a matter of time. So if I were you, I'd get a good lawyer and start thinking about what kind of deal you can make that keeps you off death row."

"I've said all I'm going to say to you. You have your list of names. They will confirm that I was in Kenosha the night Wald was executed. Now if you'll excuse me, I have a lot of work to do."

Regan stood and said, "We'll be seeing you."

CHAPTER ELEVEN

In the car, Beckman said, "What if his alibi checks out? What if he was in Wisconsin?"

"If he was, he was," Regan said. "Like I said, I think he had someone do it for him. You know about Charles Manson, don't you?"

"Yeah, I read the book."

"Manson was convicted of the Tate/ LaBianca murders and he wasn't even there. The joint-responsibility rule. He ordered it done."

"I know. But they got the people who did the actual murders *first*. We don't have that. What broke that case is one of the women who did the killing bragged about it to people she was in jail with."

"Maybe we'll get that kind of luck."

"Maybe," Beckman said. "But . . . I don't know. I don't know if I'd put Vernon May in the same category as Charlie Manson. Manson said he wanted to start a race war.

But killing a bunch of rich Hollywood players wasn't going to start any sort of race war. I think he just wanted to kill people. I'd say Manson has more in common with Hitler than May."

Regan said, "I don't understand that."

"I don't know if it's something anyone can understand. I've been thinking about Hitler and the Holocaust since I was a teenager. I've read books about it and studied it and I still don't really understand it. You believe in God and the Devil. I'm not sure I do. But if I did, it would seem like the Devil came up from hell and pretty much had his way in Germany for about twelve years. A guy I knew in the Army, his father worked for a big corporation that had offices in Germany. I met the father. He was a good guy. Protestant. Typical Republican businessman. Liked to have a few drinks at the country club, tell a few dirty jokes. No one could accuse him of being a bleeding-heart liberal. He spent five years in Germany in the early seventies. He said they were awful people."

"The Germans?"

"Yeah. He said the word he heard most there was *impossible*. He didn't have to explain to me what that meant."

"That's what Vernon May said."

"Right. Impossible. My buddy's dad called them 'the Nazis next door.' He said most of them thought the Jews had just been *moved.* He said, 'Moved where? To the country?' And I used to think that way too. That anti-Semitism and the Holocaust was just a German thing. But now I don't know."

"What do you mean, you don't know?"

"Do you know that before Hitler came along, if you were a Jew in Europe, Germany was probably the *best* place to be? The *least* anti-Semitic. The German Jews succeeded in arts and commerce far more than any other European Jews. If you were living in Europe in 1920, you would probably expect France to be the one that would persecute the Jews. Or Russia. Germany was supposedly the most advanced."

"But the French didn't do it. Neither did the Russians."

"They didn't have a Hitler to lead them."

"Do you hate Germans?"

"Of course. You don't forget something like that. And it wasn't that long ago."

Regan shook his head. "I don't understand you, Beckman. Weren't you disgusted by May?"

"Oh, yeah. I wanted to kill him back there. But is he the real thing? Or is he just some

89

loser wanting attention? Putting on a Nazi uniform to be somebody. Is he a mass murderer in the making or is he just playing dress up? I don't really know. That's why I contrast May with Manson. Manson was an original. That's what made him more frightening than May."

"I don't understand."

"What I mean is, what Manson and Hitler wanted was just to murder. Manson didn't have Hitler's evil genius, he just had the evil. But they weren't that much different. Like Hitler, Manson had a hypnotic power over his people. Manson killed and the police caught him and tried him and put him away like any other criminal. But Hitler put the criminals *in charge.* When he was done, the system itself was criminal. Wickedness was encouraged and rewarded, good punished. A veritable devil's paradise. Manson couldn't pull that off."

"But all those people," Regan said. "The Germans doing that to the Jews. Willingly. Happily. I just don't think Americans would do that."

"Don't be so sure," Beckman said, thinking of burned villages in Vietnam. He had seen it himself. The North Vietnamese were no better, of course, but then it was their country. He left knowing that savage propensities were not limited to Germans.

"You're wrong," Regan said. "We wouldn't do that."

"It's not really a question of whether or not you would do it. It's more of a question of whether or not you'd keep your mouth shut if you knew it was being done. Or if you suspected it was being done. Your neighbor's taken away. You don't know where, but you got a pretty good idea. And deep down, you know you're never going to see him or his family again. You can speak up, you can ask questions, but if you do, chances are good they'll take you away next. And not just you. Would you speak up if you knew you would be risking the lives of your wife and children? Your brother, your sister? I'm not sure I would. And those were my people."

"The Jews, you mean."

"No, not just the Jews. The German Jews. That's where my father came from. He came to America before the war. But he loved Germany. That was his home. Till the day he died, he looked down on Eastern European Jews. Said some awful things about them. We used to fight about it. There were times I actually wondered if he would have been content if Hitler had simply left the German Jews alone."

"That's terrible."

"Yeah, it is."

"No, I mean that's a terrible thing to say about your father. That's your father."

"Yeah, that's him."

"Your generation, you don't give your parents the benefit of the doubt. The respect they're due. He never said what you accused him of."

"No, he never said it out loud." Beckman shrugged. "What difference does it make now?"

"It makes a difference. A man should honor his father. It's in the Old Testament."

"Yeah, I know the Commandments," Beckman said, his annoyance at Regan's tone showing. "Anyway, this business of Hitler isn't really about him. I used to think, okay, Hitler wanted to kill all the Jews. And that's true. But say he had killed every Jew in Europe, he wouldn't have stopped there. He also killed all the gypsies and homosexuals he could find and about two and a half million Russian POWs. Even his own people began to be horrified by him near the end because they figured out that, for him, the killing wasn't a means to an end, the killing *was* the end. And he damn sure wasn't going to stop with the Jews. After the Jews, he would have probably targeted the Catholics.

And then the Poles and then whoever he put in his sights."

"I don't know if I misunderstood you earlier, but did you refer to Hitler as a genius?"

"He *was* a genius. An evil, destructive genius. We like to deny that because it's easier to believe that what happened was a result of historical forces at work. What we don't want to admit is that *he* was a historical force. We don't want to admit it because it's too horrifying to contemplate it. He was much more than just a rage-filled anti-Semite. He was a much bigger monster than that."

"But you said you don't believe in the Devil."

"I'm not sure what I believe. I know that monsters exist and I certainly believe in the existence of evil. All these studies of Hitler and the Holocaust and talk of 'never again' did nothing to prevent Stalin, Mao, and Pol Pot from slaughtering their millions. The only thing we can do to keep them from rising up is sustain a democracy and law and order."

Regan said, "Is that why you became a police officer? To protect democracy and keep order?"

"I'm not sure why I did it," Beckman said. "Even now."

CHAPTER TWELVE

When they got back to the station, Regan found a message on his desk.

He said, "Wald's funeral is tomorrow. Or I guess it's a funeral, but they're not burying him. They're going to bury him in Israel."

"Yeah, I already knew that part," Beckman said, annoyed. He was starting to wonder if Regan ever listened to him. "What time is the service tomorrow?"

"Ten o'clock. It's in Skokie." Regan handed the address to Beckman.

Regan said, "It's not being released to the media, thank God. So hopefully we won't see May's gang there."

Beckman said, "How did you get this information?"

"From Wald's brother in-law. Pretty soon, isn't it?"

"The tradition is to bury the body as quickly as possible. Is he okay with us being there?"

"Yeah," Regan said, "he's okay with it. So we'll leave here about nine, okay?"

"Okay."

After he left the station, Beckman stopped at the homeless shelter and showed the photo of the John Doe to the employees at the counter. They didn't recognize him, but told him they weren't at the shelter all the time, only nights. Beckman said he would check back tomorrow afternoon. He thanked them and trudged through the snow back to his Plymouth. He checked his watch. It was only six thirty. And that meant he still had time to go to his mother's house to celebrate his stepfather's birthday. Shit.

They were halfway through the meal when he got there. Beckman's mother, Sylvie, sat next to her husband Albert. Beckman's brother, Martin, was there with his wife, Natalie, and their three boys.

Doctor Albert Pintoff owned a big ranch house in Lake Forest. He was a balding widower with a thriving urology practice. He had a grown daughter who was in medical school herself and a condominium in Miami Beach. Beckman had mixed feelings about Albert. At root, Albert was not the sort of man Beckman would choose to like.

But Albert treated Beckman's mother well, which couldn't be said for Beckman's own father. Sylvie's wardrobe had improved with her second marriage.

Beckman's brother was about the same height as Beckman, but he was heavier. Marty Beckman was forty now, seven years older than his little brother. Beckman believed that they might have been closer if they had been closer in age. Marty Beckman had done everything right: married a Jewish girl right after he graduated college, opened a dry cleaning store, had three children. There had been no sowing of wild oats for him. He worked hard and he tithed to his temple. He and his wife, Natalie, were respected members of United Hebrew. Beckman remembered a time when he liked Natalie. Back when she was his big brother's teenage girlfriend who wore jeans and sweaters and sat on floors and smoked cigarettes. She'd gotten plumper and meaner as she got older. Or maybe she always was mean and he'd been too young to see it.

Beckman took his coat off and rubbed his nephews' shoulders and mussed their hair.

His mother said, "Where is Elyse?"

"She couldn't make it," Beckman said.

"Not feeling well?" Sylvie said.

"No, not particularly," Beckman said, somewhat surprised at how easily the lie rolled off his tongue.

"The poor thing," Sylvie said. "This snow keeps everyone in and they get sick with the germs."

"Yeah," Beckman said. "Happy birthday, Albert."

"Thank you, David," Albert said. "I hear you've been assigned to the Wald murder."

Beckman wondered how Albert could have known that. Had it been in the paper? Beckman looked at his three nephews sitting at the table, the oldest one thirteen years of age. He made a gesture to them and looked at Albert, hoping Albert would drop the subject in front of the children.

Albert said, "Well?"

"Yes," Beckman said. "I don't think we should discuss this in front of the children."

"Ah, they're okay. So it's your investigation?"

"It's not mine. I'm one of the detectives assigned."

"Terrible thing," Sylvie said.

"Yeah," Beckman said.

Albert said, "Do you have any suspects?"

"I really can't discuss it."

"Oh, come on."

"We're working on it, Albert."

"Just terrible," Sylvie said.

Albert said, "You wonder if it's going to start all over again."

Beckman looked at his nephew Adam, six years old and wearing the Yankees ball cap his father had given him. Maybe too young to understand or be frightened, but Beckman was still angry at Albert for raising it.

Beckman said, "I don't know about that, Albert."

"You don't know," Albert said. "You're not old enough to know. They're marching in our neighborhoods and murdering our people."

Beckman looked over to his brother and gestured to his sons. Marty picked up the cue and said, "Boys, why don't you go watch some television."

After the boys left the table, Beckman said, "I don't think there's any reason to panic. We're working on it."

Natalie said, "What about that Nazi? Are they going to arrest him?"

Beckman said, "I really can't talk about it."

"Why not?" Natalie said. "We're family."

"I can't really talk about it. If what I say is repeated, it could compromise the investigation. So all I can tell you is that we're working on it."

Natalie said, "You don't trust us?"

Oh shit, Beckman thought.

Natalie said, "You finally get to work on a case that means something and you won't talk about it with your own family?"

"All homicide investigations are important, Natalie."

"Yeah, but these are our people."

"There were five people killed. Nathan Wald was not the only victim."

"What about the one named Futterman?" Natalie said. "Wasn't she Jewish?"

"Her name was Helen Futterer, not Futterman, and I don't know if she was Jewish or not. Would you care more if she was?"

Marty said, "David, don't be rude. She's just asking."

Beckman sighed and excused himself from the table.

In the kitchen he opened the refrigerator to see if there was any beer. There wasn't. Nor was there any whiskey. He took the empty coffee pot to the sink and began to fill it with water. After he started the coffee brewing, he looked at a Jewish community newspaper on the kitchen table. A story was circled, which said in part:

Jewish rock musician, Howard Newfeld, will perform at a free concert noon Sunday.

Newfeld, popular with those who have attended Jewish conventions and summer camps, last performed at Ravinia's September 20th on his "Road to Eden" Sukkot tour.

Beckman wondered why the article was circled. He'd never heard of this Jewish rock musician before and he doubted anyone outside the Chicago Jewish community had either. Maybe Albert knew his parents.

His mother came in.

"Is something wrong?"

"No, Ma. I'm just tired."

"You look tired."

"I'm okay. Ma, who's Howard Newfeld?" He held up the newspaper.

"Oh. He's some kind of singer. Natalie's going to have him perform at Caleb's bar mitzvah. You heard of him?"

"No. So Natalie couldn't book David Lee Roth?"

"David Lee Roth? Is he related to Sid and Shirley Roth?"

"No, Ma. I was just making a joke."

"Your jokes I never get."

Beckman smiled. His mother was a tiny woman. About five feet and around a hundred pounds. Attractive for her age, more attractive than her daughter-in-law. The second marriage looked good on her. With Albert she had found a contentment and comfort she had not gotten with Beckman's father. God knows she deserved some happiness after the shit he put her through with his serial philandering. A selfish, mean-spirited first husband and a son whose jokes and life choices she never understood. But she loved David and Marty equally.

"Ma," Beckman said. "I'm sorry I was rude to Natalie."

"Ach, she'll be all right. Sit down, I'll pour the coffee."

Beckman did as he was told and as he watched his mother get the coffee cup down from the cabinet, he felt a tremendous guilt for lying to her about Elyse. The way she'd said, "the poor thing" after he implied she was ill, not doubting him in the slightest. She couldn't imagine that her son would lie to her. Beckman thought, *tell her now.* But then thought, no, it's Albert's birthday and why ruin it?

Sylvie poured the coffee black. Then she opened the refrigerator and pulled out a cake with chocolate icing. Then she searched for birthday candles. She was always more comfortable moving and doing things.

She said, "Marty's opening another store."

"Oh, yeah. Where?"

102

"In Evanston. He said he found a location that can't lose."

"That's great."

"He said he needs someone to manage it."

"Oh? I'm sure he'll find someone."

"He was thinking maybe you might be interested."

Beckman smiled. "He didn't say anything to me about it."

"He said something to me. He would pay you thirty thousand a year to start. Give you part ownership. It's a good opportunity."

"I think if he wanted to give me that, he would have told me himself."

"You're wrong. He's afraid to talk to you about it."

"Why should he be afraid?"

"How should I know why he's afraid? He talks to me, you talk to me, Natalie talks to me. No one talks to each other. Would it be so bad?"

To talk with Marty? Beckman thought. Then realized that wasn't what she meant. Beckman said, "To work at a dry cleaner's? I don't know. Kind of dull, I would think."

"They've made a good life."

"I know that, Ma. I don't look down on him."

"He doesn't look down on you."

"Yeah? I think his wife does."

"Natalie is who she is. You want her good opinion, all of a sudden?"

Beckman shrugged.

"And," Sylvie said, "it's not like you'd have to be working for her."

Beckman knew *that* wasn't true. Natalie would always hold the job over him. *Look what we did for you.* Not that it mattered because he knew he would never take the job anyway. Not even if Marty offered him a hundred thousand a year. The work would bore him to tears and, worse, would bring him into Marty and Natalie's orbit and likely permanently fracture the already tenuous relationship he had with his brother. In times past, Natalie's sons had seen the gun on his belt and expressed the interest in police work that most little boys would, but Natalie made it very clear — in front of Beckman — that no son of hers was ever going to be a policeman. And at least one of them took heed. Beckman felt guilty at the realization that he had started to develop a vague dislike for his oldest nephew, the one who would soon be bar mitzvahed. The boy had memorized the names of the Jewish senators and congress-men and all the stats of the sainted Sandy

Koufax. And was it Beckman's imagination, or had the boy started doing the same sort of eye rolls and disapproving head turns his mother did? A learned sneering. Beckman wavered between annoyance and pity for the boy, for he knew the boy merely wanted to please his mother by being a good Jew and a good son. The boy was smart and chances were good that he would become the doctor his mother wanted him to be and Beckman wondered if the boy had lost the ability to think for himself or had willingly surrendered his independence too easily.

The irony was, Beckman himself would have discouraged the boy from becoming a police officer if the boy ever expressed an interest. Any smart cop would do that. Yet coming from Natalie, it was an insult. To her, cops were dimwitted thugs who couldn't cut it in the private sector. She felt the same way about people in the military. And that was another irony. Natalie sometimes said things that Beckman quietly agreed with. The war in Vietnam *was* wrong. Some cops *were* brutal, racist, and anti-Semitic. But Beckman didn't feel she knew enough to air such opinions. The police department, for good or for bad, was *his* tribe and he didn't like outsiders running it down.

It was, of course, the fat sister syndrome — you can call your own sister fat and ugly till the cows come home but an outsider better not even think about it. Similarly, there are plenty of Catholics who enjoy a good joke about priests going after little boys in the confessional. But let a non-Catholic make such a crack to a Catholic and a fistfight will likely ensue. So it was with Jews and the cops. The police force was his fat sister.

Beckman said, "It's not a good idea, Ma."

Sylvie said, "You want to remain in this? This police business?"

"I don't know. For now, yeah."

"For now. Everything is for now. You don't finish law school for now. You and Elyse don't have children for now. Nothing about tomorrow. You're what, thirty?"

"Thirty-three."

"Thirty-three. When are you going to start thinking about your future? When are you going to make some decisions?"

"You act as if I haven't, Ma. In any event, you know I love you."

"Ach. I don't understand you." Sylvie finished lighting the candles on the cake. She picked up the cake with two hands. "Go and open the door for me, go on. And come

106

and sing happy birthday to Albert."
Beckman obeyed.

CHAPTER THIRTEEN

Beckman drove down Lake Shore Drive back into the city. The wind blew a deathly chill off the lake. The gusts powerful enough that Beckman needed to keep two hands on the wheel.

Beckman listened to the news on the radio. North Vietnamese–backed Cambodian insurgents announced the fall of Phnom Penh. Pol Pot was now hiding. Watergate criminal John Mitchell was released on parole after serving nineteen months in a federal penitentiary. The mayor of Chicago promised that all the trains would be running soon and that the City of Big Shoulders was going to be better than ever. Beckman shook his head and turned the dial to another station. Bee Gees singing "Jive Talkin' " and Beckman thought, right. Thought not even black people said that anymore.

Beckman didn't lock the car after he

parked it. He was afraid he wouldn't be able to unlock it the next morning because the lock would be frozen. Only a lunatic would venture out on this cold night to steal his police radio. If they did, he'd tell the department he had locked the car anyway. The Plymouth itself didn't have much life left in it, the Chicago winters having already rusted out much of the wheel wells. The city was hard on cars.

Beckman walked up the steps and unlocked the door to his apartment. He walked in, closed the door, and took his gloves and coat off. The apartment was warmer than usual. Then he noticed the light coming from the kitchen.

Beckman's heart quickened as he reached for his .38. He had killed men in Vietnam and didn't want to kill anyone again. As a police officer, he had never shot anyone. Only twice had he even drawn his gun, but that had been it. But he drew it now as he saw the light emanating from the kitchen.

Beckman spoke in a loud and firm voice that he hoped would hide his fear. He said, "Okay. I've got a gun pointing in your direction. Come out of there with your hands up."

Elyse walked out, holding her arms at chest level. She was in slacks and a sweater, her scarf still around her neck.

She said, "Has it gotten that bad for us, David?"

Beckman put the gun back in his holster. "Jesus," he said. "You scared me."

"*I* scared you," Elyse said. "You were pointing a gun at me."

"Sorry. I met with some — some pretty nasty characters today. They've got me a little spooked." He didn't want to tell her he'd met with Nazis. Odds were, she'd say he was exaggerating. She'd never found his work that interesting or even credible.

Elyse said, "I guess I should have called first."

"Yeah, you should have. Is everything all right? I mean, is there some kind of emergency?"

"Everything's okay. I came by because I wanted to talk. Is it all right if I go back to the kitchen to get a beer?"

"Sure. Sorry."

She went back to the kitchen and came out with two bottles of Old Style. She handed him one as they sat on the couch.

Elyse Beckman had never been beautiful. But she had always been attractively cute and when she laughed she was adorable. When she was younger, she and Beckman had shared the same brand of faux self-hating humor common to adolescents. She would call close friends "Jewish whore" to their faces. Her dark hair was shorter now. She had given up the long, feathered-back look. Even now, Beckman missed the girl with that hair.

Elyse said, "You've lost weight."

"Oh? Well, I've been eating less junk food since I left narcotics."

"That's good. But I think you're too thin now."

"No more home cooking either."

She smiled at that. A familiar smile, almost warm. They both knew how she hated to cook.

Elyse said, "You work late tonight?"

"Not exactly. I was at Ma's. Albert's birthday."

"Oh. How are they?"

"The same."

"And Marty and Natalie?"

"They're all right." He decided he would not tell her about the dry cleaning offer. He didn't want another subject to argue about. "Caleb's bar mitzvah is coming up."

"Oh, that's right. I suppose I should go."

"I think you should," Beckman said. "But I haven't . . . Elyse, I haven't told them yet."

Elyse sighed. "You should have told them, David. I'm not going to change my mind."

"I know. I'm not asking you to."

"You should have told them."

"I will —"

"It isn't right for you to make me tell them. Then I look like the bad guy. What if I run into your mom or Natalie?"

"I'm going to tell them, Elyse."

"When? At Caleb's bar mitzvah?"

"I will. Before then. I promise."

"You promised a lot of things."

Beckman sighed. He really didn't want to argue with her. "I don't think I broke any promises to you, Elyse."

"You said you were going to be a lawyer."

"I said I was going to law school. I still am."

"It's been years. You're not interested in finishing. Oh, what difference does it make? You're not going to change."

"No, probably not."

By her expression, he could see that she had hoped he would disagree with her. Hoped he would tell her he would change, starting now. His affirmation wounded her and her face broke.

It was brief, though. She had never been one to sob. She brushed away her own tear and said, "Shit. You know what I brought here tonight? Our final divorce decree. Everything we agreed to. I was going to come in here like Barbara Stanwyck and say, 'Here.' "

Beckman smiled. "With authority?"

"And how," she said. "I thought you'd plead with me to stay." She smiled and said, "But you're not one to plead, are you? You're so . . . proud, David. So stubborn. I used to know what you were thinking."

"Ah, Elyse. You still know me," Beckman said, not being truthful.

"Not so much. It seems we both let each other down, huh?"

"You never let me down."

Elyse shook her head. She pulled the divorce papers out of her bag and handed them to Beckman. "Don't lie, David. You were never much good at it."

Beckman read through the document. Their years together reduced to seven pages of division of assets and debts. There wasn't much of either. She would get the yellow '76 Camaro that had six payments left on it.

Beckman said, "Looks okay to me. Just sign here?"

"Yeah."

He handed it back to her. She put it back in her purse and said, "Good thing we didn't have any kids, huh?"

"Ah, Elyse."

"Sorry. Bad joke." She got off the couch. "I'll have my lawyer send you a file-stamped copy."

"Okay. Elyse, it's bitter cold outside. Why don't you stay the night?"

Elyse smiled uncertainly. "What do you have in mind? You know we haven't been together in months. It might be kinda weird, the two of us."

Not just weird, Beckman thought. But painful. For him anyway.

"No," he said, "not that. It's just that it's dangerously cold out. You take the bed. I'll sleep on the couch."

"Is that in the decree? Sorry. No, I'm going to go."

Beckman got his coat. "I'll walk you to the car. Make sure it starts."

"It'll start," Elyse said. "You bought a new battery for it last month. And a new set of snow tires."

"You have to around here," Beckman said, aware of how mundane his words were. Saying something to say something.

Beckman stood by the Camaro as she turned the key in the ignition. The engine caught on the first turn. Beckman gave her a thumbs up. She rolled down the window.

She said, "You're not even curious, are you?"

"What do you mean?"

"About whether or not there's someone else. Whether or not I have a lover."

Beckman made some sort of gesture. Oddly enough, he wondered if it was even any of his business. They had drifted that far apart.

Elyse shook her head and rolled the window back up. Then she put the car in gear and pulled away.

Chapter Fourteen

Regan and Beckman parked across the street from the synagogue. Soon after they arrived, Esther Wald's brother came out to talk to them. He was a bearded man of about forty and he was dressed in black. His name was Daniel Epstein. Regan rolled down the window of the Nova.

Epstein said, "We're about to start. Do you mind staying out here?"

"Not at all," Regan said. "We weren't planning to intrude."

Epstein said, "Okay. I'm sorry, but my sister doesn't want any outsiders there."

"We understand," Regan said. "You'll tell us if you see a stranger?"

"Sure."

Regan said, "We've got a couple of patrol cars in the area. Skokie Police Department."

"We didn't ask for that."

"I know you didn't," Regan said. "We'd just like this to be peaceful."

Daniel Epstein looked uncertainly back to the temple. Then he turned back to the cops and said, "Can I talk to you for a minute?"

"Yeah," Regan said. "Get in the back. You don't want to stand out in the cold."

Epstein closed the door after he got in. Regan turned the heater fan up.

Regan said, "What's on your mind?"

Epstein said, "I told you before, I'm not from here. I came here from Buffalo after I heard about the shooting. That's where we're from, Esther and I. She fell in with Nathan after hearing him speak in New York."

"Right," Regan said.

"My parents, they're survivors of the Holocaust. This has been very hard on them."

Beckman turned in his seat. "Did they like Nathan?"

"No," Epstein said. "They didn't. They did not support what he did. But that's not the point. They want me to bring Esther and the boys back to Buffalo with them. This whole thing has been very frightening to them. They want it to stop. They don't want any more of this."

"Neither do we, Mr. Epstein," Regan said. "If you want her and her children to come back to Buffalo with you, I don't have any problem with it."

"So I presume she's not a suspect?"

Regan said, "Are you an attorney, Mr. Epstein?"

"As a matter of fact, yes. Does it show?"

Regan said, "A little. Criminal defense?"

"No. Personal injury. I've made a good living because I'm pretty good at it. But no, I don't do criminal work. But if Esther's a suspect in this thing, I'd just as soon you'd go ahead and tell me."

Regan said, "She's not quite at the top of our list, Mr. Epstein. Do you have any reason to think she should be?"

"No reason at all. I've lost touch with my sister over the years, Sergeant Regan. Ever since she became enthralled with Nathan Wald, she's more or less dropped her own family. She found us too soft and accommodating, I guess. Though we're all practicing Jews. I guess we weren't militant enough for her."

Beckman said, "Daniel, are you relieved that Nathan's dead?"

Epstein caught Beckman's expression in the rearview mirror. "That's quite a thing to say to me, Detective Beckman. Esther told me about you."

Beckman said, "Did she now."

"Yes."

"Did she find me too soft and accommodating as well?"

Epstein smiled. "Something like that," he said. "I don't know if you can understand someone like my sister or Nathan. But I think you can. I don't think they're exactly strangers to you."

Beckman said, "How do you mean?"

"Esther and Nathan were more threatened by people like you than by anti-Semites. That's why she was so rude to you the other day. Yeah, she told me about it."

Beckman said, "It's not a concern."

"Okay, then," Epstein said. "But to answer your question, yes, I am a little relieved that Nathan's gone. Not because I hated him. I didn't. He could be very charming, even to me. But he was a man who was attracted to danger as much as he was the spotlight. Esther never really figured that out. Anyway, now he's gone and we want her and the boys back safe with her family. We don't want any more of this."

Regan said, "Why are you telling us this, Mr. Epstein?"

"I'm telling you because I want you to encourage her to leave this town. Maybe even scare her into doing it."

Regan said, "I think you overestimate our influence. You're her brother."

"She won't listen to me. Maybe she'll listen to someone in authority. She likes strong men."

"It's not really my place, Mr. Epstein."

"I'm asking you for a little help, Sergeant. I've been helping you."

Regan sighed and said, "I'll do what I can, Mr. Epstein."

"Thanks," Epstein said.

He got out of the car and walked back across the street.

Regan said, "He seems like a good man."

"He's wasting his time," Beckman said. "She's not going to go back with him."

Regan shook his head and said, "Man, you're hard. He's trying to keep his family together. What's wrong with that?"

"People don't like to change. She married Wald for a reason. Her brother thinks he can take her back to Buffalo and have her marry a dentist and start all over again. It's too late for that."

"Well, I'm still going to say something to her."

Beckman shook his head. He didn't want to have this conversation with Regan. An Irish Catholic lecturing a Jew about family ties.

Regan said, "Beckman."

"Yeah."

"Something I don't understand. Epstein said that the Walds were more threatened by people like you than by anti-Semites. What did that mean?"

"I don't know." Beckman turned the heater fan to a lower setting. "Okay, I do know. At least, I think I do. People like Nathan Wald worry that Judaism and the Jewish people will become, well, diminished by a secular civilization. If not extinguished."

"Secular. You mean, nonreligious?"

"Sort of. But religion isn't entirely it. It's as much cultural as anything else. Wald once said something to the effect of the real danger not being the Gentile's icy rejection of Jews, but rather what he called their 'seductive embrace.' "

"You mean that you'll assimilate?"

"Yeah."

"Like a Dubliner moving to London and liking it?"

"Yeah, maybe. But it's probably more complex than that. More than once, I've been told that when a Jew marries a Gentile, Hitler wins."

"Really? How?"

"I don't know. Marrying outside the faith, diluting the blood, turning your back on your own. I don't know."

"Do you go along with that?"

"No. I've never believed that. But Wald did."

Regan took a Swiss Army knife out of his pocket and opened out the stubby piece of steel that functioned as a beer-can opener. With the point he began to pare his finger-nails.

"Well," Regan said, "being tribal isn't exactly limited to the Jews. I had a grand-father who thought we shouldn't be fighting alongside the English in the Second World War. Never mind the Germans, he thought the British were the foulest race on the earth. God, that man could hate."

Beckman said, "Was he a cop too?"

"No. He was a crook. A small-time one, at that. Running beer for Deanie O'Banion's outfit on the North Side. He never amounted to anything. Bitter, stupid, and angry to the end."

Beckman almost smiled at the man. Some-thing about the matter of fact way he passed judgment on his own granddad. Irish, yes, but little sentimental blarney from him. That was the beauty of being a cop. It made it just about impossible to hold onto false, romantic notions. You ended up thinking every race had its share of assholes, even your own.

■ ■ ■ ■

Approximately ninety minutes later, the family came out of the synagogue. The detectives watched as Mickey Shaivetz walked Esther Wald to a car and put his hand on her back. They watched as she stood by the door of the car and as Shaivetz touched her on the arm before she got in. Small things, but experienced detectives notice body language. They know it conveys more truth than words.

Regan said, "Are you thinking what I'm thinking?"

"I don't know," Beckman said. "She's got a few years on him."

"Ah, she's got a certain something. For him, anyway. I think we're going to have a little talk with the boy."

CHAPTER FIFTEEN

Beckman wanted to question Mickey Shaivetz at the synagogue, but Regan said no. They followed Shaivetz to the Wald house and watched Shaivetz walk Esther Wald into the house. Beckman said, "let's hit him now," and Regan still said "no." Beckman fidgeted in the car and, sure enough, Regan said, "Patience, lad" and Beckman said, "Oh, shit." Fucking Irishman talking in his singsong voice when he was in a good mood because he thought he was onto something. Beckman, still a young cop, wanted *action*. They weren't on surveillance, for Christ's sake. If they were going to question the guy, they should question him.

But then ten minutes later, another car pulled up and some people got out with Esther Wald's children. They led the children to the front door and let them in and walked back to the car. A few minutes after that,

Mickey Shaivetz came out and walked down the street to a yellow Toyota Corolla.

They followed him three blocks and then pulled right up behind him at a traffic light. They saw him look at them in the rearview mirror. Then he turned around and looked at them again. Regan got out and walked up the driver's side of the Toyota.

Shaivetz rolled down the window. "What do you want?"

They sat with their coats on at a Dunkin' Donuts. Regan's hat and gloves were on the next table. He had paid for Shaivetz's coffee. In the background Neil Diamond and Barbra Streisand sang "You Don't Bring Me Flowers."

Regan said, "We never got much of a chance to talk the other day."

Shaivetz said, "What would I have to say to you?"

"I wanted to know if you were with Nathan the night he was killed."

Shaivetz hesitated. Then he said, "Not that night, no. I was with him during the day."

"Tell me about that day."

Mickey Shaivetz smiled. "It was cold. I remember that."

Regan stared at him for a moment, unsmiling. Regan said, "That's pretty funny,

125

Mickey. What else do you remember? And let's start with the morning."

"All right. That morning, I got up at seven. I met Nathan at our office on the North Side at eight-thirty. He was on the telephone from about nine to eleven. After that we talked about a speech he was scheduled to make."

"Where?"

"At Washington University. The one in St. Louis."

"They let him speak at universities?"

"Why wouldn't they? He spoke at a lot of places. To spread his message and raise some money."

"You talked about a speech he was going to make. Then what?"

"We had lunch at Sonnschein's Deli. Then we went back to the headquarters. He made some more calls. I worked the phones too. Then, around four o'clock, he left."

"Where did he go?"

"I don't know."

Regan frowned.

"I *don't*. He didn't tell me everything he was doing."

Regan said, "Was he a . . . secretive man?"

"Well, I don't know what you mean by that."

"Sure you do. Did he like girls?"

"He was married with two kids."

"Right. But he did see other women?"

"That's none of your goddamn business."

"Actually, it is. If he was, it's obviously material to this investigation. I mean, how could it not be, Mickey?"

Beckman said, "Mickey?"

"Yeah."

"It seems like there's something you want to get off your chest."

"No."

Beckman said, "It seems like there is. I think you'd feel better if you told us what you know."

"There's nothing to tell."

Regan said, "The best of us can be tempted. And a charismatic man like the rabbi . . . well, it would only be natural that women would be attracted to him."

"He was not fooling around. I don't care what anyone says."

Regan said, "Anyone says. What do you mean? Have people said that he has?"

"No."

"What do you mean, no? You just said 'I don't care what anyone says.' So who's been saying he was running around?"

"You misunderstood me. I never heard anyone say anything."

"Did you see anything?"

127

"No."

"No girls coming by headquarters?"

"No."

"Any female friends?"

"No."

"You know, it would be better for everyone involved if you told the truth about this. What I'm saying is, it's not something we would have to tell his wife about."

Shaivetz flinched. Then he said, "I've told you the truth."

Regan sighed. He said, "You talked about Nathan making speeches. Did he make much money from that?"

"Not much. Enough to get by."

"How much? Roughly."

"I really don't know."

"You worked for him, didn't you?"

"Yeah."

Beckman said, "He was the president of the Alliance. Who was vice president?"

"There was no vice president. No board. Esther did the secretarial stuff. And there was me."

Regan said, "That's not what she said."

"Who?"

"Mrs. Wald. She said she knew very little about his business."

"Well . . ."

"Well what?" Regan said. "Did she lie to us?"

"No, she wouldn't lie. And I don't know what she told you. I know I'm not going to take your word for it."

Beckman said, "Now that Nathan Wald is dead, who's in charge of the Alliance?"

Shaivetz said, "Well, I don't know, really. I guess I am for the moment."

Regan said, "When will that change?"

"Well, we'll hold a meeting and we'll have an election. And . . . you know . . ."

Beckman said, "And you'll be elected or someone else will be elected."

"Yeah."

"And then who will go make these speeches and collect these speaking fees Nathan did?"

Shaivetz turned in his seat for a minute. "I don't know," he eventually said. "I suppose I will."

Regan leaned back and shook his head as if this conversation saddened him. Maybe it did. He said, "I don't know, Mickey. I understand Rabbi Wald was quite a talented speaker. Very few people have that gift."

"I know how to speak, Sergeant."

"Sure, sure, Mickey. But can you *move* them? That was his talent."

"I helped him. I helped him write his

speeches. I was very much part of the program. And don't forget our membership. We have thousands of members."

Regan said, "And you to lead them?"

"Yeah."

"I see," Regan said. "Is that what you wanted?"

Shaivetz looked at Regan and then at Beckman. He smiled again and then forced out a laugh.

He said, "You guys must think you're pretty smart."

Regan made a gesture with his hand. A shrug.

Shaivetz said, "I did not kill Nathan. Do you understand me? I did *not* do that."

"Kill Nathan?" Regan said. "Kill Nathan Wald? Who said you did?"

Shaivetz said nothing.

Regan said, "Is that why you think we're questioning you?"

"I . . . I don't know."

"What gave you that idea?"

"I don't know."

"Do you think you *should* be?"

"No."

"I mean, this is silly, but you can account for your whereabouts the night of the murder, right?"

"Yes. I was at home in my apartment."

"Where's that?"

"In Skokie. The Hi-Pointe apartments."

"Were you alone?"

"Yes."

"Friend, girlfriend . . ."

"Alone."

"So no alibi."

"No. But . . . no, I was alone."

Regan said, "You seemed like you were about to change your answer. Is there something you want to tell us?"

"No. I was alone."

"Doing what?"

"Reading a book."

"What book?"

"It's called *Dawn.* By Wiesel. Have you read it?" A smug smile then on Shaivetz's face.

"No," Regan said. "What's it about?"

"It's about a Jewish patriot who's forced to execute a British soldier. It's about a struggle you don't know anything about." Shaivetz was looking at Beckman when he finished.

Regan said, "Sounds interesting. You know it reminds me of something. Let's see . . . Oh. Were you and Mrs. Wald sleeping together?"

Mickey Shaivetz almost dropped his coffee. ". . . what?"

Beckman put his face between his hands as if he were about to sneeze. He did not want Shaivetz to see him grin.

Regan said, "Were you and Esther Wald sleeping together?"

"How can you — how dare you ask such a question?"

"Just a question. Were you? Or should I say, are you?"

"How *dare* you."

Regan raised an eyebrow. "There's no shame in it, son. She's an attractive woman."

"You're indecent. You think this is funny?"

"Not at all. But I do need you to answer me. And before you do, know that I'm going to find out the truth anyway."

"No."

"No, you're not going to answer me or no, you weren't sleeping with her?"

"No, I did not sleep with Esther."

"You sure?"

"I would know, Sergeant. Jesus, you people."

Regan said, "Oh, don't play the outrage card with me, son. I'm better at this game than you are. You follow?"

"Yeah, I follow."

"Now. One more thing, would you say you and Esther are friends?"

"I don't know what you mean by that, but

yes, we are friends."

"Did she ever tell you that she and Nathan were having problems?"

"What do you mean, problems?"

"You know what I mean. Problems with their marriage."

"She never told me that."

Beckman said, "Apart from what she told you or didn't tell you, did she seem unhappy with him?"

Shaivetz sighed but didn't answer. His expression seemed to answer the question, but the detectives wanted something more.

"Did she?" Regan said.

"I don't know," Shaivetz said. "Maybe."

Regan said, "Maybe what? Be more specific."

"Maybe once or twice she complained about him not being home enough. But it didn't mean anything."

Regan said, "Did she ever in any way indicate to you that she thought Nathan might be running around on her? Come on now."

"She never told me that."

CHAPTER SIXTEEN

When they got back to the city, Regan stopped at an Irish pub called Muldowney's for lunch. He did not ask Beckman what he would like to eat. He just said, "Let's have some lunch." Beckman had never been there before.

They took seats at the bar. A shaggy, white-haired bartender shook Regan's hand and said, "Tommy, what do you know?"

"Not much Jimmy. How are the boys?"

"Getting along fine. My oldest is at Gordon Tech now."

"Oh, that's a good school."

"We're hoping he'll take an interest in engineering."

"I'm sure he will. Jimmy, this here's Mr. Beckman, one of our new detectives."

The bartender took in the non-Irish name. Then he shook hands lamely and said, "What'll you have to drink, sir?"

Beckman said, "A Tab, if you have it."

"We don't. Will a Pepsi be okay?"

"Sure."

"A Guinness for you, Tom?"

"Just a half, Jimmy. And I'll have the stew."

"And you, sir?"

Beckman looked at the menu board to his right. "I'll have the pastrami on rye. And never mind the Pepsi, I'll just have a cup of coffee."

"Suit yourself."

Beckman took the place in. A black-and-white portrait of Michael Collins behind the bar. On the back wall pictures of Beckett, Yeats, J. P. Donleavy, and some fat guy with his arm around Jackie Gleason.

Beckman pointed to it and said, "Who's that with Gleason?"

The bartender set Regan's Guinness on the bar and said, "It's Brendan Behan. He's only one of Ireland's most famous playwrights."

Regan said, "Easy, Jimmy. We got a civilian here."

Beckman said, "Was he one of the writers for *The Honeymooners*?"

The bartender bristled and Regan smiled and rested his hand on Beckman's wrist. In a quiet voice, Regan said, "Respect the local gods, David. You're on our turf now."

Beckman smiled back, raised a hand, and

said, "Sure." They had both made their points.

The bartender left them and Regan said, "You're a young intellectual, aren't you? You ought to give the Irish poets a try. You might like them."

"I'm not an intellectual."

"Intellectually curious, then. Though that's not a bad thing in a detective. Ah, the Irish lionize Behan because he wrote a poem about Collins there and because he was a lovely drunk. Drank himself to an early death entertaining the likes of Jackie Gleason and Groucho Marx. The drunken Irishman, drinking when he was thirsty and when he was not, becoming a caricature and making all the wrong people laugh. A waste of talent."

"This poem he wrote about Michael Collins, do you know it?"

"I used to. But I can only remember a little bit of it now. Let's see . . . 'For all you did and would have done, my enemies to destroy, I'll prize your name and guard your fame, my own dear Laughing boy.' More about himself than Collins, really."

"The Irish called Collins 'Laughing Boy'?"

"That's what Behan's mother called Collins. She loved him."

" 'Prize your name and guard your fame,

my own dear Laughing boy.' I like it."

"Do you now?" Regan said. "Well, they say all policemen eventually become Irish. Even the black ones."

Regan sipped his Guinness. "Now let's talk about that other Mick. Mickey Shaivetz. Would you agree we can cross him off our list?"

"No I would not."

"Why not?"

Beckman said, "Well, he strikes me as a rather nasty piece of work. And he had motive."

"What motive? The woman?"

"No, not the woman. I don't see that at all."

"Don't like the woman, do you?"

"No," Beckman said. "But that's not the point. I just can't see Mickey being attracted to the rabbi's wife."

"You can't see *yourself* attracted to her," Regan said. "But I know what I saw. He feels something for her."

"An affection, perhaps. Maybe even pity. But not an attraction."

"Well, that's not how I saw it. The way he looked at her when he escorted her to the car. His interest was more than that of a little brother. But that aside, you say he had motive."

137

"Yeah. Well, maybe. I don't think Shaivetz much liked Wald. Maybe he knew something about him that we don't. I mean, look at him. Do you see any remorse?"

"Not exactly. But that's not much to go on."

Beckman said, "May I speak frankly?"

"Sure."

"I think you misjudge Shaivetz. You see, perhaps, a harmless little Jewish boy. But don't forget these guys bombed places. They advocated violence. Nathan Wald and Mickey Shaivetz should not be confused with your typical college student rabble-rousers."

"And what about Vernon May? Do we put him in the clear?"

"Oh, shit. No, of course not."

"You think May is harmless?"

"No, I said I didn't think he was the next Hitler. I never said I thought he was harmless."

"May is our man. Not Shaivetz."

"Tom, how can you know that? You think you can look into Shaivetz's eyes and say, 'He's not a killer.' It's not that simple. Besides, you were the one who said we should talk to him in the first place."

"I know that."

"To be frank, at first I thought it was a

waste of time. But after we talked with him, I've been thinking he's hiding something."

"After talking with him," Regan said, "I feel he didn't do it."

"But he's not telling us all he knows. Anytime a suspect lies, we should investigate further."

"Look, I think he lied to us too. But every suspect, every witness I've ever interviewed has lied about something. Everybody lies sometime. Doesn't mean they gunned down five people at a subway stop."

"All right, but don't ask me to write off Shaivetz as a witness."

"Have I asked you to do that?" Regan said. "Do I check your daily activity reports?"

The bartender set their food on the bar.

Beckman said, "No, you haven't."

"Okay, then. Thanks, Jimmy." Regan returned his attention to Beckman. "Have you got an I.D. on the John Doe yet?"

"No."

"Okay. After we get back to the station, I want you to interview the people who lived with the two girls. See if you can find anything there."

"Keough and Halloran already interviewed them. They were the ones who informed them of the deaths."

"I know they did. I read their reports too. But they did it quickly and they did it at the same time when they informed them of the murders. I want you to do it thoroughly."

CHAPTER SEVENTEEN

Catherine-Anne Corbett's roommate was a college student named Mary-Beth Hanley. She was twenty-five years old and was also a nurse at St. Mary's Hospital. She answered the door in light-blue scrubs and a zip-up hooded sweatshirt that said "Loyola." She was petite and carried herself well and Beckman was sorry to see a young guy sitting on her couch watching Dr. J and the Sixers playing the Lakers.

Beckman told her who he was and what he was there for. She led him past the apartment living room and into the kitchen. She invited him to sit down and asked him if he wanted a cup of coffee.

Mary-Beth Hanley said, "I guess it's good you caught me here. I'm working the four to midnight shift tonight at the hospital."

Beckman said, "I know you already talked to some other police officers. I just wanted to double-check some things."

"It's okay. But I don't know what else I can tell you."

"Was she coming home directly from work that night?"

"Yes."

"And that was her regular train?"

"Yes. Once in a while, she'd take a cab home. But cabs are expensive. She didn't like to walk alone to the train station."

"She was with her friend, though, that night."

"Yes."

Beckman said, "The other detectives, did they ask you if your roommate knew this man?" Beckman placed a photo of Nathan Wald on the kitchen table.

The girl studied it and said, "No. They didn't ask me."

"Have you seen him before?"

"No. Was he one of the victims?"

"Yes."

"Was he the first one shot?"

Beckman looked at the girl. Twenty-five, still young, but then nurses were very often matter of fact about life and death. They formed hard shells and joked about mortality to stay sane. They were like cops in some ways.

Beckman said, "We don't know. What do you know about him?"

"Only what I read in the paper. After . . . after it happened."

"I'm sorry for your loss."

"It's okay. I'm sorry too. We weren't . . . Cathy and I weren't very close. I liked her, but we were more roommates than friends."

"Was she closer to the other girl?"

"Yeah. They were talking about getting a place together."

"Was it unusual for her to be at that place at that time that night?"

"No. Like I said, that's the usual way they would have gone home."

"Do you know if she had any people in her life who might have done something like this? An ex-boyfriend, someone from the hospital?"

"You mean, someone who would want to take her life?"

"Yeah."

"No. She didn't have a boyfriend or an ex-boyfriend. There were no psychos in her life."

"What about Helen Futterer?"

"I didn't really know her."

"Did Catherine-Anne say anything about Helen having a boyfriend or someone bothering her?"

"I know Helen was seeing a guy for a while, but he turned out to be kind of a rat.

I met him once at Faces. Have you been there?"

"I understand you have to have a membership to get in."

"Yeah, like I would have a membership. We got in because Helen's boyfriend had a membership. Or a lot of coke." She smiled. "Oh, sorry."

"That's okay."

"That's not my thing, you know. Not cocaine. I was just making a bad joke."

"It's okay, really. That's not . . . it's not what I'm interested in. What was the guy's name?"

"His name was Richie La something . . . LaFevers. That was it. Richie LaFevers. He was a trader for the Chicago Mercantile Exchange. The Chicago Merc, he called it. You know, one of those types."

"What do you mean?"

"I mean, he told us he made $60,000 last year and he's only our age. You know, a show-off."

"Sure."

"You're writing his name down."

"Yeah."

Mary-Beth Hanley frowned. "What I said earlier, about the cocaine. I don't know that he does that. I think he does, but I'm not sure. I just don't want to get someone in trouble when I'm not sure."

"You're not going to get him in trouble. I don't do that anymore."

"Excuse me?"

"What?"

"You said you don't do that anymore. Do what?"

Beckman thought, *oh shit.* He'd slipped. He'd revealed himself. Maybe because he felt comfortable with the girl. He hadn't slipped when he was in *the Life.* Working undercover in narcotics and vice, hanging out with lowlifes and drug dealers and pimps, being in places where slipping could get you put in the trunk of a car. But he slipped with a young Catholic nurse who put him at ease with who he was and what he was doing.

Beckman said, "I used to work in narcotics. I don't anymore. That's all."

Mary-Beth Hanley looked at him.

Beckman said, "I don't."

"It's okay," she said. "I guess I trust you. And I know I don't do that sort of thing."

"Good," Beckman and smiled at himself. He had never been the Joe Friday type. Giving lectures to the young on drugs and patriotism.

The Hanley girl regarded him, openly, and

said, "I can see why they picked you for that."

"Can you," Beckman said, his head down. He didn't want to engage her on this. He didn't want this thing turned on him.

But the Hanley girl said, "Yeah. You don't look like a police officer."

Beckman looked at her again and this time noticed the pale green of her eyes. Then he thought, *I'm divorced.* Like he had forgotten about it already. Or he had forgotten that he had been married. Maybe that was why he had slipped earlier and told the girl he used to be a narc. In his early thirties now and he was starting to shed parts of himself. The ex-narcotics officer, the ex-husband of a woman he had lost touch with years ago.

Mary-Beth Hanley smiled and said, "But I guess you've heard that before, huh?"

"A few times," Beckman said. "This time you went to Faces, is that the only time you went out socially with Helen?"

"Yeah. That was it. Like I said, it wasn't exactly my scene. A lot of girls in Halston dresses and guys with gold chains around their necks. It made me feel parochial."

"Most of us are parochial," Beckman said.

"But few admit it," the girl said. "Would you like some more coffee?"

"No thank you."

146

"I'm going to have some."

Standing at the kitchen counter, the girl said, "On the news, they said that Cathy's purse and money weren't taken. Is that true?"

"Yes, that's true."

She shook her head. "So fucked up. Why would someone do something like that?"

"I don't know, Miss Hanley."

"I knew her from Loyola. Sometimes we'd go to the student mass together on Sunday nights. She was . . . very naïve."

"What do you mean?"

"I don't know. One time at college, she left her dorm unlocked and someone went in and took her stereo. Probably another student. And she was so . . . *wounded* by it, you know? Like she couldn't believe there were people out there who would steal."

Beckman said, "Some people are like that."

"I know. But they usually don't become nurses. She never should have tried. To become a nurse, I mean. Her parents pushed her into it. This would have never happened if she hadn't tried to become a nurse."

"Well . . ."

Mary-Beth Hanley smiled grimly. "God, listen to me. Now I'm blaming her parents.

Car wrecks, cancer, falling off roofs — I've seen people die from all sorts of things. It's all luck. Good luck, bad luck. Random . . . wickedness. There has to be something more than that, don't you think?"

Beckman didn't answer her.

"Oh," she said, "I don't know why I'm bothering you with this." She put her nurse face back on. "Is there anything else?"

"Just one more thing. Was it just the two of you living here?"

"Usually. Well," she said, gesturing her head to the living room, "Ben stays sometimes."

"And he's with you?"

"Yeah. Well, sometimes . . . yeah."

"What's his full name?"

"Ben Martin. He's a resident at the hospital."

"A doctor?"

"Yes."

"Okay." Beckman was suddenly self-conscious. He believed he had asked her for professional reasons. "Well, I guess that's all."

At the door, she said, "I'm sorry I wasn't much help."

"You were."

"No, I wasn't. But call me if you think you need something else. You have my number, don't you?"

"I do. Thank you again."

As she closed the door, Beckman heard a roar come from the television set. Dr. J had scored on a reverse lay-up.

Chapter Eighteen

He wondered if he had lied to the girl about Faces. She had asked if he had been there and he had said you have to have a membership to get in. Not telling her he'd never been there, but implying he hadn't and letting her believe he hadn't. Beckman had gotten good at lying when he worked in narcotics and vice. Though, at the time, he thought of it more as acting a part than lying. But now that he was out of it, he realized, no, it was lying. Lying to get the job done and lying to keep from being killed. And what was the job at the end of the day? Arresting pimps, seizing drugs, closing down whorehouses, and scaring off johns, and the day after you did all that all the sleaze would just pop up somewhere else. Like playing Whac-A-Mole. It was a game and the honest vice cops who were good at their jobs would admit that they got off on the rush the work provided and perhaps didn't think so much about the greater good, if such a thing could be said to exist. Acting, deceiving, wheeling and dealing. It could be very thrilling for a couple of years until the black moods came and the deepening sense of despair and degradation threatened to overwhelm you. There was a reason they didn't let cops stay under too long.

Yeah, he had lied to the Hanley girl about Faces. He had been there a couple of times back when he was in the Life. Hanging out with coke dealers and party girls watching straight guys in polyester suits and gold chains trying to be Tony Manero on the dance floor but none of them as good on their feet as the blacks or the gays. Beckman drove flash cars back then that vice had seized from horse dealers or pimps: Thunderbirds, Cadillacs, Buick 225's, and the like. It helped to keep him in character. He had lied then to a lot of people and he had lied tonight to the Catholic scrub nurse with the pale green eyes and cute little behind and the young doctor boyfriend on the couch, and then . . . and then later he had told her he once worked in narcotics because he had felt bad about lying to her. As if that would make up for the lying. Why had he done that? Who was she that he should be straight with her? Or was it just because she had been straight with him, telling him all she knew about clubs and coke snorters like Richie LaFevers?

Beckman didn't look for Richie LaFevers at Faces because he doubted he could get in without telling them he was a police officer. Also, it was too early for LaFevers or anyone else to be there. The place didn't fill until at least eleven. He called dispatch and asked for LaFevers' address and then drove to an expensive high-rise apartment on the Gold Coast. Beckman showed the doorman his police identification and told him he needed to speak with LaFevers right away. The doorman escorted him to the elevator and went back to his *Sun-Times*.

The apartment on the eighteenth floor was answered by a slick looking, thin man of about thirty. He wore a V-neck cashmere sweater with a silk shirt underneath. His feet were bare. Beckman flashed his I.D. again and asked if he was addressing Richard LaFevers.

"Yes," LaFevers said. "What's this about?"

"Helen Futterer."

"Oh God. She was one of the people at the subway, wasn't she?"

"Yeah. Can I talk to you about it?"

"Er . . . can you give me just a minute?

My friend needs to get dressed."

"Sure."

Beckman gave him a couple of minutes to hide his drugs. A record player was turned off and Beckman heard an exchange of voices, the tones urgent but indecipherable. LaFevers came back to the door and let him in.

It was a beautiful apartment. Spacious and modern with a view of the lake. And high enough up that you could feel the force of the wind against the windows and sometimes the building itself. White shag carpet on the floor and about three thousand dollars' worth of stereo equipment against the wall. A *Playboy* pad.

Beckman looked at the glass-top coffee table and saw the telltale traces of white powder. Probably left over from earlier because LaFevers didn't seem coked at the moment.

LaFevers asked him to have a seat and asked him if he would like a drink.

"No, thanks," Beckman said. "I'll just ask a few questions and be on my way. How long did you know Helen?"

"Oh, I met her . . . let's see . . . at Ravinia's last summer. No, it was September. We hung out a few times, nothing serious."

"You dated?"

153

"I wouldn't say dated. Hung out."

"Were you sleeping with her?"

LaFevers shifted his position on the couch. He wasn't ready for that.

"No," he said. "She was just a friend." LaFevers smiled uneasily and said, "You sure you don't want a drink?"

"Yeah, I'm sure."

"Do you mind if I get one?"

"Not at all."

LaFevers was nervous and trying to hide it with action. He made a point of facing Beckman when he stood at his bar and put ice in his glass, then pouring scotch on top of it. All of it a little too quickly.

"Yeah," LaFevers said, "she was a buddy. Pretty much every time we were together it was in groups of people. A nice girl. Probably too nice for the crowds we run with."

Beckman said, "She was pretty, though."

"Oh, very pretty. She could have been a real looker if she took the time to work on it. Pretty good dancer, though not great. Terrible that something like that had to happen."

"Pardon?"

"I mean, it's tragic, of course."

"What makes you think it had to happen?"

"Did I say that? Jesus, I'm sorry. I guess it wasn't really accidental, was it? What I meant was, I'm sure it didn't have anything to do with her."

"Why are you sure?"

"Helen was a nice kid. She wasn't mixed up in anything bad. She was on her way from work that night, wasn't she?"

"Was she?"

"That's what I understand."

"You weren't involved with her, yourself. Is that what you said?"

"Not sexually, no. I didn't think of her that way."

"Was she seeing anyone else?"

"I really wouldn't know."

A girl walked out of the bedroom between Beckman and LaFevers. She wore a silk nightie that fell just beneath her behind. A pert little behind at that. Beckman almost drew breath. A girl of about nineteen or twenty with thick, chestnut hair and a smashing little body. She looked Beckman right in the eye and said, "Hello."

"Hi."

"Are you the policeman?"

"Yes." Beckman decided to remain in his seat. Partly because he knew the girl expected him to stand.

He could see that her entrance made LaFevers uneasy. She walked to bar and said, "Pour me one, darling."

155

LaFevers poured her one and gave her some sort of disapproving look. She ignored it and carried her drink over to the couch where she sat down. Close enough now to Beckman that he could see she had nothing on beneath the nightie.

She said, "I'm Renee."

"Nice to meet you."

"You haven't told me your name."

"David Beckman."

"Are you a detective, Mr. Beckman?"

"Yeah."

LaFevers said, "He was asking about a girl named Helen Futterer. You don't know her."

Renee kept her eyes on Beckman. She said, "No, I don't remember meeting her. Do you mind if I put some music on?" She was directing her question to Beckman.

Beckman said, "As long as it's not too loud."

"Yeah," she said. "Someone might call a cop."

"That's very funny," LaFevers said.

She made a point of bending over as she searched through the records. Not like she was onstage or anything, but enough to draw attention. Beckman thought, she sure knows how to work it. She put Crosby, Stills, and Nash on the turntable. "Carry On" came out of the three-foot speakers at high volume and then she turned it down.

Renee turned around and said, "What are you here for?"

LaFevers said, "He's investigating the subway murders. Helen was one of the victims."

"Oh. That thing where all those people were shot?"

"Yeah," Beckman said.

The girl looked at him steadily and said, "Getting anywhere?"

Beckman had dealt with whores and pimps by the bushel. But even he was struck by the cold way this girl addressed her question. Young, beautiful, high-breasted, and heartless. Everything would slip with time but the meanness would remain.

Beckman said, "We're working on it, Miss —"

"Renee."

"What's your last name?"

"Aiken. A-I-K-E-N. You want my address and number?"

"Do you live here?"

"Yes."

"Then I have that already. Did you know Helen?"

"Nope. Never met her." She smiled at him and said, "Anything else?"

"No, I guess that's about it."

Beckman said to LaFevers, "Can you tell me where you were the night of the murders?"

"Yes. I was in Aspen, actually. The airline would be able to confirm it."

Renee Aiken said, "That's true, he was."

Beckman said, "Did you go with him?"

"Nope."

"Okay," Beckman said. To LaFevers he said, "I wasn't asking you because you're a suspect. But if you can tell me what airline it was, I can put it in my report and you'll be out of it."

"It was United to Denver. Left the day before on the two fifty-five flight. I got back that Sunday night on the red-eye." LaFevers smiled again, a little easier this time, though he was still trying to put on a show. "If I'm lying, I guess you'll find out, huh?"

Beckman gave him a thin smile, but didn't answer.

CHAPTER NINETEEN

The restaurant manager escorted Peter Mandel to the kitchen. Mandel inspected the stove tops and opened the ovens and peered inside. He even looked at the hands of the cooks. The head chef did not know Mandel and stepped forward to stop this fat little bald man from invading his space. The manager stopped the head chef and told him to keep quiet. Mandel was a nice man and a very generous tipper.

After he was done with his inspection, Mandel said, "Thank you, Evan."

The manager said, "So you'll be dining with us?"

"Yes."

Mandel walked up to the chef and said, "I hope you'll forgive the intrusion." Mandel's tone was smooth and easy, the Polish accent detectable but soft. Mandel pulled a twenty dollar bill from a money clip and said, "May I? For your trouble."

Mandel was not vulgar with money. He knew some chefs took offense easily and Mandel liked to keep most relations affable. This chef was not offended and he liked the look of the crisp bill. The chef looked to the manager and the manager nodded.

The chef took the bill and thanked Mandel.

Mandel went to the dining room and the manager said to the chef, "Don't get mad. Mr. Mandel never eats in a restaurant unless he inspects the kitchen first. It's nothing personal."

The chef didn't understand it. The little bald man was in one of the most exclusive French restaurants in Chicago. The soup alone was six dollars. Did he expect to find rat droppings in the kitchen? The chef could not know that Peter Mandel had once spent several months of his life covered with lice.

The manager said, "He's got a thing about germs. *Dreads* them. I understand he won't even touch alcohol. He only drinks bottled water. And he insists the bottle be opened at the table."

Born in the summer of 1919, Peter Mandel was fifty-nine years old. The son of a moderately affluent physician in Lvov, Poland, Mandel had been a handsome boy with thick black hair and athletic grace. The German invasion and the war changed all that. He had been bald and ugly since his early twenties, the victim of years of malnutrition. The starvation of the war years had ruined his metabolic balance. Since the war, he had been unable to contain his appetites. He was a fat man, almost bug-like in appearance.

Also, his eyesight was poor. Rarely was he seen without his dark tinted glasses.

With him tonight was a girl of twenty-three. Her name was Sally and she wore an emerald green dress Mandel had bought for her. Mandel had met her at a club. He saw that her wrist was bare and then he exercised one of his usual approaches.

"I see you don't wear a watch. That's a shame. A beautiful young lady like you should have a watch. You need to know what time it is. You don't want to be late for your appointments, do you?"

He then produced a twenty-two-carat diamond watch and asked that she try it on. The girl did. Peter told her how much it became her, how flattering it was to her delicate wrist.

"I *insist* that you keep it."

The girl did keep it, unaware that Peter Mandel bought such watches in bulk. Mandel felt no shame at the exchange. He had been engaging in such transactions for most of his life. And he could not buy what was not being sold.

Besides, most of the young girls who involved themselves with Peter did not regret it. He was unattractive to be sure, but he was generally polite, always generous, and he had good table manners. He was civilized and cultured. He did not ask for gifts to be returned when the relationship was over.

Some would call girls like Sally a "soft" prostitute. Not working street corners, but selling themselves just the same. But Mandel wasn't a man to judge women. Or men. He took people for what they were. And he liked prostitutes. He had befriended them and even respected them. He saw them not as predators or even as victims, but as scrappers and survivors. Fellow survivors. He had seen hardship up close. He had seen women in postwar Europe sell themselves for a bar of chocolate because they were hungry. He had seen men in Soviet labor camps murder for a piece of bread. Mandel had learned that morals were a luxury for people fortunate enough to afford them.

Sally said, "How's your food?"

"Good," Mandel said. Probably one of the

best French dinners he'd had in America. Mandel liked good food. But even after twenty-five years in Chicago, he was still homesick for the distinctive smells of Polish food. Homesick, too, for the sound of the Polish language. Chicago had the largest Polish American population in the United States. Mandel had tried to fit in to the city's Polish community, but they had not let him in. As a boy in Poland, he had thought of himself as Polish, rather than Jewish. But the Germans and the Russians said he was a Jew and treated him accordingly. Later, when he fought for the Polish 2nd Corps against the Germans, he realized the Poles thought of him as a Jew too. His own countrymen. In a way, that was the most painful blow.

Nor had the Chicago Jewish community accepted him. He was a man of power and wealth and considerable ability. And he was charming and usually pleasant company. But he was considered "disreputable." They said the usual things: *slumlord, pimp, hustler, shady character,* and so forth. A shylock. A stereotype they didn't want around. He didn't belong in either community. He knew it, but he hid the resentment and hurt.

After dinner, Mandel and Sally stood outside the restaurant until the valet brought his new Cadillac Deville to the curb. It was a '79 model with metallic blue paint and a dark-blue vinyl top. Mandel had never bought a German car.

They drove to the apartment Mandel kept for Sally on the Near North Side. When they got inside, Sally checked the messages on her answering machine. The first one was from a guy she used to work with at The Brassary. The second one was from Renee Aiken.

Sally turned around to see Mandel staring at her.

"What?" she said. "That's just Timmy. I used to wait tables with him. What? He's a fag. Can't you tell by his voice?"

Mandel said, "I don't care about him."

"Then what?"

"It's her."

"Renee? I know you and her used to have a thing. I don't care."

"I don't want you hanging out with her."

"Oh, come on, Peter. She's cool."

"She's trouble."

"Why? 'Cause she likes to fuck black guys?"

"I don't care about that."

"Oh, you do too, Peter. Look, I know how you are about blacks. You get along with them, you don't like people calling them

164

niggers, you feel sorry for them. But when they go after white girls, they're animals. Right?"

"No —"

"You guys are all alike. Liberal, love-your-brother bullshit until they came after *your* women."

"No, I don't care about her doing that. What she does is her business. Renee and I are still friends."

"Then why don't you want me hanging out with her?"

"Because she's trouble. She likes trouble."

"Oh, I don't know . . . Yeah, okay, maybe she's got a thing for dangerous types. For chrissakes, she's twenty years old. What do you expect?"

"I expect you to show me some respect."

Sally Ryan walked over and put her hand on Mandel's cheek.

"I respect you, Peter. And I'm grateful to you. But you told me at the beginning that I could have my own life. My own friends."

"I didn't mean her."

"You met me *through* her." She put her arms around Mandel's neck and kissed him on the cheek.

Mandel reached up and pulled her arms off.

"No," he said.

"Peter, come on. It's not like we talk about you when we're together."

Mandel looked at her.

"Well, maybe a little bit. But it's nice things."

Mandel smiled and shook his head. "What does she want to do?"

"She wants me to go to the B.B.C. with her tomorrow night. You told me you have a meeting tomorrow night anyway."

"The B.B.C.?"

"Yes."

"And that's all?"

"Yes."

"And you promise to be home by midnight?"

"I promise."

"Okay."

Sally kissed the old man again. Soon they were in the bedroom with the lights off.

Mandel left her apartment two hours later. He usually did not stay the night with her. One time he had and had awakened her with his uncontrolled sobs. She shook him out of his nightmare and asked him what he had been dreaming about. He didn't tell her. She said he had frightened her, a man his age crying like that. He still didn't tell her. He never told anyone about his nightmares.

Mandel parked the Cadillac at the Taft Gardens apartment complex. He left the engine running so that he could keep the heater on. The windchill was about twenty below zero. The cassette deck played a tape of classical music. Mahler's Fifth. Recorded by Leonard Bernstein conducting the Vienna Philharmonic Orchestra. Devoted Mahlerians had mixed feelings about Bernstein. But Mandel had nothing but admiration for him. Some said Bernstein was a queer and a political naif, but Mandel didn't care. It took a tough Jew indeed to go into Hitler's Vienna and bend their orchestra to his will.

Mandel had himself played the piano when he was a boy. His parents had never encouraged him to make a career out of music, but they had left him with an appreciation of it. After the war, he had even allowed himself to wonder if he could get the piano back. But he never got back to Poland, yet alone Lvov. The Poland he knew was gone, bartered away by the western powers. Lvov was now part of the Soviet Union. Mandel could be sentimental at times, wondering if acquiring his childhood piano would have made things better.

One thing he had acquired since the war was the Taft Gardens apartment complex. Unlike the piano, it was not a thing of beauty. There was nothing garden-like about it. A Brutalist structure, built in 1956. A monolithic brick of eighteen stories, poured concrete unrelieved by fanciful decoration. It would not look out of place in present-day communist Warsaw. Once there had been lawns near the entrance, but they had been paved over to save maintenance costs. Once there had been sanitation service. Now rotting garbage stacked up in clogged trash chutes. Windows were boarded up, basic utilities were left unrepaired. Mandel had forgotten how long ago he'd quit thinking about it.

Headlights reflected in the rearview mirror. A Lincoln Continental slid up next to the Cadillac. The Lincoln's lights went off with its engine. A black man got out of the Lincoln and walked around to the passenger side of the Caddy and got in. The black man held a bible.

His name was Leon Murray. There was a thick file on him at the Chicago Police Department. He was believed to be the leader of the original Gangster Disciples. The file photo had been snapped in the early seventies, Leon's superfly days, when he wore what police called a "felony hat." Wide-brimmed, garish fedora. Leon didn't wear the hat anymore. Fashions had changed. Now Leon wore glasses and cut his hair short. Neat and clean.

But Leon was still the same man. He was never without a knife or a gun.

Mandel said, "How was Florida?"

"It rained a great deal. But the food was good."

"Try the seafood?"

"I had some crab. But it wasn't as good as what I had in Baltimore. You been to Baltimore?"

"Nope."

"It used to be a nice town. Now it's looking to become the next Detroit. But they got this mayor, a white man, he says he's gonna name a brother chief of police."

"Really?"

"Yeah. I think he means it too."

"Well, it's about time." Mandel said, "I heard about Ronnie. I'm sorry about that."

Leon Murray nodded. Ronnie was his cousin. He'd been shot to death on Christmas day by his wife.

"Yeah," Leon said. "That was some bad shit. But Ronnie should have known better."

"What do you mean?"

"Lynette had caught him before, messing around. And she told him if she caught him again she was gonna gut-shoot him. And she did."

"I thought it might be something like that."

Leon said, "Thing was, she caught him with a white lady. Maybe she'd a done it if she'd caught him with a sister, but I don't know."

"You blame him?"

"I didn't say that. I'm just saying he should a known better. Some brothers who've gotten over, gotten into some big money, naturally they start flashing it on the creamies. And that's trouble, man."

Leon had told Mandel more than once he didn't approve of interracial relationships. He said that the day Muhammad Ali started chasing white pussy was the day he stopped rooting for him. Mandel had said, "But Ali's part white." Leon said that wasn't the point.

Mandel took an envelope out of his coat pocket and handed it to Leon. Inside the envelope was ten thousand dollars, the second payment. Leon put the envelope into his bible and closed it.

Leon said, "You haven't said anything, but I'll tell you."

"Yeah?"

"I'm sorry it was five instead of one. I didn't plan that."

"All right," Mandel said. "Can you tell me what happened?"

"I'll tell you. I was tailing Wald on the train. My plan was to take him after he got off the train, but on the street. Night that cold, I figured it'd be easy to get him alone on the street. But when we got off the train, he turned around and looked at me and . . . he knew. I don't know how, but he knew I was there for him. He started to run on the platform and I popped him. There were witnesses and . . ." Leon shrugged.

"I understand. There were witnesses."

"I'm sorry, man. But I couldn't risk going back to jail."

"I said I understand."

"All right." Leon nodded. "I see you next week then."

Leon Murray went back to his Lincoln. Leon did not count the money. At least not in front of Mandel. Mandel had never shorted him. Not because he feared Leon would kill him. Mandel knew there were worse things than dying. Mandel had never shorted Leon because he liked and respected him.

Sally had said that Renee had an attraction to dangerous men. Peter Mandel shared

171

that attraction. Not a physical or sexual attraction. Mandel liked women. They flattered and amused him. Arousal was secondary. But he also enjoyed the company of rough men. Perhaps because of his own physical shortcomings, he was drawn to brute strength. He was often surrounded by misfits with criminal tendencies. Flawed, dangerous people who had strength. He gave them money and they in turn gave him some semblance of friendship.

Leon Murray was a criminal, but he was not a misfit. In his world, he was formidable. After Mandel first bought a controlling interest in the Taft Gardens, he found out the apartments were besieged by gang wars. In his first year of ownership, there were eleven homicides. The city was threatening to shut the whole thing down. That was when Leon Murray approached him and told him he could solve all his problems.

Normally, a man in Mandel's position would have pegged Leon as a shakedown artist. Which was a fair assessment. But Mandel was not a normal man. And he detected in Leon Murray a shrewdness that went beyond muscle and showed something of an entrepreneurial spirit. He also sensed the natural traits of a leader.

Mandel said, "Tell me where you're from."

Leon said, "Mississippi."

Mandel said, "I didn't think you were from Chicago."

Leon told him that he was born into a family of sharecroppers. One of ten children to a father who had beat him. At age fifteen, Leon was thrashing pecans out of trees and selling them in Jackson. He said he knew even then that he was too smart for that. So he went north with a friend and became part of what would later be called the Second Great Migration of black Americans from the south. Others in that group sought industrial, union jobs, entry into the middle class, and an escape from the cruel, casual bigotry of the south. Leon Murray became a criminal.

Mandel told Leon a little about his own migration. Not to gain his sympathy, but to let him know that perhaps they weren't so different. Mandel knew how some blacks distrusted Jews more than other white people. Leon didn't buy it; he knew they were different. But he came to understand Mandel was a man he could do business with.

Murray's Disciples took over the Taft Gardens. Rival gang leaders were bought off or thrown off a roof. The message went out: the Taft now belonged to the Disciples.

In exchange, Leon Murray got a small share of the rents. Mandel always believed you got better loyalty paying percentages than a flat rate. Order was maintained.

Mandel was not sorry about Nathan Wald. In his mind, Wald had caused his own death. Mandel regretted that other people had been killed. But experience had taught him that life was to be regarded cheaply.

Chapter Twenty

Regan said, "The airline confirmed it?"

"Yeah," Beckman said. "He was not in town. And LaFevers has never been arrested. He's no killer."

"I didn't think he would be."

They were at the station, facing each other over their desks. Regan stirred the sugar in his coffee cup.

Beckman frowned and said, "You didn't see the guy."

"I'm just agreeing with you," Regan said.

"You sent me to check on him."

"I sent you to interview more witnesses. You did two interviews. Keough and Halloran didn't know anything about this LaFevers. You did good."

"LaFevers was a dead end. I think I wasted my time. We don't know any more now than we did before."

Regan shook his head. "What do you think homicide is? You turn up stones and find nothing underneath and you move on."

"And hope you get lucky."

"It ain't luck. It's work."

Beckman said, "You still think it's Vernon May?"

"Yeah. I think he's behind it."

"If you think that, why did you send me to interview those witnesses?"

Regan looked at the younger detective. "Because we need to check everything. You think I sent you there to amuse myself?"

"I don't know."

"What do you mean, you don't know? Five people were murdered. You think I want to waste the department's time sending you on a wild goose chase?"

"I didn't say that."

"I know what I'm doing," Regan said. "And I already told you, you did good work."

"Yeah, you told me."

"You don't want this assignment? There are detectives who would love to have it."

Beckman sighed. "Yeah, I know, Tom. Detectives better than me."

"I didn't say better. I meant more experienced."

"Oh, well, thanks."

"Look, more experienced doesn't necessarily mean smarter. You're smart enough."

Beckman said, "You know, that's the second time you've told me I'm smart. What do you mean by that, exactly?"

"Smart. It's a compliment."

"Doesn't sound like it."

Regan stopped stirring his coffee and looked up. He smiled and said, "What do *you* mean?"

"Well, I don't know."

Regan said, "Do you think by calling you smart I'm making some sort of anti-Semitic remark?"

"Yeah, maybe."

"What, do you think I look at you and think, 'There's the smart Jew.' "

"Well . . ."

"Well, what?"

"Okay," Beckman said. "Forget I said it."

A telephone rang at another desk. A detective picked it up and answered it. A moment passed and the detective said, "Does that include the rust proofing?"

Regan said, "Look, I respect you. Okay? You got good instincts for this work. I see that. But I'm gonna tell you something and believe it or not, I'm telling you *because* I respect you."

"What?"

"Do you know why you got this assignment?"

"Not exactly."

"You don't know?"

"No, I don't know."

"You got it because you're Jewish. I didn't ask for you. You were assigned to me. You were assigned to this high-profile case because someone at the mayor's office thought there needed to be a Jewish detective working the case. You're here for political reasons."

Beckman shook his head. "That's . . . that's not . . . no one told me that."

"Why *would* they tell you that?"

For a moment Beckman didn't say anything. He looked at the older detective and tried to see contempt. But he didn't see contempt.

Regan said, "I'm no saint, I know. When I first became a cop, I said 'nigger' all the time. Everyone did when I started. But I don't do it anymore. I don't even like my kids saying it. But sometimes I *think* things I'm not proud of. I struggle with things, okay? And any man who tells me he's never had a bigoted thought I know is a liar."

"All right, Tom."

"No, let me finish. If I resent you being here, it's not because of who you are or what you are. It's because you haven't earned the right to work what most cops would consider a plum case."

Beckman was quiet for a few more moments. Then he said, "Okay, maybe you got a point. Maybe. But did you ever look at it another way?"

"How?"

"Did you ever consider the possibility that we're never going to solve this damn thing? That a year from now we'll still be interviewing people like Richie LaFevers and Mary-Beth Hanley and we won't have a goddamn thing to show for it. And then these people upstairs you refer to will be able to say, 'Hey, what do you want from us? We put a Jew on it.' My point is, I don't think anyone did me any favors."

Regan laughed. "You might be right about that, young fella. They didn't do either of us any favors."

Beckman said, "Look, Tom. I asked you before if you wanted me to transfer off the case, but I didn't really mean it. This time I do mean it. If you want me replaced, I won't fight you on it."

"So you think it's a loser now? You think it's going to hurt your chances for career advancement?"

"That's not why I'm offering to transfer. Really."

"I'll ask you directly then. You want off?"

"No. I want to stay with it."

"Then stay with it."

Regan looked at his watch. He said, "Okay. We're leaving in a half hour."

"Where are we going?"

"Kenosha. We're gonna interview a bunch of Nazis."

It was Regan's case. Beckman was just assisting him. Whether detectives admit it or not, every detective develops a theory of his case. And when that theory is formed, the detective — consciously and unconsciously — works to keep that theory healthy. Facts and evidence consistent with the theory are sought out and welcomed. Facts and evidence inconsistent with that theory might be ignored. Regan's theory was that Nathan Wald had been killed by Vernon May. Either by May himself or by someone working for May. Certainly, Vernon May had motive. He hated Jews and witnesses had seen Wald punch May in the face.

Driving up the interstate to Wisconsin, Beckman considered the position he was in.

Regan had told him he had earned his respect. Perhaps begrudgingly, but that was better than nothing. Maybe now Beckman was free to speak his mind and form his own opinions about the case. But Beckman didn't feel he was free to form his own theories. Tom Regan was an unusual man. He shared some things with his younger partner, but only some. Beckman believed Regan only opened up when it was in his interest to do so. There was something of the clever Irish politician in Regan, never fully revealing what he was thinking. Beckman couldn't help feeling he was being outsmarted.

Regan said the prime suspect was Vernon May. Okay, say May had been the killer. What did they have? No witnesses. No weapon. Maybe not even enough to get a warrant to search May's premises. And even if they did, would May be dumb enough to keep the weapon he had used? Beckman had been a police officer long enough to know that being a suspect wasn't enough. Jimmy Hoffa had disappeared four years ago. City, state, and federal officers were *still* investigating it and they had nothing. Everyone suspected mafia boss Anthony Provenzano. And as Hoffa had smashed a bottle over Provenzano's head and witnesses had heard Provenzano threaten to tear Hoffa's heart out, there was little doubt about motive. But no one had any proof that Provenzano had actually killed Hoffa. They hadn't even found Hoffa's body.

Strangely enough, in 1976, Provenzano was seen playing golf with Richard Nixon. A couple of years after that, Provenzano went to prison for killing some other mobster. With Provenzano in prison, maybe nobody cared anymore about Hoffa.

Hoffa, *shit.* Beckman was annoyed and trying not to show it.

He said, "What do you mean, we're interviewing a bunch of Nazis? Are we going to their homes or what?"

Regan said, "Nope."

"Then what?"

"We've got eight subjects waiting for us at the Kenosha Police Department."

"Are you shitting me?"

"Nope."

"How did you manage that?"

Regan shrugged. "I made a few calls. Wisconsin Department of Justice. Kenosha County Sheriff's Office helped out too."

"And they got these neo-Nazis to agree to come in and answer questions?"

"Some pressure may have been applied."

Beckman said, "So you've got clout with some people up north." Beckman was impressed, but he didn't want to admit it.

Regan shrugged.

And Beckman said, "Is this what you were doing while I was running down John Does and interviewing roommates? Lining this up?"

"Are we going to go through that again?"

"When you were going to tell me about this?"

"I told you this morning."

"I guess I should be glad you're bringing me along."

Regan laughed and said, "So now you're feeling sorry for yourself?"

"No," Beckman said, though he probably was.

"By the way, have you run down that John Doe?"

Beckman sighed. "I'm still working on it."

They rode the rest of the way in silence.

They shook a lot of hands at the Kenosha Police Department. The Kenosha police chief asked them if they wanted coffee. An investigator with the Wisconsin DOJ asked Regan how his family was. The DOJ investigator had worked with Regan before and seemed to look up to him. Beckman envied Regan for the deference and respect he received from these men. He overheard the DOJ investigator tell the Kenosha chief that Regan was the "real McCoy." The investigator told Beckman he was lucky to be working with the best homicide detective in

Chicago and Beckman said, "Yeah, that's what I hear." The investigator smiled, oblivious to the young detective's petulance. All of the Wisconsin officers were glad to be involved in a high-profile murder. It boosted their egos and relieved them from the tedium of routine police work. It made them feel important.

Beckman said, "How many?"

"Eight."

"Do you want to split them up?"

"Of course."

"No, I meant, I'll interview some and you interview some."

"No," Regan said. "We do them together."

Beckman decided this was no reflection on his abilities.

They were there for seven hours and did not break for lunch. They interviewed the witnesses separately and asked them about the meeting of American Nazi Party on the night in question. The witnesses were mostly farmers. Most of them were heavily in debt, overextended and fighting off bankruptcy. They were frightened of losing their farms and livelihoods. Vernon May had told them it was the fault of the Jews.

They were consistent in their stories, though. They told the Chicago detectives when Vernon had arrived and when he had left, what he had been wearing and what he had said. Halfway through the interview with the fifth witness, Beckman began to feel that they were telling the truth. When they finished with the eighth, he had no doubts left.

CHAPTER TWENTY-ONE

Vernon May joined the John Birch Society when he was twelve years old. At fifteen, he attempted to join the Mormon Church. But he was thrown out of the youth group when he started a fight with the youth minister. He dropped out of high school his senior year and enlisted in the Marines. The Marines did a background check on him and found out he'd changed his name. They let it pass. He was at Camp Pendleton for a year, then was deployed to the Marine Corps Air Station at Yuma, Arizona. He hated Yuma, hated the desert. It was too vast. It gave him too much time to think. He read a lot during the downtime. *Which Way Western Man?* and then *The Turner Diaries. The Turner Diaries* led him to *Mein Kampf.* He was an intelligent young man, but he had no social ability to edit his thoughts. He said what he was thinking. He gave voice to his vision.

Had he been sent to a war or battle, he might have proven himself to be a courageous soldier. But he never got the chance. Without war to focus on, he started fights with the men in his platoon. He was not accepted. He became known as the odd little soldier who told anyone who would listen that the Americans fought on the wrong side in the Second World War. Vernon said they should have been fighting alongside the Germans against the communists. He told his commanding officer he would refuse to sit at a table with a nigger or a Jew. They discharged him for insubordination. His executive officer would later say that Vernon May was crazy. His NCO told people he just couldn't keep his mouth shut.

If Vernon was hurt by the dishonorable discharge, there was no evidence of it. He believed he was meant for better things. He believed that he was destined for greatness. His only regret was that he had not been able to serve in combat as Hitler had in the first Great War. He would have been content to have fought as a mere corporal as the Führer had done.

Sitting at his desk now, Vernon still believed in destiny. He believed that Nathan Wald's death was proof of divine intervention.

Herndon, his lieutenant, appeared at his desk. He was holding a newspaper called the *Chicago Jewish Reader.*

Herndon said, "Commander, I think you should see this."

The newspaper was turned to a story that Herndon had circled. It read in part:

Detective David Beckman is investigating the slaying of Rabbi Nathan Wald. Beckman attended Block Yeshiva High School and served two tours of duty in Vietnam. Beckman's stepfather, Dr. Albert Pintoff, said that the detective is working for the Chicago Police Department while he attends law school.

Herndon said, "He's a Jew."

Vernon said, "I should have known."

CHAPTER TWENTY-TWO

On the way back to Chicago, Regan said, "Yeah, okay, the alibis look solid. May was in Kenosha the night of the murder. But did you notice the witnesses couldn't account for all of May's people? He could have sent one of them to do it."

Beckman said, "Yeah, he could have. Maybe he did. But we still don't have shit."

"It's too bad the shooter didn't use a machine gun. If he'd used a machine gun, FBI might have a chance of tracing it to the owner."

"It wasn't a machine gun."

"I know that."

"It was a semiautomatic pistol."

"Yeah, I know that."

Beckman said, "We agree on one thing, don't we? That the shooter was there to go after Wald."

"Yeah, we agree on that."

"Doesn't it also make sense that the

shooter only intended to kill Wald, then? He went to kill Wald but somehow screwed up and had to kill four witnesses. The other four witnesses didn't have any enemies."

"We don't know about —"

"Yeah, I know, we don't know about the John Doe. I'm working on it."

"Okay. Okay, maybe Vernon brought someone in from out of town to do it for him. Maybe someone from Wisconsin. Someone from a rural area. One of these farmers. Has him kill Wald and then go back home."

"The way the mob does?"

"Yeah."

"I don't know," Beckman said. "I think the killer knew the city. Knew where the El trains stopped."

"You don't know that."

"No, I don't know that," Beckman said. And thought, *neither do you.* Fucking Regan. A normal detective would have taken the day's events as a setback. All eight of the witnesses confirmed that Vernon May was in Kenosha the night of the murder. But Regan thought it confirmed that May was behind the murders. The point being that May had *planned* to be out of town because he knew it was going to happen. Regan had said it was all too convenient.

Like May had had the alibis waiting for the day when the detectives came knocking on his door.

Perhaps there was something to that line of thinking, Beckman thought. May had seemed pleased to share the trip to Kenosha with them and not much else. Not much else besides a lot of ugly anti-Semitic shit. Maybe he wanted them to think he was a crank who needn't be taken seriously. Or maybe he liked to talk about his beliefs.

Later that night, when Beckman returned to his apartment, he realized he didn't want Regan to be right about May. Because if Regan *was* right and May *was* behind the killings, there stood a good chance that May was going to get away with it. Which meant that Vernon May was not just some pathetic little hater in Cicero, but a clever and crafty dangerous killer.

And what do you do then? Beckman thought. What do you do if you know there's a neo-Nazi killer out there who's going to go scot-free? Do you wait for him outside his home and put two bullets in his head as he walks to his car? It's what the Israelis did to the people behind the Black September murders. The idea appealed to Beckman in an Old Testament sort of way and he didn't

191

like that it appealed to him. He was a police officer, not a commando, and his duty was to enforce the law . . . He knew that, and yet . . . and yet, couldn't it be argued that killing Vernon May would *save* lives? Would prevent other Jews from being murdered? What was he, after all? A Jew who happened to a cop, or a cop who happened to be a Jew?

He walked up the steps to his apartment, unlocked the door, and let himself in. There was one message on his answering machine.

It was from his mother. She sounded very upset and she asked him to call her back as soon as possible.

Beckman thought of Albert and Marty and Marty's kids. He hoped nothing was wrong.

His mother answered the phone and said, "I called Elyse today."

Oh, shit.

Beckman said, "You did?" Thinking maybe there was a chance he was still in the clear.

"I called her at work. She told me about the divorce."

No chance.

"Ma."

"She didn't tell me you were divorcing or having problems or thinking about divorcing. She said you were divorced."

"Ma —"

"Divorced. Finished."

"Ma. I was gonna tell you."

"When? At dinner the other night? You knew then, didn't you? People don't decide to get divorced and then get divorced in a couple of days, do they?"

"I'm sorry."

Now his mother was crying. It should not have surprised Beckman. He had been dating Elyse since they were in high school. A part of his life for more than twelve years. A part of his mother's too, as his mother saw it.

"Mama, I'm sorry."

"*How can you do this?* You've been together since you were kids. You don't do this."

"Mama. We didn't do it to you. We haven't been happy for a long time."

"Who said you deserve to be happy? You made a commitment to each other. She was part of our family."

Elyse had tolerated Beckman's mother more than she had liked her. Though she was not above forming alliances with his mother when it suited her needs. *Sylvie, tell him to finish law school. Sylvie, do you know David's friend Herbie Edelman has his own practice now and is making ninety thousand*

193

dollars a year? Sylvie, he's got so much potential. Can't you talk to him? And so forth.

Beckman said, "She wasn't . . . she wanted this too. Probably more than I did."

"So you know what she wants?"

"Better than you."

"Don't talk to me like that. I'm your mother."

"Sorry."

"What is it? Huh? She didn't like being married to a policeman?"

"I don't think so, Ma."

"You just had to do it, didn't you?"

"Do what, Ma?"

"You had to have your way. Big, macho policeman busting heads instead of making a decent living. Now you've lost your wife. A good Jewish girl. You happy now?"

Happier, Beckman thought. But he couldn't say that to his mother.

"Mama, it's better this way. Elyse would be happier married to someone else. I probably would too."

"Oh, fine. Everyone gets to be *happy*. I see. That's what it's all about. If it feels good, do it. Your father and I were married twenty-eight years. We never asked to be happy. We stayed together till death did us part."

"That's admirable, Ma."

194

"Don't be smart! We stayed together because that's what decent people do. You don't leave just because you're unhappy!"

Beckman exhaled. "Mama? If Papa hadn't died when he did, wouldn't you have eventually divorced him? If you had the option? If you could have?"

"No!"

Beckman heard the phone slam down. His mother had hung up on him. Beckman didn't blame her.

CHAPTER TWENTY-THREE

In the morning, he thought, well, it's out now.

His mother would tell his brother and the rest of the family and he wouldn't have to. He thought of his sister-in-law, Natalie, and the smug, satisfied smile she would be wearing the next time he saw her. *Elyse finally wised up, huh? You should have seen it coming. I know I did.* Then Beckman thought, man, what is wrong with you? Worrying about the bad opinion of fools. The hell with Natalie. He had put his ex-wife in an awful spot and, worse, he had hurt his mother. Not just by getting divorced and hiding it from her. But mostly by saying those ugly things about his own father. Why had he done that? To let her know she wasn't so goddamn perfect? Christ, it wasn't her fault her husband and his father had been a jerk. Was Sylvie to be blamed for staying with him until he died? What was she to do? He was supposed to take care of her. Why punish the living? Why punish her after she had survived?

Beckman walked across the street to the take-home Plymouth. He started it and put the defroster on full blast.

He would have to call her later. No. He would have to call Elyse first and apologize to her. Take the beating over the phone and then ask Elyse how Sylvie had taken it. Which was chicken shit, of course, but he knew he would do it anyway. Later he would call his mother and apologize to her for the things he had said. And she would say, what things? Pretending the awful marriage to the awful man had never happened along with all the other awful things. *What things?* And Beckman would promise himself not to say it again. Sylvie complained that her sons communicated with each other through her, her burden to bear. But no one was supposed to talk to her about her burdens. Not the real ones.

After letting the car warm, Beckman pulled out into the street. A few moments later, a white Chevy van pulled away from the curb and followed him. Two men were in the van.

Beckman was pouring his morning coffee

when the squad's secretary handed him a message. It was from Mary-Beth Hanley. Beckman returned the call from his desk.

"This is Detective Beckman, returning your call." He grimaced at the sound of his own formality.

Mary-Beth Hanley said, "You sound so serious."

"Oh. Well, you know. It's morning." He didn't know what else to say. He hoped she was calling him to ask to meet her for a drink.

She said, "Well, it is business, I guess. You said to call if I remembered anything else."

"Right. Did you?"

"No. But last night, Richie LaFevers was brought into the emergency room at St. Mary's. I didn't treat him, but I know he's there."

"Really? What happened?"

"Well, I'm sort of bound by a physician-patient confidentiality. Even though it's an ER patient. But . . . I think he was beat up."

"By who?"

"I don't know. I don't think the staff knows. He said he fell, but it doesn't look like he fell."

"I see."

"Anyway, it probably doesn't have any-thing to do with anything. But . . . I thought

I'd tell you."

"He's still there?"

"Yes. Room 515. But you didn't hear it from me."

"Okay."

"Seriously. I could lose my job."

"I didn't hear it from you. Thank you, Ms. Hanley."

"You can call me Mary-Beth."

"Thank you, Mary-Beth."

"Take care."

"You too."

Beckman hung up the phone, clinging to her *take care* and feeling stupid for doing it. He thought of the pretty Catholic nurse with the doctor boyfriend who might be her rich husband someday and thought, *what are you doing to yourself?*

Beckman looked across the desk at Regan.

Regan said, "Got something?"

"Maybe. The nurse I interviewed said Richie LaFevers is in the hospital. She thinks he was beat up."

Regan shrugged.

Beckman said, "I think it's worth looking into."

"Okay," Regan said. "You can handle that on your own, can't you?"

"Yeah. I'll see you later."

■ ■ ■ ■

Beckman had been a cop long enough to know when someone had been the victim of a methodical beating. Richie LaFevers had one eye swollen shut and contusions about his cheek and jaw. His left hand was in a cast. *The Price Is Right* was on television.

He lay in a hospital bed frightened and angry. He told Beckman he wasn't allowed to have visitors and even if he was, he wouldn't want to be visited by *him*.

Beckman said, "Take it easy, Richie. The worst of it's over, isn't it?"

"I don't know what you're talking about."

"Someone beat you up. Why don't you tell me about it?"

"No one beat me up."

"Your hand is broken."

"I told them. I fell."

"Where did you fall?"

"I fell getting out of a cab on State Street."

"And used your hand to break the fall?"

"Yeah."

"But still fell on your face?"

"Yeah."

"That's not what happened, Richie."

"Well that's all you're going to get out of me. So why don't you get out and let me get some rest?"

"Someone did this to you. Why don't you tell me about it? I can help you."

Richie LaFevers snorted.

Beckman said, "You got problems? A gambling debt? The wrong friends? Whatever it is, it can't be that bad. Just tell me about it and you'll feel better."

"My problems are none of your business. And whatever they are, they have nothing to do with your investigation."

"How do you know that?"

Richie pretended to look at the television set. The curtains opening up on a yellow 1979 Monte Carlo.

Beckman said, "How do you know they have nothing to do with my investigation?"

"They don't."

"I have a feeling they do. Richie, I know when a man's in trouble. You're in trouble. Now I can help you if you'll let me."

"You want to help me? Leave."

He saw Mary-Beth Hanley at the administration desk. She was in blue scrubs. She saw him coming and walked toward him. Beckman realized she didn't want him talking to her in front of the other staff.

She said, "Finished?"

"Yeah. Unfortunately."

In a low voice, she said, "Let me walk you out."

She got on the elevator with him and pressed the lobby floor button for him. The doors closed and they were alone. The girl smelled pleasantly of fresh soap and Beckman remembered that nurses were discouraged from wearing strong perfumes.

The girl said, "I'm sorry if it seemed like I wanted to rush you out of here. Like I said, I wasn't supposed to tell you what I knew about him."

"I understand."

"And don't worry, I'm not going to ask you what you talked to him about. I'm not looking for something to gossip about."

"I understand that too."

"Okay."

"And I appreciate you calling me."

"I don't know if it helped you."

"Every little bit helps." He realized he sounded like Regan then. But he more or less believed it now.

A few quiet moments passed and then the Hanley girl said to the elevator door, "Ben and I aren't seeing each other anymore."

She turned to face Beckman when she finished. She was vulnerable then, not trying to be sexy or coy. Apprehensive, but putting it out there.

Beckman said, "Oh. I'm sorry."

The girl was still looking at him.

"Are you?"

Beckman looked at her and said, "No, I'm not. But I don't know . . ."

"What don't you know?"

"I just got divorced. I mean, I *just* got divorced."

"And I just broke up with a guy I was seeing for about a year. But you're divorced now?"

"Yes."

"And you are attracted to me, aren't you? The way you looked at me the other night . . . I'm not reading it wrong, am I?"

"No, you're not."

"Because if I am, I'm going to feel really —"

"You're not. It's just that I'm . . . I don't know."

"If we were to have a cup of coffee," she said, "and talk. That would be okay, wouldn't it?"

"Yes. That would be okay." Beckman found himself looking at the way her hair curled behind her ear. "Better than okay. Tonight maybe?"

"I get off at six."

His heart was still fluttering when he

203

reached the car. Mary-Beth, Mary-Beth. Not Mary or Beth, but Mary-Beth. God, with a name like that, how could she not be Catholic? Call your mother and tell her about *this. Cheer up, Ma, I've got a crush on a Catholic girl. She's good-looking, she's cool, and she doesn't care if I'm not a doctor.* Wait for the sound of his mother's body hitting the floor. What did they call the children of Catholic-Jewish couples? Cashews, that was it. He'd heard that somewhat ugly term from his brother's wife. And now he could practically hear his brother saying, *haven't you done enough to Ma, already?* Beckman saying back, *for chrissakes, we're just having coffee.* Then Beckman was scolding himself, thinking he was a thirty-three-year-old man, he'd fought in Vietnam and was a police officer. Shouldn't the time of worrying about being a family disappointment be behind him?

Beckman got in the Plymouth and started it. He checked the side mirror for traffic before he pulled out. And that was when he saw the white Chevy van parked several car lengths behind him.

He'd seen it before, when he left his apartment. He checked the rearview mirror and got a better look at the two men inside the van. He'd seen one of the men before. It was at Vernon May's headquarters.

Chapter Twenty-Four

The van stayed with him through the next four stoplights, keeping some traffic between them. Beckman slowed to the fifth light as it turned amber, then pressed the accelerator just as it turned red. He pulled into a parking garage two blocks ahead. Stopped inside, reversed, and turned and drove back to the exit. A minute or so later, the Chevy van went by.

Beckman pulled out after it.

When he was behind the van, he radioed dispatch and gave them the tag number. They told him the van was registered to a man named Ernest Wheeler, twenty-seven years of age. Last known residence in Joliet, one arrest for assault and battery, no conviction as his girlfriend refused to press charges. Beckman thanked the dispatcher and pulled the Plymouth up alongside the van.

He hung the flashing red light from the

hook on the ceiling and turned it on. Then he honked the horn to get the driver's attention. The driver looked over to him. Beckman pointed and said in a loud voice to pull over. The driver couldn't hear him but the message was clear.

They made a left turn and parked under the El tracks.

Beckman parked behind them and got out of the car. He had his hand on his .38 as he approached the driver's side. The driver rolled down the window. Up close, Beckman now knew it was one of the guards on Vernon May's porch.

The guy said, "What's the problem?" His voice hard.

"Mr. Wheeler?"

"Yeah. What do you want?"

Beckman opened the door to the van. He didn't see Wheeler's hands on the wheel. He wanted to see his hands.

"Step out." Beckman looked past him to the passenger. It was the blond-haired man who had tried to prevent them from interviewing Regan. "You too," Beckman said.

The blond-haired man came around. They stood facing him, surprised and still uncertain in that moment so this was the time to take control.

Beckman said, "What are you doing following me?"

Wheeler said, "We weren't following you, boy. Seems to me you were following us."

"All right," Beckman said. "Turn around and put your hands on the van. Both of you."

If it had just been the blond-haired man, he would have done it. But the blond-haired man would take his cue from Wheeler. And it was Wheeler who stood his ground, bowed up, and said, "Fuck you, kike. You're all alone now. What are *you* gonna do?"

Beckman kicked him in the kneecap. Wheeler cried out and stumbled forward. Beckman grabbed Wheeler by the hair and kneed him in the face so hard that his head snapped back. His nose was broken on impact. Then Beckman pulled his weapon and pointed it at the blond and told him to grab that van, now. The blond-haired man did.

Beckman checked Wheeler for weapons and found a buck knife in his coat pocket. That was all he found. Then he handcuffed the blond-haired man's hands behind his back. The blond didn't have any weapons. After that, Beckman told him to have a seat on the pavement.

Wheeler lay on street, clutching himself, the blood from his face staining the snow.

Beckman crouched next to him and put the barrel of the .38 in his ear.

Beckman said, "Listen, you cracker piece a shit, I ever catch you hanging around my home again, I'll kill you. You understand me? This kike'll put a bullet in your fucking head and shove that knife up your dead ass."

Lieutenant Greg said, "What I want to know is, why didn't you call for backup before you pulled them over?"

Beckman said, "I didn't think it was necessary."

"You didn't think it was necessary? You checked them for weapons."

"Well . . ."

"If you checked them for weapons, you must have thought they were armed and dangerous."

Regan said, "Greg —"

Greg said, "Am I right?"

Beckman didn't answer him. They were in Lieutenant Greg's office. Greg was pissed off. He hadn't told them that the chief of detectives had leaned on him, but then he probably didn't need to.

Regan said, "Greg. Take it easy, huh."

Greg said, "I am taking it easy. Do you know what internal affairs would do with this? They'll say he didn't call for backup because he wanted to beat the piss out of these guys and he didn't want anyone else to stop him."

Beckman said, "That's not true."

Greg said, "We've got a citizen in the hospital with a busted kneecap and God knows what other injuries. And a witness who says that a police officer assaulted him without provocation. Internal would tear you apart."

Beckman said, "He threatened me. It was self-defense."

Greg said, "Oh, give me a break. Threatened you? He called you a name and you beat him up. You tell me, how does it look?"

Beckman said, "It's not what he said, it was his body language. It's in my report."

"Your report doesn't take care of this. Not nearly."

"I respectfully disagree."

"I see. So if some lowlife calls one of our black officers a nigger, that officer has the right to beat him up?"

Regan said, "Greg, come on. This is Chicago."

Beckman said, "I'm not asking for any favors."

"Shut up, Beckman," Greg said. "No one's going to do you any favors."

Regan said, "Look. There were two of

them. One of them had a knife. David had to control the situation before someone got hurt."

"Someone *did* get hurt. And don't give me any of that 'this is Chicago' shit, Tom. The department is not what it was ten years ago."

Regan said, "Is there a different standard for him? 'Cause I'll tell you right now, I would have done the same thing. And I'd tell IA that too."

Lieutenant Greg glared at Regan for a moment, trying to discern whether or not he was being insubordinate. Greg said, "You mean that?"

"I do."

"Okay," Greg said. "Stand by him if you want. But if May's behind this murder, Detective Beckman just made your job a hell of a lot harder. Now if we get a case against May, he's going to claim that a Jewish cop with a chip on his shoulder wants to frame him. It'll be raised at court and maybe even get the case dismissed."

Greg turned to Beckman and said, "And as for you, you are reminded that you are a police officer, not a vigilante. Leave your personal distaste at home."

Before Beckman could respond, Regan said, "Yeah, we got it, Lieutenant. Come

211

on, David."

"They came to my home," Beckman said.

"David, let's *go.*"

Outside the lieutenant's office, Regan motioned Beckman to follow him. They got on the elevator and went down to the cafeteria. It was the afternoon and the cafeteria was empty. Beckman took a seat. Regan got two coffees from the vending machine and sat down with him.

Beckman said, "Thanks."

"Don't thank me yet," Regan said. "I want to ask you about this, as your partner, and I want you to answer me as a partner: did you injure that guy because you needed to or was it because you were angry?"

"He had a knife."

"Come on, David. I'm not your supervisor. Partners don't lie to each other."

Beckman sighed and said, "Okay. I didn't know he had the knife till after I brought him down. But the thing about wanting to pat them down for weapons, that was legit."

"Yeah. Standard procedure. But is that it? Is that all it was?"

". . . maybe not. I don't know. When I saw them following me, I realized I'd seen the van before. They were parked in front of my apartment this morning. Then I realized they had been following me all day. Maybe before that too. Maybe they were parked outside my apartment with a rifle waiting for me to walk in front of a window."

"They didn't find a rifle in the van."

"But they were following me. Don't you understand? Fucking neo-Nazis were parked outside my *home.*"

"Yeah, I understand. You're a Jew and May sent these guys after you. Maybe to hurt you, maybe just to try to rattle you. Were you scared?"

"Maybe. I don't think I remember being scared. I was fucking enraged though. Yeah, I wanted to hurt them."

"I don't blame you," Regan said. "But if IA gets involved in this, they won't see things that way. What I mean is, they forget that a cop is still a man with human emotions. I look at this and say what you did was human. And justified. Maybe some genetic memory was awakened."

Beckman smiled. Not for the first time he had underestimated the older detective. Beckman said, "Genetic memory? You believe in that?"

"Yeah, I believe in it. How does the sheep-dog know how to herd sheep when he's never been around them? It's there, deep inside. Part of evolution. We remember things that happened to our . . . species, if you will, before we were born. There's no Third Reich in present-day Chicago, David. But they were sent to threaten you and maybe some part of you remembered a time when they hunted your kind. Am I right?"

"My kind."

"You know what I meant, David. I'm on your side."

"Yeah, I know that. And maybe there's something in what you say. But I'm not sorry I did it. Not by a damn sight."

"Nor should you be. But if IA questions you about it, you don't tell them common sense truth, okay? You don't for one minute let on how much you enjoyed bloodying that guy's face. You don't tell them that this stupid Jew hating, eighty IQ, piece of shit will think twice about threatening you again after what you did to him. Because those guys, they'll just use it against you. What you tell them is you saw the knife in his belt and you saw him reach for it. *Before* you kicked him in the knee and busted his face open."

"Why should I have to lie to anyone about it?"

"Because you're a good detective and you need to remain in homicide. You play your cards right, you might be a lieutenant someday. Christ, I wouldn't be surprised if you made chief of detectives. But if you want to stay in homicide for the time being, you're going to have to learn how to protect yourself. I don't mean physically because you already know how to do that. I mean administratively. You *do not* want to become one of those cops who needs the department more than it needs him."

"I already know how it works."

"No, I don't think you do. You're not working vice anymore, where they more or less let you alone. You're in homicide. It's a good job. You get to use your head and there's good overtime. Dozens of cops want to be where you're at."

"You've told me that more than once."

"Because I want you to remember it. And this time I'm telling you for your own good."

"So now you want to help me." Beckman's tone was cynical and not entirely grateful.

"I do, actually. You trying to talk me out of it?"

"No."

"Yeah, I'm trying to help you. And if you're smart, you'll listen to what I'm saying." Regan sipped his coffee and said, "I know what you're thinking now."

"What am I thinking?"

"You're thinking, they wouldn't do this to

215

me if I weren't Jewish. Jews aren't supposed to hit back. Right?"

"I didn't say that."

"You're thinking it though. The brass may want to punish you because you didn't stay in character."

"All right. Maybe do I think that. Are you saying I'm paranoid?"

"No, I'm saying you might be right. Then again, you might be wrong. Yeah, it's possible there are people at the department who think a Jew shouldn't defend himself. That he should just take shit no Irish cop would ever take."

"So then I'm not paranoid."

"Every cop is paranoid. It's a hazard of the profession. Cops are much more paranoid than any Jewish guy."

"Thanks."

"I don't know. Maybe even Greg thinks, on some level, you shouldn't hit back. And Greg's not a bad guy."

"Greg thinks I should have allowed those guys to stalk me like prey?"

"He doesn't think that consciously. But unconsciously, who knows? Greg's no Jew hater. I've known him for years and I've never heard him say anything awful. But cops are tribal and ninety-five percent of them have grown up with certain prejudices.

What's a Jew doing at the police department? Why isn't he out practicing law or running a business? Why's he have to take my place at homicide? They may not say it, but they'll think it."

"I didn't get that feeling at vice."

"I keep telling you, you're not at vice anymore. You no longer have the convenience of hiding behind a beard and dirty clothes. So when you're asked, you tell them that Wheeler was going for his knife. Got it?"

"Yeah, I got it."

CHAPTER TWENTY-FIVE

Renee Aiken grew up in McKinley Park, a working-class neighborhood in the southwest part of the city. She was aware at a young age that she was beautiful and she soon regarded that beauty as a passport to a better life. She left home when she was seventeen and took a job as a topless showgirl at a mob-owned cabaret club. In time she became acquainted with Richie LaFevers. Richie let her move in with him. They had kissed a few times, but it was clear from the beginning that his interest in her was not sexual. Richie LaFevers didn't have much interest in penetrating any woman. But he liked being around beautiful, troublesome girls like Renee. Richie liked to watch. In his apartment, he had drilled holes into one of the bedrooms so that he could peek inside and see Renee having sex with other men. Sometimes threesies. Renee knew about it and didn't mind.

Richie got a kick out of introducing Renee to rich, powerful, and sometimes dangerous men. Renee had met Peter Mandel through Richie. She had also met Leon Murray through Richie. But Richie had not tried to pimp Renee to Leon. Even Richie had limits.

On this night, Renee was scheduled to go out with a real-estate developer who was about sixty-two. Next week she would go to Jamaica with him.

Renee was wearing a red cocktail dress when she answered the door.

Peter Mandel stood there, holding his hat.

"Darling!" Renee said, and kissed him on the cheek.

Mandel took the greeting for what it was. He had practically forgotten their ugly breakup scene on Rush Street a year ago. Her throwing the keys to the Trans-Am he had bought her at his feet. A crowd of people laughing as Mandel said, "And don't bother coming back!" Mandel did not begrudge beautiful girls for such things.

Now Renee was acting gracious, asking him if he'd like a cup of tea. She had at least remembered that he rarely drank alcohol.

"No thank you, my dear. I don't think I can stay long."

"Ohhhh. Well, come in for a minute."

219

They sat in the living room. Mandel set his hat on his knee.

"It looks like you have a date tonight."

"Yes. Phil Berry. He goes on and on about business and horses, but he is sweet."

"Is he going to buy you one? A horse, that is."

"God, I hope not. He wants me to come work for him, though."

Mandel said, "And?"

"I told him I'd think about it. I'm far too young to work, don't you think?"

"I agree. Renee. What did you want to see me about?"

"Well, you heard about Richard, didn't you?"

"No. What's the matter?"

"He's in the hospital."

"Oh, no. What happened?"

"What happened is he got beat up. Your friend Leon did it."

Mandel raised a hand. "Renee. Don't."

"He did, Peter. Richie told me."

"Did you see it happen?"

"No. But Richie wouldn't lie about that."

"If you didn't see it happen, it's none of your concern. Stay out of it, Renee. I'm telling you as a friend."

"Look, Peter. I'm not asking you to get Leon in trouble. I'm not going to mess with him. What I mean is, I'm not going to threaten him."

"You couldn't if you wanted."

"I know that. All I'm asking you to do is talk to him. Tell him that Richie is going to pay."

Mandel knew what it was without asking. Richie owned Leon money for cocaine.

Leon liked money. But he once told Mandel that he had never meant to get in the coke-dealing business. Leon pimped women, but he soon found out that one trade led to another. Even Mandel, who could be self-deceptively romantic at times, knew that most if not all whores powdered their noses. Leon told Mandel, "You get rid of whores by getting rid of coke."

Richie, who was a different kind of pimp, liked to have parties. Parties where there were bowlfuls of coke. Richie knew cocaine had become the coin of the realm.

Mandel said, "How much does he owe him?"

"Oh, I'm not sure. Richie says it's only about twenty thousand. Which means it's probably about fifty."

"He shouldn't have gone to Leon."

"You're one to talk. You're more drawn to thugs than Richie ever was."

"Leon's a friend. I don't buy drugs from him."

"Well, be that as it may, Richie says that if he doesn't pay, Leon's going to kill him. You've got to do something."

"What can I do?"

"Leon listens to you."

"I hardly know the man."

"Peter, come on. You know I know better than that."

"It's not my problem."

"Peter, please. I'm asking you as a friend."

She gave him what she would consider her softest expression. Cunning and calculating, and Mandel knew it. But he never could resist acting the part of the benevolent despot.

Mandel said, "Is he going to pay his debt?"

"He will. He makes good money."

"When?"

"A couple of months?"

"How about ten thousand dollars in one month? A good-faith down payment."

"I think so."

"Tell Richard it will have to be more solid than I think so."

"I will."

"Okay. I'll talk to Leon, then. But I can't promise anything."

"Thank you, Peter."

"Oh, but I'm not finished. I want something from you too."

Renee made a face.

"No, not that," Mandel said. "It's about Sally. I don't want you calling her anymore. I don't want you hanging around with her anymore."

Renee smiled again. "Okay, Daddy. I won't call her anymore. But tell her to quit calling me."

Mandel didn't answer that. He didn't know that Sally had been calling Renee. He would discuss that with Sally tonight.

Then Renee said, "By the way, you might tell Leon that there was a cop here the other night."

"Really? You're not in trouble with the law, are you?"

"No. He was talking with Richie."

"About drugs?"

"No. He wasn't a narc. He was a detective. A homicide detective. He was investigating those murders at the subway stop."

Mandel shifted his hat in his hands. "Why would he want to talk to Richie?"

"Richie knew one of the victims. Helen Futterer. You know her?"

"No. Detectives came here?"

"Just one. His name was Beckersomething. Beckman. That was it."

Mandel remembered the name from the newspaper. There was no picture to accompany the name. Somehow he would have felt better if he knew what the man looked like.

"What did he want?"

"Fuck, I don't know. Wanted to know if Richie knew anyone who would want to hurt Helen. Richie said he didn't." Renee smiled. "He was nervous. You know, I think he'd snorted a line right before the detective knocked on the door. The detective, I don't think he was fooled."

"What do you mean?"

"I mean, I think he knew Richie was a cokehead. But he didn't care."

"Why would he not care? He was a cop, wasn't he?"

"He's looking for a murderer, not users."

"You thought the detective was smart?"

"I don't know. Maybe. He was cute. You know, one of those good-looking, dark-haired Jewish guys."

"He was Jewish?"

"I thought he was." Renee smiled again. "What's the matter with you? Are you jealous?"

"A little."

"No, you're not. Besides, I thought you loved gossip."

"Well, you know. I have a lot on my mind."

"Yeah? You falling in love with Sally?"

Now Mandel smiled. "You know me. I fall in love with all of them."

At the door, Renee kissed him on the cheek.

Driving down Michigan Avenue, Mandel considered the name. Beckman. Beckman and Renee thought he was Jewish. A good-looking dark-haired Jewish boy as Mandel had once been. His little brother, Sam, had also been dark haired. Sam was seventeen when the Germans invaded.

Peter Mandel had just entered dental school when his world was shattered. He went from feeling optimistic and assured about his future to losing everything. The Polish aristocracy had tried to appease Hitler by keeping silent when Czechoslovakia was swallowed up. But it did them no good and on the first day of September, 1939, the German tanks rolled into Poland. The Germans came in from the west and the Russians came from the east. Three million Polish Jews were sent to German concentration camps, among them Peter's parents. Peter would not know until after the war that twenty-nine out of every thirty Polish Jews had been exterminated. Years

later, he would still not be able to compre-
hend it. The nightmares that made him cry
out in his sleep were always about the day
the Germans came and arrested his parents.

The only reason Peter and Sam were not
killed along with the others was that they
were both strong and athletic. Conse-
quently, the Germans put them to work,
building a highway to the Russian border.
The two boys of an affluent Polish family
had become slaves of the Reich.

It was near the Russian border that the
brothers made their escape. Days later, they
had misgivings. Starvation and lack of
shelter put them nearer to death than they
had been when working for the Germans.
They were almost relieved when they were
captured by Russian soldiers.

But whatever relief they felt was extinguished when the Russians separated them.
Sam was put on one truck and Peter was
put on another. And no amount of crying
or screaming could stop the Russians from
doing it.

Peter Mandel had never been an intro-
spective man. Before the invasion, he had
been happy-go-lucky. Athletic and fun loving. After the nightmare was over, contem-
plation was simply too painful. Even so, he
believed that when the Russians took Sam

away, his soul died. That he was a survivor, but no longer human. He was not to feel that pain again until he discovered what Nathan Wald had done to him.

The Russians sent Peter to a labor camp in the Arctic Circle. There, he slaved for Stalin instead of Hitler, bringing down trees and dragging them to the river's edge. There were no fences at this prison because to escape was to freeze to death. There was no food or shelter for hundreds of miles. Thousands of Polish prisoners died anyway. That part of the earth was never meant to support life. It was there that Mandel saw men kill each other over a scrap of bread or for rags adequate enough to wrap their feet in. It was there that Mandel was beaten so savagely and regularly that it made him sterile. It was there that Mandel learned how expendable life is and that moralizing was a luxury for those who could afford it.

Mandel had a talent for surviving. But even he knew he would have died in that Russian camp if not for Adolf Hitler. That was the irony. Hitler saved his life.

Hitler saved Mandel's life by declaring war on the Soviet Union. The German invasion of the Soviet Union changed alliances. Just like that, the Russians were on the side of the Americans and the British instead of the Germans. Pursuant to an agreement between the exiled Polish government and the Soviets, Mandel and many other Poles were released from the prison camp and sent to the Polish 2nd Corps. By 1942, he was fighting alongside the British in the Middle East.

Mandel believed at that time that he was a Pole first and a Jew second. He also believed that being a soldier in the Polish 2nd Corps would gain him respect. He was wrong on both counts. Most of the officers in the Polish Army thought that the Jews were cowards and not capable of being good soldiers. Mandel and the other Jewish survivors were constantly berated in front of the other men. Few of the Polish officers could believe that any of the Jews *wanted* to fight. In a way, this rejection and scorn was more painful to Mandel than the physical hardships he had endured as a captive slave. The Germans and the Russians had been his declared enemies. But the Poles had been his friends and neighbors. He could not believe that his own countrymen held him in such low regard. Never did he hear from the Poles any expression of sorrow for the Jews. Forgotten was any contribution they had made to Poland's arts or commerce or way of life. Indeed, some of the

Poles *blamed* the Jews for what the Germans did to Poland. As if they had brought it on.

Mandel saw it, rightly, as a betrayal. And the experience left him with a distrust for all humanity that, despite his seemingly friendly disposition, he never would shake. Outwardly, he was warm and quick with a joke. Inwardly, he seethed with resentment and humiliation.

When the war was over, Lvov was swallowed up by the Soviets. It was no longer part of Poland. Mandel was left with no country, no family, no ability to father a child, and no friends. At the age of twenty-six, he was balding and ugly and looked forty.

Often, after being subjected to insults from the Poles, Mandel would tell himself that he would go to Israel after the war. A homeland where he would always be welcome. But when the time came, he rejected Israel. If asked why he didn't repatriate to Israel, he would probably not be able to explain it. Perhaps it was because he had grown up in a nonorthodox home where neither religious faith nor Jewish identity had been stressed. Or maybe it was because he had come from an affluent family. Or it may have been the fact that, on some level and in spite of all that had happened, he was a bit of a snob who still liked to think of himself as a Pole who happened to be Jewish.

In any event, he did not go and in 1947, he found himself in Chicago with about two-hundred dollars sewn into his clothes. He worked, he saved, he built, he spent, and he pursued the good life. Women, good food, clothes, cars. He survived.

He never married. In part, because he knew he would never want to limit himself to one woman. In part, because he knew he never would be able to produce children.

Now he thought about the Jewish detective who had questioned Richie and Renee. The detective didn't seem to have gotten anywhere. Asking if some girl named Helen that Richie knew had had any enemies. The detective was way off the path. That being the case, Mandel thought, why was he worried about it? Was it because the detective had questioned someone that he — Mandel — knew? Or was it because the detective was a Jew?

For some reason, the detective being a Jew nagged at Mandel. Mandel had ordered the death of a Jew and now he was being hunted by a Jewish cop. Not in Israel, but in Cook County, Illinois, where Jewish cops could likely be counted on two hands. What were the odds of that? Mandel was not a religious man, but he did have a vague belief in gut instinct or what the Indians called bad medicine. He felt no guilt about Wald's murder. Yet he was troubled by the fact that a Jew was now pursuing him. A Jew who, based on Renee's description, bore a physical similarity to Mandel as a young man. And maybe might still look like had he not been deformed by starvation and horror.

Chapter Twenty-Six

Mary-Beth said, "It *is* private, yes."

"I know that," Beckman said. "We can leave it alone."

"It's not that I mind telling you," she said. "It's just that . . . I'm uncomfortable sharing too much with you this early. You tell people a lot about yourself and then later you realize you may not hit it off and that you'll always be strangers. And then you've given something away. You know what I mean?"

"Yeah, I know that feeling," Beckman said. "But it's not like we're at a singles bar."

"No, it's not. And I suppose you should know why it ended." Mary-Beth Hanley smiled. "I suppose it does have something to do with you."

They were sitting at a diner near Milwaukee Avenue and West North. Trains rattled by every few minutes. Beckman had finished his corned beef sandwich, not realizing how hungry he had been.

He was glad he was here with the girl and not at a dimly lit bar where he wouldn't be able to see her expressions and hear what she was saying.

Beckman said, "You sure?" He had trouble believing she would dump a medical resident after meeting him only once.

"Well," Mary-Beth said. "I don't mean you, exactly. A couple of days ago, we had a patient at the hospital fall off a bed and break her arm. And it was Ben's fault. Not that that was so terrible. Things like that happen all the time, unfortunately. She was strapped into her bed and Ben unstrapped her to give her a shot. And then he got distracted by something and he just forgot to strap her back up. She was very, very drunk and very big. Ben just forgot. But when he was questioned about it, he blamed the nursing staff for it."

"You?"

"No, not me. He didn't blame me. It wasn't my floor. The point was, he wouldn't take the heat for it. This happened before you came to my apartment. But I didn't find out about it until after. What I mean is, I didn't find out Ben had dodged the blame for it until later. Anyway, I confronted him about it. Not at work, but outside of work.

And he more or less admitted he'd screwed up. But he didn't see anything wrong with putting it on the nursing staff. He said it had nothing to do with me. I told him it had everything to do with me. Anytime a physician blames a nurse for something he did wrong, it affects all of us. He didn't get that."

"I see."

"Well, anyway, it started me thinking about us. I mean, me and him. He's not a bad guy, but he really didn't see anything wrong with what he'd done. And I realized that this is who he was. He was becoming or had become your typical young doctor, arrogant and self-assured about everything. And I wondered if we really had any future together."

"Did you think you did before? Have a future, I mean."

"I don't know." She hesitated, touching her coffee cup. "I don't know. Maybe. I don't know if I was ever doctor's wife material." She smiled. "They generally prefer prettier women."

"You're very pretty."

"Thank you. I'll choose to believe that."

"I mean it."

She smiled and Beckman wondered if she was actually blushing. She said, "I'm not showgirl pretty. They like that. You know, when I was in college, I started out premed. I had the grades. Do you know I had the second highest score on my organic chemistry final?"

"Really?"

"Yes." She turned her head in a sort of self-mocking haughty gesture. "I was going to go to medical school myself. But around my junior year, I realized I didn't really want it. It was a lot of work to become a doctor and, well, I just didn't really want it that much."

"You can still go to medical school, can't you?"

"Yeah. If I change my mind. Anyway, my junior year I switched my major to nursing. And I don't regret that."

"Even with this incident with your boyfriend?"

"He's not my boyfriend anymore. But . . . no, no regrets. I like being a nurse. I like the work. But I don't like people assuming I'm dumb. Or that they can blame me for their mistakes just because I'm not an M.D."

"But Ben didn't blame you for his mistake."

"He would have, though. If he didn't know me."

"Maybe."

"No, no maybe. He would have. You know, I told a girlfriend about it and she told me to forget about it and not screw up a good thing. And then I realized my girlfriend thought I was hoping to marry Ben."

"And you were insulted by this?"

"Of course! I didn't not become a doctor just so I could marry one. Is that what you think too?"

"No. I don't know you well enough to think that."

"Whether you know me or not, I would hope you wouldn't think that."

"Okay. I don't think that."

"Now you're just trying to be nice."

"I don't. Really."

"Okay. I believe you. You know, the girls who *do* do that, who set their sights on that, they don't realize it's work too."

"I don't understand."

"Being the wife of a rich doctor. The wife of any rich man. They marry for money, but you don't actually *get* the money. Yeah, you get the nice things. The clothes, the Cadillac, the nice house in Lake Forest, kids in private schools, all that. But it's not really yours. You're just sort of renting it. And they always have to keep up, always have to compete with other doctors' wives. It's not going to make you happy."

"You're very perceptive."

"Oh, not really. I've seen it up close."

"What do you mean?"

She sighed. Then said, "My father's a doctor."

"Oh . . . And your mother . . . ?"

"Is someone I don't want to be."

"Oh."

"Yeah. Oh. Do you think I'm awful?"

"No. Why would I?"

"Talking about my own mother that way. It's not very respectful."

"No, I don't think badly of you. I understand. Probably better than you know."

"Sorry," she said. "I think I've said too much. How about you? You have parents?"

"Yeah. My mother. My father died a few years ago. My mother's remarried. She's happy."

"Well, that's good."

"Yeah, Albert's a good man." He seemed to want to persuade himself. "My mother deserves a good man."

"Is something wrong?"

"Oh. Well, sort of. I said something unkind to my mother last night."

Mary-Beth said, "Why?" She didn't ask what he'd said.

"I was upset. She called because she had

found out I was divorced. I hadn't told her. I know . . . the divorce wasn't finalized until a couple of days ago. But I hadn't told her it was coming. I hadn't even told her Elyse and I were having problems. We'd been having problems for years. I thought my mother could see that. I guess maybe she didn't. Elyse and I should have probably split up two years ago, but we were both afraid of letting our parents down. The Jews can be . . . well, I'm not going to use the word 'touchy,' but they can be hard on their own when they split up with a Jewish spouse. In a sense, we're one big extended family. And my mother thinks I'm self-hating or something."

"Do you think you are?"

"What?"

"Self-hating."

"Oh," Beckman laughed. "We all are to some degree. As a friend of mine used to say in college, 'Can you blame us?' I've always thought that anyone who says they've never had an anti-Semitic thought might just as well say they've never had a cold. And that includes us. Anyway, I guess I sort of blamed my mother, unfairly, for staying with Elyse as long as I did. But that was wrong. It wasn't my mother's fault. It's my fault for marrying too young. Ultimately, we're responsible for our actions, aren't we?"

"I think so. Did you think that before you became a policeman?"

"I think I did. Anyway, what I said to my mother was something about my father. Her husband. I . . . criticized her for staying with him as long as she did. But it wasn't fair. She didn't really have any choice."

"What, you didn't like your father?"

"He wasn't easy to like. He was selfish, bitter, and kind of mean. He was never a huge success and I think he felt he should have been. He chased a lot of women and he didn't really care how much it hurt my mother. Or us. So, no, I didn't really like him. And when he died, I was shamefully relieved."

"Did he abuse you?"

"No, not physically. He would insult us. I think he envied us in a way, resented us."

"Why?"

"I don't know. Maybe because he was afraid we would succeed where he had failed. I don't think being a father much appealed to him."

"How did he die?"

"A car wreck. He was hit by an eighteen wheeler on the Dan Ryan. It was the truck driver's fault."

"Does your mother miss him?"

"Oh, not remotely. I think my brother mourned his passing. But my brother's a very dutiful type."

"And you?"

Beckman didn't answer her.

"Thank you for driving me home," Mary-Beth said. "I've never been in a police car before."

"I washed the vomit out of the back just for you."

"Yeah, it is a little utilitarian. You must have done a good job cleaning though. I don't smell anything. But, wait, there would only be vomit in a patrol car, right? One with lights on top."

"Yes."

"You did that already, right?"

"Yes, I've done years in patrol. I may go back to patrol if things don't go well."

"What do you mean?"

"Nothing."

"You said you worked in vice for a while?"

"Yes."

"What was that like?"

"It was fun for a while. Got to drive a nicer car, that's for sure."

"Did you arrest prostitutes?"

Beckman laughed. "What are you asking

me that for?"

"I don't know. I'm just curious."

"I arrested a few. That wasn't something I liked doing, though."

"Why not?"

"Because — wait — you're not asking me if I slept with any, are you?"

"No. Well, maybe a little."

"Well, not that I feel I have to tell you everything, but no I didn't."

"Okay."

"We see them all the time in vice. Movies, television, they usually make them look a lot cheerier and cleaner than they are in real life. Usually, they're badly abused people. Young, battered looking, and quiet. Most of them are quiet."

"Aren't a lot of them addicted to drugs?"

"Most. And once they're hooked, they'll do anything to get a fix. So it's not exactly flattering to be approached by one. Odds are, you're one of twenty that day. They're very sad and exploited people."

"But didn't they choose that?"

"No. I don't see it that way. Girls from healthy, stable, loving families don't become prostitutes. They're broken, not bad."

"You sound like a liberal."

Beckman turned to look at her smiling in the dark. Teasing him now.

He said, "Do I? Most cops in vice felt the same way I do. They'd have a coronary if anyone called them a liberal."

"You think Carter will get re-elected?"

"I haven't the slightest idea."

"Have you heard that Steve Martin joke? He says Ronald Reagan's going to bring this country back to what it once was: a large mass of ice."

"That's pretty funny."

"I thought it was. But . . . I don't really follow politics that much either. My father does. Like most doctors, he thinks anyone to the left of Goldwater is a communist and is going to socialize medicine, whatever that means. Ben's starting to say the same things my father does." She turned to Beckman. "I'm sorry. I'm not going to talk about Ben."

"It's okay."

"I wasn't in love with him, you know."

"You don't have to tell me that."

"Yes, I do."

Beckman was uncomfortable then. Because she had put it out there. He was not used to women like this. Women telling him their real feelings and him having to decide what he should do with them. With Elyse, conversation had always been difficult. A series of avoiding subjects that could start fights. But Mary-Beth Hanley was not a fight starter. He wondered what he should say now to the girl who had just told him she was not in love with the doctor who probably reminded her of her father. He could avoid it by going back to politics, of course, though that would be cowardly.

He said, "Yeah, uh, most of the cops I know are going to vote for Reagan. I've told a couple of them that Reagan would probably outlaw police unions. But they don't seem to care."

She smiled at him then, seeing that he was nervous and wanting to change the subject.

She said, "How about you?"

"Well, I haven't decided who I'm going vote —"

"No, I don't mean that. I mean, has your work changed the way you think about politics? Or life?"

"I don't know. Maybe."

"Well, you expressed some sympathy for prostitutes. Did you feel that way before you became a cop?"

"No. I guess I didn't think about it much. Regarding the prostitutes, the way I feel is the way I think I have to feel."

"I don't understand. You *have* to feel that way?"

"Yes. Because I can't . . . you can't let yourself think that it's all dirty. That it's all

243

shit. If you start thinking all the people you meet on the job are filthy and bad inside, then after a while you starting asking yourself if you're filthy and bad inside too. If all humanity is that way. And you can't live like that. Every cop has to guard against it."

"With some forgiveness and understanding?"

"Yeah. I guess."

"Do you pray?"

"No. Do you?"

"Sometimes. Working in medicine makes people religious. I'm not sure why. But most doctors and nurses I know are religious. And most lawyers I know aren't."

They drove in silence for a while. A light snow descended on the streets and Beckman set the wipers on intermittent.

Mary-Beth Hanley said, "I guess we're a little different, aren't we?"

"Not so much," Beckman said. "Hanley. Is that an Irish name?"

"Yes," she said. "What are you smiling at?"

"Nothing," Beckman said, but he was thinking about what Regan had told him the other day at the pub. Every cop becomes Irish sooner or later.

Beckman said, "I'd like to see you again."

"I'd like that too."

CHAPTER TWENTY-SEVEN

Mandel said, "Have I ever told you what to do?"

Leon said, "No, but —"

"I haven't, have I?"

"No. But you interfering."

They were sitting in the back room of one of Leon's clubs. A mid-level house, catering to up-and-coming hoods and wannabe executives. Leon's ladies were in the front room: three spade hookers and one Vietnamese girl who affected broken English, all of them about two notches below prime. Business was slow so they sat and smoked and watched *General Hospital* on television.

Mandel said, "When have I ever interfered in your business?"

Leon said, "You doing it now."

"I'm asking you a favor. That's all. You don't want to do it, there won't be any hard feelings."

Leon Murray considered Mandel. Leon

had grown up hating white people. When he became something of a success in crime, he dealt with Italian mobsters and he didn't much like them either. The wops seemed to hate the blacks the most, maybe because deep down they feared they were related to them. But Leon had always like Peter Mandel. Mandel spoke to him right and true. Mandel never talked down to him.

Another thing: Mandel never seemed to be afraid of him. And that was a strange phenomenon, an old white, flabby dude not being afraid of him. Leon was no stranger to suffering, but he sensed that Mandel had gone through some really bad shit at one time and now wasn't really afraid of anything. Like there was nothing more that could be done to him that hadn't already been done.

Leon said, "I know why you're here."

"Of course you know. I told you."

"No, you didn't tell me who sent you. It was that bitch Renee, wasn't it?"

"She has nothing to do with this."

Leon shook his head, his sympathy genuine. "Peter, what you want to get mixed up with that girl for? She ain't worth your time."

Mandel smiled. "Now you're interfering in my business."

"Look, the man owes me money. Man's got to pay. He's a big boy."

"Richie's a boy, all right. You're right about that."

"It's his problem."

"I know." Mandel sat back and relaxed. "Okay, I'm not going to lie to you. He didn't send me here. And neither did she. But, yes, she did ask me to help him out."

"Okay, then." Leon liked that Peter usually told him the truth. "He say he got the ten thousand?"

"No. I'm going to talk to him about that."

"Well, I'm going to tell you right now, I'm not taking the money from you. It's got to come from him."

"Point of pride, Leon? Haven't we always agreed never to let pride get in the way of a good deal?"

"That's your philosophy, man, not mine. And it ain't pride. It's business. Richie lets you pay his debt, even part of it, he's going to run at the mouth and let people know he stiffed me. He do that and I *have* to put him down. Do you see that?"

"Yes, I understand that completely."

"All right," Leon said. "I'll give him some time. A little. But he's going to pay the debt in full, not partial."

"He will. If he doesn't, you do whatever

you have to."

"Okay. And you can say you did what you could to help."

Leon shook his head again. "You know you just about the smartest man I ever met. But when it come to the fuzzies, you just don't want to do any thinking." Leon smiled to let him know he was being friendly. "Take my advice and forget about that girl."

Mandel smiled back, but didn't reply. On his way out, he gave friendly goodbyes to all the whores.

CHAPTER TWENTY-EIGHT

Regan said, "It's good news."

Beckman said, "Yeah, I guess it is."

Beckman said that, but he wasn't sure. Regan could see that he wasn't sure and he frowned. He was disappointed.

They were at their desks. Regan was preparing a warrant to search the premises of Ernest Wheeler, the neo-Nazi Beckman had put in the hospital. Regan's sleeves were rolled up because he found it easier to type that way.

Regan said, "He lives with his mother in Melrose Park. What we're going to do is wait for him to leave, then search the premises. Law says he doesn't have to be there when we search."

"I know that," Beckman said.

"Figured it be better to do it while the man is gone to one of his Nazi meetings. Fella like that surely has an arsenal on the promises. No point in being shot at."

"I agree. But . . . you think you can get a judge to sign it? I mean, we really don't have anything on him."

"He was following you, wasn't he? And something else: the witnesses say they saw Vernon May in Wisconsin the night of the murder. But no one said they saw Mr. Wheeler."

"Yeah, it's something," Beckman said.

"You disagree?"

"No, I don't disagree."

"You don't feel strongly about it."

"No. It's not that. It's just that I don't think Vernon May's that dumb."

"A couple of days ago you said he was dumb. That we — that I gave him too much credit."

"I know I said that. But . . . I don't think May would send Wheeler to kill Wald and then send Wheeler to follow me. It's just too risky. Why put Wheeler out in the open like that?"

"Maybe he sent Wheeler to kill you too."

"We don't have any proof of that."

"Proof? We're just getting a search warrant."

"There were no guns in the van."

"Did it ever occur to you that he was marking you? Tracing your movements, planning an assassination?"

"Maybe it did then. Maybe. But now . . . I don't know."

Regan said, "I don't understand you. In any event, it's a break and we're going to exploit it."

Regan asked him to hang around the station while he ran the warrant to the judge's chambers. Regan said the plan was to catch the judge right before he went to lunch, catch him on the run. He said he needed Beckman to stay here and man the phones in case any of the Wisconsin police officers called about Wheeler. Beckman didn't buy that. He suspected Regan didn't want him along because he was bad luck or something. All because Beckman had trouble believing that Ernest Wheeler had been the subway killer.

Beckman read a story once about an American soldier who was captured and held prisoner by the Japanese during the war. A big Japanese guard had given the soldier daily beatings with a golf club. The Japanese would say, "You still alive?" before each beating. He was enjoying himself. Then the war ended and the American army brought the American soldier into an office where the Japanese guard was held. The Americans handed the American soldier the golf club and said, "Here you go." For a moment, the American soldier didn't understand. They had to tell him it was opportunity to exact vengeance. He said he wasn't interested. The American officer who had handed him the golf club was disgusted.

Beckman understood though. Once he had put Wheeler on the ground and his fear had abated, he had no interest in Wheeler. No interest in hurting him anymore. To a degree, he didn't even see Wheeler anymore. He was just another thug with a knife.

Maybe Regan's instincts were right and Beckman's were wrong. Maybe Wheeler was the shooter. But Beckman had trouble seeing it. It just didn't make sense for Vernon May to have the killer of Nathan Wald follow the detective who was investigating that murder. May couldn't be that dumb.

So now he was back to his John Doe. Because Regan thought he was too thick to see what was at the end of his nose.

Beckman stayed at his desk. No one called from Wisconsin. But a vice cop named Ray Wilson called and told him he might have something for him if he wanted to come down to his office and talk to him about it. Better yet, they could meet outside county jail because that was where the witness was.

■ ■ ■ ■

Beckman felt a stab of envy when he first saw Ray Wilson outside the massive gray structure that was the Cook County Department of Corrections. Ray Wilson was in a leather jacket and a yellow t-shirt; his hair was down to his shoulders and he had about three weeks of growth on his face. He was standing next to a Lincoln Continental Mark V with baby-blue paint and a vinyl top. Ray Wilson was still in "the Life."

Ray winced at the sight of Beckman's shitty police issue Plymouth and at his sport coat, knit tie, and short hair.

Ray Wilson scrunched up his face like Marlon Brando, close to tears as he said, "Look how they massacred my boy."

Beckman sniffed the air and said, "What's that — Jesus, man, when's the last time you bathed?"

"Still wishing you were me, huh?" Ray said. "Christ, I saw you crossing the street and thought you were going to try to sell me life insurance."

"Onward and upward," Beckman said.

Ray said, "Sorry I can't shake hands."

Beckman saw then that his hand was in a cast. "What happened?"

"Let's get inside and have some coffee. I'll tell you about Scotty Maine."

Ray still chain-smoked while he talked about his work and he gulped cups of coffee down like lemonade. And Beckman thought, he's still the same. Then he wondered why he should feel different if Ray was still the same. If he *was* different now that he was in homicide, he hoped that Ray wouldn't notice it.

Ray told him how the vice squad came across Scotty Maine. And Beckman remembered that was part of being in vice too. How talking about the job after it was done was part of it. A need to let the steam escape. But also a chance to re-experience the rush that came with the Life.

Ray said, "You remember Gene Dennison?"

"The police impersonator?"

"Yeah."

"What about him?"

"We finally popped him."

"Arrested him?"

"Yeah. And this time it's going to fucking stick." Ray grinned. Again, Beckman felt the stab of envy.

Beckman said, "You were in on the bust?"

"Yep."

"Shit," Beckman said. "I wish I could have been."

"Well, you know, they need your talents over at, ah, where is it they put you?"

"Fuck you. Tell me about it."

Ray told him. Gene Dennison ran a gang in West Chicago that made good money scamming old homosexuals with money. They would send a young chicken to seduce the rich queer and then bust in and make a false arrest on sodomy charges. Then they would offer to let the mark buy his way out of it. Gene Dennison had once taken fifty thousand dollars off a retired Navy admiral.

What helped Gene Dennison in his work was that he *looked* like a cop. Much more so than Ray Wilson or Beckman. He had the square face and the bull shoulders and the weary, seen-it-all expression. He was an expert forger and his fabricated search warrants were barely distinguishable from the real article.

Scotty Maine was one of his recent chickens. Scotty was nineteen, but could pass for fourteen. Perfect bait for old men who liked young boys. But Scotty and Gene had gotten into an argument about something and Gene had beaten him up. That was when Scotty went to Chicago vice and offered to help them bring Gene Dennison down.

Ray said, "Naturally, we were suspicious. We've been onto Scotty and Gene for some time. But we never had any witnesses who were willing to testify against them. Which is understandable. But Scotty would fuck us over same as he would Gene. But . . . we just couldn't pass it up."

"So you set up a sting," Beckman said.

"Yeah. Morty was the guy who pretended to be the mark."

"Morty?" Beckman laughed, wishing again that he could have been there.

"Yeah. We put this gray wig on him and this flat cap and glasses. And, you know, we had to make him look like he was rich otherwise Gene wouldn't have gone for it. We got him a limo. And we got him these two hundred dollar shoes — Gene always looks at the shoes — and we had him pose as some fag producer from Hollywood. We booked three rooms at the hotel. The one where Morty was we had completely wired. We had a video camera in the wall. And we had the rooms on both sides. The bitch was, we had to rely on Scotty to set it up. I had to *trust* this little fairy. I had to be nice to him. You know how it works."

"Yeah, I remember."

"But he came through. About eleven o'clock, Scotty shows up with Morty. Poor

Morty, he strips down to his underwear, you know, to make it look good. Scotty of course takes all his clothes off. Pete and I and three other cops are in the next room watching, trying not to laugh. And then, bam, two minutes later, in walks Gene and some musclehead he's got working for him. Immediately, Gene grabs Morty by the throat and throws him on the bed, shows him his fake badge, and tells him he's going to jail for twenty years. The muscle's kicking Morty in the leg. Scotty puts his pants on and Morty starts crying and a couple of minutes later Gene made the offer."

"How much did he want?"

"Sixty thousand. I guess he figured a Hollywood producer could make that easy. Morty has him repeat it. 'Sixty? I don't know . . .' And then Morty says the code word, 'Okay, you win, officer.' And that was when we busted in and arrested them."

Beckman said, "That how you broke the hand?"

"Oh, yeah. Naturally, I was the one who had to tangle with the muscle. He stepped on my hand at some point. But we got Gene Dennison."

"Sorry I wasn't there."

"I'm sorry too. Better your hand than mine."

"And what about Scotty Maine?"

"We weren't going to file any charges against him. He cooperated with us. But three nights later, narcotics caught him trying to run the same con on another faggot from Gary. He thought he could do it on his own, the stupid shit."

"And now he wants to trade."

"Yep. He thinks we're friends now. I don't know that he's got anything *to* trade. But he told me he read about the subway thing in the newspaper and he thinks he knows who your John Doe is."

CHAPTER TWENTY-NINE

Scotty Maine lighted a Winston red, inhaled it, and grinned. His blond hair was pushed back behind his ears, one of which had a ring in it. His sleeves were rolled up and he wore a red bandanna around his neck as a scarf.

They were sitting at a table in the detainee visiting room. Scotty had one knee propped against the table. Beckman sat back in his chair, his posture relaxed so he wouldn't look like someone from the State's Attorney's Office.

Scotty said, "Raymond here thinks he's got me in some sort of bind. But it's all a misunderstanding."

Ray Wilson smiled and said, "Okay, Scotty. Whatever you say."

Beckman said, "I don't know what they got on you. Doesn't really concern me. But you're the one who called the meeting."

"I'm just trying to be nice," Scotty said.

"Same as before." Scotty looked to Ray. "How's Morty?"

"Morty's good," Ray said.

"You tell him I said hey."

"Sure."

"Well," Beckman said, "let's hear what you got."

Scotty smiled again. He said, "I read in the paper about this subway thing. Says the John Doe had a tattoo, right." Scotty pointed to his left shoulder. "Here, right?"

"That's right," Beckman said.

"A flower and a sword."

"Yeah."

"And I thought to myself, I know that guy. And then I read that the police thought he may have been in the Navy and I thought, yeah, I *know* I know that guy."

"Where do you know him from?"

"I saw him at the hospital. We both had the same problem. Hepatitis. He got it from a dirty needle, you know, community needle. Me too. I told him if there was one thing worse than jail, it was to be stuck in a hospital for six weeks, weak and sick and wishing you were dead. He said he wouldn't know about that. I said to him, come on, man, don't tell me you never been in jail. He said he hadn't. He said he'd done six years in the Navy and he didn't think

260

anything could be worse than that. Until he was in the hospital. And I remember that tattoo. 'Cause it was beautiful, man. Beautiful work. And I asked him where he got it because I wanted something like that for myself. He said he got it in the Philippines."

Beckman said, "When was this?"

"About a year ago. Maybe ten, eleven months ago."

"What was his name?"

"Now, hold on a minute. What are you going to do for me?"

Beckman shrugged. "Ray and I are friends. You be good to me, he'll be good to you."

Scotty said, "I thought Ray was my friend too. I helped him set up that bust. They wouldn't had nothing without me. And now I'm here on some bullshit charge."

Ray said, "Ah, Scotty. Come now. We never you gave authorization to do whatever you wanted. You're here because you fucked up."

"Fucking cop gratitude for you," Scotty said. "Maybe I won't remember things so good when you want me to testify in court."

"We got it all on tape, audio and video," Ray said. "We don't need you."

Beckman said, "Hey, cut the bullshit, huh? We're not talking about that now. We're talking about something else. You got a name?"

261

"What are you going to do for me?"

"Not much I can do for you if you don't give me a name. You do that and I'll call the prosecutor myself and tell him you been a good boy."

"And what will he do?"

"That's up to him. What do they got you on?"

"Solicitation," Scotty said.

"Extortion," Ray Wilson said. "Attempt to defraud and maybe even kidnapping."

"Kidnapping?" Scotty said. "Are you fucking kidding me? That guy wanted it so bad he could taste it. I mean, did you get a look at him?"

Ray Wilson said, "We can talk to the State's Attorney, persuade him to reduce it to solicitation. You'll be out on bail tomorrow."

Beckman thought that would probably happen anyway, presuming Scotty Maine got a halfway decent lawyer. Beckman and Wilson were bluffing with a pair of sevens and they both knew it. Scotty Maine would know it too if he stayed in county for a few more days and spoke to anyone who knew anything.

Beckman said, "So what do you say, Scotty?"

"All right," Scotty said. He leaned forward

like it was something of real value. He said, "The man's name is Lester Wayne."

Beckman wrote it down. "You spell it like John Wayne?"

"Far as I know," Scotty said.

"Where did he live?"

"He stayed at this hotel on Lincoln Avenue. Fucking dump."

"What address?"

"I don't know the number. It's across the street from a bar called the Orion."

Beckman said, "Did he like boys?"

Scotty smiled. "He *said* he didn't. Said he wasn't queer. But, yeah, he liked boys. Younger than me. He used to be a teacher until they fired him."

"He was a schoolteacher?"

"Yeah. Junior high school. He taught shop. Metalwork. But they caught him in the shop room with one of the boys and shit-canned him. Didn't go to jail because the kid's parents didn't want to press charges. But man, them people at the school, they knew. The boys at his school called him M-Lester Wayne."

"He told you this?"

"Yeah."

"When did that happen? When did they fire him?"

"About five years ago. He's been wandering the streets since then."

"User?"

"Yeah."

"What sort?"

"He was off the horse after that trip to the hospital. Then he got into coke, some. Mostly he just drank rye. He was one of those guys that was already dead but just hadn't lied down."

"What he was doing on the subway that night?"

"I don't know. Really, man. If I did, I'd tell you."

"Did he have any enemies?"

"You mean, people who'd want to kill him? No, I don't think so."

"You said he molested kids, though. What about that?"

"Teenagers. And who's to say what they wanted?"

Beckman resisted an urge to punch Scotty Maine in the mouth. He said, "Boys with fathers. Did any of them ever threaten Lester?"

"No, man. Look, I gave you his name. I don't know who killed him. The papers said the Jew was the one they were after."

"Hey," Ray Wilson said. "Watch your mouth."

"It's all right," Beckman said. To Scotty,

he said, "He was a user, huh? Who did he buy from? Who did he get it from?"

"Man, I don't know."

"Bullshit," Ray said.

"Man, this is Chicago. You kidding me? He could have got it off any street corner."

Beckman said, "All right, Scotty, you gave me a name and I keep my agreements. But I want you to think about what kind of bad people Lester knew and I want you to think about coming up with some names. Because I know you're going to fuck up again and you'll be right back here asking for another favor. So start thinking about making a down payment."

"No, man, I'm done. I'm through fucking up."

"We'll see you around," Beckman said.

Driving back to the station, Beckman felt good. They had a name now for the fifth victim. The hole was filled. He wasn't sure it would lead to anything. He tended to think it would not, but it would give him some satisfaction to be able to put it in his daily activity report and tell Regan about it. Hell, Regan might even be impressed. But then Beckman remembered the lead had basically dropped into his lap. Ray Wilson had called him and told him about the lead.

Beckman hadn't found it himself. Beckman pictured Regan nodding his head, mocking him for his diligence. *So you answered a phone call from an old friend at vice. That's brilliant police work.* Beckman realized he'd have to preface it some way with Regan. Start by admitting he got lucky. Start with that any good detective knew he had to have a good network to get anywhere, particularly with other cops. Misfits and rogues who didn't play well with others didn't make good police investigators, despite the image that was perpetuated in movies and television. But if he said such things to Regan he would sound defensive, so he wouldn't say them. Regan had made him sensitive about being too cocky and taking credit for things. He couldn't relax around Regan the way he could around Ray Wilson or the other guys he had worked with at vice. He wondered if he'd be happier back at vice where his co-workers had forgotten he was a Jew or otherwise didn't care. At vice they knew he was capable and cool and nobody second-guessed him. Ray Wilson had told him they missed him and when was he going to come back? Beckman said he was happy with his new assignment and Ray had said, "Right," not believing him.

Beckman was still overthinking his conversation with Regan when dispatch reached him on the radio and connected him to the sergeant himself.

"David," Regan said. "We got the search warrant. I want you to meet me at Wheeler's house."

CHAPTER THIRTY

Ernest Wheeler returned to his mother's house while the police were searching it. His mother was on the porch shouting at a uniformed police officer. Wheeler ran to the porch and the police officer had to push him back. Wheeler flew back at the officers and soon three of them had wrestled him to the ground on the front lawn.

Regan walked out on the front porch and said, "I see our friend has returned."

Beckman came up behind him. He saw that Wheeler was facedown now, an officer cuffing his arms behind his back, his belly hanging out of his shirt. Beckman took no pleasure in it.

Beckman had arrived after Regan. There were two other detectives there going through the house. For some reason Wheeler's mother had decided to yell at the uniformed officers they'd left outside.

Now Regan looked at Beckman and said,

"Disappointed?"

"No," Beckman said.

"Let's go back to the basement."

The basement was where they had found the guns. A Colt .45 semiautomatic, a shotgun, an AK-47, and, of course, a long-barreled Smith & Wesson Model 29 with the .44 Magnum load.

Regan said, "Sales of these things went through the roof after *Dirty Harry* came out. Now every lowlife thinks he has to have one."

Beckman said, "The subway killer used a nine millimeter."

Wheeler lived in his mother's wood-paneled basement. His bed was there and he even had his own little refrigerator in which they found a .357 revolver. Loaded and ready, like a mercenary's. They found back issues of *Soldier of Fortune* amidst copies of *Hustler* and *Oui*. They also found a lot of Nazi porn: black-and-white photos of Wehrmacht soldiers and Tiger tanks, adventure-like stills of Hitler, Rommel, Heydrich, and Himmler. He even had one of Klaus Barbie, the Butcher of Lyon. Like a kid collecting baseball cards.

Beckman felt his detachment stretching away from him. Christ, what kind of man would gather pictures of such monsters? A

group of twisted psychos bent on extermi-
nating a race. What would drive a man in
present-day Chicago to worship such things?
He had expected to find pictures of Hitler,
but Barbie? Wheeler admired the whole roster.

The police went through the drawers, the
underside of the bed, the closet, and the
army foot locker. They went through baskets
of clothes in the laundry room — which was
next to Wheeler's bedroom — and they
went through the box of laundry detergent.
They found the Bulgarian Makarov pistol
in the pocket of a long coat hanging on the
back of a door.

Regan said, "We have a nine millimeter."

When they went back outside, Wheeler was
still there. He was on his feet with hands
cuffed behind his back. He saw detectives
carrying boxes out with his guns in them.
Then he saw Regan carrying the plastic
evidence bag with the Makarov inside.

Wheeler focused his attention on Beckman.

"You! You fucking kike! You did this!
You're gonna burn, man. All of you are
gonna fucking burn!"

CHAPTER THIRTY-ONE

Renee was surprised when Richie told her she didn't need to come along. She didn't think Richie had it in him to meet with Leon alone. Richie's face was still bruised from Leon Murray's fists. She knew the beating had scared him. But Richie looked her in the eye with an attempted fixed stare and said, "I can handle myself."

Renee looked back at him and said, "Shit. How many Valium did you take?"

"Just one," Richie said. "It's for the pain."

For the pain, her ass. And Renee thought he'd probably dropped two or three. Renee said, "Look, Peter's already got it worked out. All we have to do is meet him and give him a down payment."

"I don't need you to be there," Richie said.

"I know you don't," Renee said, lying. "But I think it would be better if someone drove you."

Richie didn't argue with her anymore. She

could see he was relieved.

They met Leon Murray at the abandoned
lots of the famed Union stockyards. The
yards had been shut down since 1971, made
obsolete by the age of decentralized meat-
packing. All that was left was the big concrete gate and barren fields. The yards were
now a mere part of the Chicago landscape,
a town that hid itself in winter.

Renee drove Richie's Porsche 928. They
parked the car between two discarded,
rusted-out trailers and kept the Porsche
running while they waited. On the radio
Carly Simon sang "You Belong to Me."

A Lincoln Continental appeared. Leon
shut the engine off and got out. Richie and
Renee got out of the Porsche. Richie left
the Porsche running.

Leon sighed, taking in the sight of Renee
Aiken. There she was in her jeans and knee-
high boots and fur jacket. Like she was in
Dallas or some shit. What was she doing
here?

Richie smiled and said, "Hey, Leon. Glad
you could make it."

Leon resisted shaking his head. The girl
was staring at him now, giving him attitude.

Leon said, "It's cold out, Richie. You got
something for me?"

"Yeah."

Richie walked over and handed him an envelope. Richie stepped back while Leon went through it. His heart raced but he was out of hitting range when Leon looked up.

"Leon —"

"There's three thousand dollars in here and some change. What the fuck's going on?"

"Listen —"

"The man said you'd bring ten. I agreed to that."

"Yeah, I'm —"

"You lied to the man?"

"No. No, now listen. See that car there? It's worth twenty-eight thousand dollars. It's yours until I pay you in full. Not just the ten thousand."

Leon actually laughed. The man was amusing him.

"Richie, what am I gonna do with that?"

"It's brand new. Practically."

"I already got a car."

"But this is a Porsche. You get to have it until I'm paid up."

Now Leon was insulted. Give a nigger a shiny toy and he'll be pleased. The stupid shit white people thought.

Leon said, "I'll bet you don't even own it."

"Yeah, it's mine. I mean, sure, there are some payments left."

Leon remembered what his mama had once told him. When you lose your temper, count to five before you hit anyone. Leon counted to five and said, "Richie. I'm going to do you a favor. Out of respect for a friend. No, not you, you're not my friend. I mean Peter. I'm going to give you till tomorrow to come up with seven thousand dollars. You don't do that, I'm going to have to hurt you. And the next time, it'll be bad, you understand?"

Renee said, "Oh, why don't you cut the shit?"

Richie paled as Leon turned and seemed to consider Renee for the first time.

Leon said, "Pardon?"

"You heard me," Renee said. "You ain't going to do shit. He'll pay you when he can. You push too hard and we'll just go to the cops and turn you in."

"Oh, Christ," Richie said, and now he was white with fear. "Leon, she didn't mean that."

Leon crooked his head at Renee, his expression at first curious.

"Shut up, Richie," Renee said. "We're not buying the hard-ass black guy routine today, Leon. Peter told you to lay off us and that's what you're gonna do. Now you want the Porsche or not?"

Leon pulled a pistol out of his coat pocket and shot Renee three times in the chest and torso. Richie turned and started to run to the Porsche. Leon shot him in the back. Then Leon walked over to him and shot him in the back of the head.

Leon looked over at the Porsche. It was still running. Shit, he thought. The man had offered to give it to him as collateral. He could drive off with it now if he wanted to, but that would be stupid. He didn't like the color anyway. Yellow. Like some kind of fucking banana. But in unnerved Leon to see it running. So he took a handkerchief out of his coat pocket and walked over to the car. Holding the handkerchief, he opened the door to the car and turned the engine off.

CHAPTER THIRTY-TWO

Regan said, "His mother is saying he was home that night with her. She said they watched television together."

Lieutenant Greg said, "Yeah? You don't believe that, do you?"

"Oh, no," Regan said. "She's quite a piece of work. She said to me, 'Are you one too?' You know, a Jew."

"They learn it young," Greg said.

Beckman said, "Not always." He said it more to himself than to the other police officers in the lieutenant's office. But Lieutenant Greg heard him mumbling.

"What's the matter, David?"

"Sir?"

"Do you have a problem with this?"

Beckman said, "I don't know. I don't think the evidence is there."

"Never mind the evidence for now. Do you think Wheeler's the guy?"

Wheeler was in county jail now, arrested

on charges of assaulting an officer and unlawful possession of firearms. The State's Attorney's Office had filed an application to revoke his parole. Wheeler had been on probation for breaking and entering. He had not been arrested or charged with the murder of Nathan Wald.

Beckman said, "I honestly don't know."

Greg said, "What about what he said?"

"What do you mean?"

"The 'you're going to burn for this.' "

"That's just anti-Semitism," Beckman said. "A pissed-off loser mouthing off. I've heard it before."

Regan said, "You expressed reservations earlier because you didn't think Vernon May would be dumb enough to put him out in the open after ordering him to make the hit. Right?"

Beckman wondered if he should be mad at Regan for repeating what he'd said to the lieutenant. He decided he shouldn't be.

Beckman said, "Yes. I still think that."

"Fair enough," Regan said. "But isn't it possible that Wheeler acted on his own? That he did it without May's okay."

Beckman said, "To impress May?"

"Maybe. Or maybe he just wanted to do it on his own. Swept up by the things May had said to him."

"Yeah," Beckman said. "It's possible. But there are no witnesses that put Wheeler at the subway stop. No evidence."

"None yet," Regan said. "We're just theorizing. But we do have evidence. We have a gun that's been fired. A nine millimeter."

Beckman said, "Yeah, we have that. But the man had a lot of guns. He was bound to have a nine millimeter among his stockpile."

Lieutenant Greg said, "You're kind of a glass half empty guy, aren't you?"

"I'm not even sure there's a glass," Beckman said and regretted it. "We got a guy that hates Jews and has a lot of guns."

Greg said, "Are you bothered by something else?"

"What do you mean?"

"I mean, are you having second thoughts because you knocked him on his ass?"

Beckman sighed. "No, that's not it."

"Are you worried about that coming up in a trial?" Greg asked.

"No." Beckman was beginning to become uncomfortable with this conversation. "I'm just not sure he's the guy."

Regan said, "So we talk to him. We offer him a deal."

"If he gives up May?" Beckman said.

"Yeah."

"I doubt he'll go for that," Beckman said. "Besides, he's already lawyered up. He's not going to talk to us."

Regan said, "Let him sit in county for a couple of days. He'll change his mind."

Greg said, "Take a rest, David. Time's on your side."

CHAPTER THIRTY-THREE

The bodies of Renee Aiken and Richie LaFevers were not discovered until the next morning. A truck mechanic found them there and called the police. Their bodies were frozen and the blood from their fatal wounds had dried.

The police notified the next of kin. After that, the names of the deceased were given to the media. Sally, Mandel's girlfriend, saw it on the six o'clock news and immediately called Mandel to tell him.

Mandel put down the phone in his office and sat back in his chair. Renee gone. And Richie too. He was shocked by the news, but not devastated. He had never much liked Richie, whom he had always suspected of being a closet homosexual. Richie liked hanging around women because he did not have to compete with them and Richie believed he had some sort of Svengali-like ability to improve them. Richie also hated to be alone. Richie liked to tell people he would turn Renee into another Pamela Harriman. That Renee would one day be the wife of a senator or a multimillionaire industrialist. Mandel never deluded himself with such notions. He took Renee for what she was: an ambitious girl from McKinley Park who was fun and promiscuous and had some taste. He admired her for her mercenary nature and lack of scruple. He had not loved her, but he had liked her very much. Now she was dead.

Mandel had met Renee through Richie and he did not hesitate to offer her what he knew she wanted: money, comfort, and the brief illusion of glamour. Truth be told, he had never had much of a sexual relationship with Renee. She had performed oral sex on him a few times, but they had never had intercourse. Mandel was not a virgin, but he had only had sexual intercourse with a handful of women. His attraction to women was genuine, but his phobia of venereal disease was as strong as his fear of contaminated food. Besides, Renee's taste in men ran to the rough and the dangerous. Mandel did not object to her sleeping around. He only asked that she be discreet and not humiliate him. It was a good deal for a girl who wanted to have nice things and an apartment and not have to work. But in time, she screwed it up and made a very public display of dumping him.

Another man in Mandel's position might have taken a grim satisfaction in hearing of her death. But Mandel wasn't like that. With few exceptions, he was not a man to hold a grudge. Within a few months of their split, Mandel had regained his fondness for Renee. His only dispute with her was her continuing friendship with Sally. There was no need to worry about that now.

He had little doubt that Leon Murray had killed her and Richie. Either Leon had done it or he had sent someone to do it. Mandel was conscientious enough to know that in some way he had inadvertently caused it. Perhaps Leon had killed them to make a point to Mandel. That he would not be told what to do. Or, more likely, Leon had killed them for his own reasons. Maybe Richie had told Leon to go fuck himself. Or, more likely still, Renee had. Renee had never really been afraid of anyone. Mandel had long suspected that trait would get her into trouble one day.

Leave it alone, Mandel thought. She's gone now and there's nothing you can do about it. Leave it alone.

He was still telling himself that when he walked out of his office and got in his Cadillac to drive to Leon's club.

Leon said, "If you want to ask me, just ask me."

Mandel said, "I'm not asking you."

"Then what did you come down here for?"

"I just want to know if you know anything about it."

Leon Murray smiled. "Peter, you ever kill anyone?"

Mandel shifted in his chair.

Leon said, "I mean, directly."

"I think you know the answer to that."

"If you ever do," Leon said. "If you ever have to, don't tell anyone. You didn't tell anyone about Wald, did you?"

"No. You know I didn't."

"Do I?" Leon said. Leon's eyes were wide open and Mandel detected something that might be a threat.

Mandel said, "Are you suggesting I told Renee about Wald?"

"Well, I don't know," Leon said. "I know that girl's got a mouth on her. Say you did tell her. It's something you don't really have to worry about anymore, right?"

"I did not tell her about it. I did not tell anyone."

Leon stared at him for a few more minutes. But Mandel didn't flinch. Leon wondered what it would take to make this man afraid.

Finally Leon said, "Well, it wasn't me that put the bitch down. Or her faggot friend. The man owed me money and I had it from you he was going to pay. So now I'm not going to get my money."

"Okay, Leon."

"Anyway, I told you the lady was trouble. More likely she got him killed than anything."

"I understand, Leon. I told you I wasn't going to interfere."

"Yeah, you told me. But in case you change your mind, remember what I did for you. Police show up at my door asking me questions, it's not going to be good for either of us. You understand that too?"

Mandel stood up. If he was scared, he didn't show it.

"You've made your point," Mandel said.

CHAPTER THIRTY-FOUR

It was after six when Beckman left the station. It had been a long day and he had earned some overtime. He didn't know there was much else that was good about it. Regan and Lieutenant Greg seemed to think there was light at the end of the tunnel because they had a neo-Nazi in the county jail who might be willing to confess after a couple of days. Beckman didn't like the vibe at all and he wasn't sure why. Now he could go home and get some sleep, but he sensed that he was too tired to sleep. Or that his thoughts wouldn't allow him to sleep. He could have gone to a cop bar to unwind, but he had never been much of a drinker and he knew he didn't want to discuss the subway case with a bunch of cops. They would sense his lack of confidence in the Wheeler arrest and maybe even resent him for it. As Regan continued to remind him, there were several cops who wanted to be in his place.

He thought of Mary-Beth Hanley and thinking of her, realized he was lonely. He had been lonely in his marriage too, but that was a different kind of lonely. The worst kind, where you feel like you're married to a stranger. Friends and people with psychology degrees would tell him it was too soon to jump into a relationship with another woman, but he was human and he realized he didn't have much control over such things.

Then he thought of what he had told Mary-Beth, what he had shared with her, and realized he had something else to do.

Albert, his stepfather, answered the door. He frowned at Beckman and Beckman knew that his mother had told him about the divorce.

Albert said, "What do you want?" His tone was bordering on hostile.

Beckman suppressed a smile. For perhaps the first time, he admired Albert. Albert was angry at him for hurting Sylvie. Beckman knew then that Albert really did love his mother.

Beckman said, "Albert, I want to talk to my mother. Is she here?"

"Yes, she's here. I don't know if she feels

like talking to you right now."

"Will you ask her? Please."

Albert stared at his stepson for a moment. Then he backed up and let him into the house. Albert looked down at the floor and said, "She's in the kitchen."

Beckman walked in and looked at Albert.

Albert said, "Go on." He was going to stay out of it. And Beckman thought, God help me, I may even grow to like this guy.

Sylvie was at the sink washing dishes. She turned when Beckman walked in and stood by the kitchen table. Sylvie's face registered a mixture of pain and anger and perhaps relief.

She said, "What do you want?"

"I just wanted to talk to you," Beckman said.

"We already ate dinner."

After a moment, Beckman said, "Well, I . . . I'm not really hungry."

"You already ate, then?"

"No, Ma."

"Sit down then. I'll make you a fried baloney sandwich."

Beckman had liked fried baloney sandwiches as a child. He had lost his taste for them around the age of nineteen. Now he said, "Okay."

Sylvie got a small frying pan out of the

cupboard and set it on the stove. Then she got the baloney out of the refrigerator and bread out of the box.

"Ma," Beckman said, "I'm sorry."

"What are you sorry for? You already told me you were sorry. You're sorry you got divorced and lied to me?"

"I'm sorry I lied to you. And I'm sorry I let you down."

His mother turned from the stove. "What was it? Another girl?"

Christ, Beckman thought. Another girl. What else would she think, having been betrayed herself so many times?

"No, Ma. There wasn't another girl. That's not what the problem was."

"You sure?"

"Yes."

"You lying again?"

"No. There was no one else. We just weren't happy."

"I don't know what to say."

"Ma, look at me. Don't you think you'd know if I were lying?"

She looked at him for a few moments. He had lied to her before, of course. Hiding the fact that he and Elyse were separating, then hiding the divorce itself. He didn't want her to think he was an adulterer on top of all that.

"Okay," she finally said. "But if there wasn't another woman, why?"

"I told you why. Mama, times are different. Life is short. People realize they made a mistake and they're miserable, they get divorced."

"People got divorced in my time too, you know. Your generation didn't invent divorce. They just didn't do it for breakfast."

Beckman laughed. She could be funny, his mother.

"Yeah, laugh. You're unmarried and childless and I have a son who's divorced."

"Well, there are worse things."

She didn't respond to that. She shook the pan around over the stove's flame.

Beckman said, "Ma? Ma. What I said about Papa. I didn't mean that. Will you forgive me for saying that? Please."

Sylvie scooped the sandwich out of the pan and onto a plate. Then she set the plate on the table in front of him. She stopped at the table and looked at her son. She dipped her head then, just a little, and her eyes squinted. He realized that was as much a response as he was going to get from her. It was enough and more.

She said, "You want a glass of milk?"

"Yes, please."

■ ■ ■ ■

It was almost ten o'clock when he returned to his apartment. He turned on the news. The Chicago mayor was still trying to justify the city's anemic response to the snowstorm. Challenger Jane Byrne was now ahead of him in the polls. The Dow Jones Industrial Average closed at 833. The Shah of Iran had fled Egypt. Saddam Hussein was consolidating power in the Middle East and was expected to become president of Iraq sometime in the summer. The YMCA had filed suit against the Village People for libel and slander over the song "YMCA." The State of Ohio finally settled the lawsuits brought by the families of the students killed at Kent State in 1970. And U.S. intelligence reports indicated that China had massed troops on the Vietnamese border and were prepared to invade.

Beckman laughed at that one. "Fuck," he said. "You can *have* it."

Beckman turned off the television and dialed Mary-Beth Hanley's number. The phone rang four times and he was afraid he would wake her. But she answered on the fifth ring.

"Hello."

"Hi, it's David. I didn't wake you, did I?"

"Oh, hello. No. How are you?"

"I'm fine. I just wanted to call and . . . check in, I guess."

"Check in?" She laughed. "Do you work for me?"

"No. I don't know. I wanted to see if I could see you tomorrow."

"Yes, I think it's still okay. If I don't have to work late."

". . . still?"

"You already asked me. The other night, remember?"

"Oh. Yeah."

"Is everything okay?"

"Yeah."

"Did you call your mother?"

"No. But I did go by after work tonight."

"How did it go?"

"Good, I think. She doesn't seem to hate me anymore."

"She never hated you. If you don't mind me asking, what did you tell her?"

"I told her I was sorry for what I said about her and my father."

"Did you talk about it then?"

"Talk about what?"

"Your issues with your father."

"Oh God, no. I just said I was sorry."

"You could have explored it a little more.

It might have been healthy to discuss it. For both of you."

"I doubt that."

Beckman heard the girl sigh. "You're not exactly modern, are you?"

Beckman said, "I thought I was."

"You're not. Not even close. But it's not a bad thing. Maybe it's not too bad a thing."

"Okay, I guess."

"And it's good you apologized to her."

"I know." After a moment, he said, "Thank you."

"For what?"

"For — I don't know, for pointing me in the right direction."

"I didn't do that. Will I see you tomorrow?"

"I think so."

The conversation made him feel better. After they said goodbye, he turned the television back on to watch *The Tonight Show.* Johnny Carson joked about Lee Marvin's palimony suit. Then he interviewed George Peppard and Valerie Perrine who brought four very big dogs on stage with her. Everyone on the show seemed at ease.

Beckman fell asleep sometime during the *Tomorrow* show, Tom Snyder interviewing one of the Watergate conspirators who was promoting a book about his involvement and subsequent contrition. Beckman woke up to the sound of the television humming its off-air signal and turned it off and went to bed. He slept reasonably well. Then around seven a.m. his phone rang and he answered it.

"Beckman."

"Beckman, this is Sergeant Stevenson. We got a call from county jail. Ernest Wheeler, is he the guy you and Sergeant Regan arrested?"

"Yeah."

"He's dead."

Chapter Thirty-Five

Beckman and Regan met with the deputy sheriff at Cook County Jail. He told them what he knew so far.

Ernest Wheeler was put into a holding cell with an inmate named Kelvin Deion Jackson. Kelvin had been arrested for the murder of a liquor store proprietor who Kelvin had shot twice in the face after he found out there was only sixty odd dollars in the till. Kelvin was suspected of three other murders as well, mostly rival gang members. Kelvin Jackson, age twenty-two, knew he was going away for life and felt he had nothing to lose by killing a white cracker while he was in county. Indeed, Kelvin believed — rightly — it would help his reputation at the state penitentiary.

Regan said, "How?"

The deputy sheriff said they had been on clean-up duty together. Kelvin broke off a piece of a broomstick and beat Wheeler to death with it. Wheeler did not die immediately. The incident had happened last night. Wheeler died in the infirmary approximately six hours later.

Beckman said, "Did Kelvin Jackson know what Wheeler was in for?"

The deputy sheriff sighed and said, "We all knew. But the problem was, this Wheeler couldn't keep his mouth shut. He said he didn't want to be put in a cell with niggers."

Beckman said, "If you knew he was having trouble keeping his mouth shut, why, *why* didn't you take steps to protect him?"

The deputy sheriff said, "We didn't expect that. Do you know how many inmates we got here?"

"Jesus Christ," Beckman said. "This is fucking unacceptable."

"You're the one who put him here," the deputy sheriff said.

Lieutenant Greg called them in later. Beckman expected them to be bawled out. It didn't happen. Greg told them it was bad luck, but said it wasn't their fault. Greg said, "It's too bad you didn't have time to get a confession out of him."

Regan said, "Well . . ."

Beckman said, "We're not sure he's the killer."

Greg said, "You got something else?"

Beckman didn't answer him. Regan looked at the floor.

Greg said, "That's what I thought. Work with what you got, gentlemen."

He cleared them out of his office. In the hall, Beckman said, "Work with what we got. Just what does that *mean*?"

"Lower your voice," Regan said.

Beckman followed Regan out to the stairwell. There was some semblance of privacy there.

Beckman said, "Is he asking us to wrap this case up? To pin it on Wheeler?"

"He's not going to ask us directly," Regan said. "You might say he's encouraging us."

"You want to go along with that?"

"Now hold on, David. When you say 'go along,' it sounds like I'd be going along with some sort of lie. I don't think I would be. I think Wheeler's our boy."

"But I'm not sure."

"You don't believe it? Okay. But if I do, there's nothing wrong with me clearing this case. And I am lead detective."

"That's not . . . I don't think I can do that."

"No one's asking you to do anything. If I'm wrong, it's my responsibility. Not yours. You come out okay either way."

"I'm not looking to come out okay. I want to solve this murder."

"What if it's already been solved? What if Wheeler is the man? You going to feel cheated somehow? You didn't get the satisfaction of making the case against him? You didn't get to arrest Vernon May for conspiracy?"

"That's not where I'm coming from."

"Listen to me: Greg wants this thing cleared, okay? But that doesn't mean he's going to tell you to write a false report. He's a good man."

"I know he's a good man. He's the lieutenant, isn't he? But he doesn't know this case as well as I do."

Regan said, "All he's doing is making a suggestion. And he's asking a fair question: do we have anything else?"

Beckman said nothing.

"Well," Regan said, "do we?"

"I found out the name of the John Doe. His name is —"

"Lester Wayne. I know. But what does that give us? Can you honestly call that a lead?"

Beckman was quiet again.

Regan said, "I'm going to tell you again: no one is asking you to do anything improper. But I suggest you take a day to think about things. And think about this: Greg wouldn't have said what he did if he didn't have backing from upstairs. And maybe something more than backing."

"You mean the chief of detectives wants this wrapped up?"

"Yeah. And if he does, odds are he's being pressured by the mayor."

"So never mind the snowstorm," Beckman said. "The Chicago police have solved the murder of Nathan Wald. The mayor gets to claim a victory."

"Oh, shocked, are we? Stop the presses, there's politics at City Hall. Oh, the humanity. Jimmy Stewart in *Mr. Smith Goes to Washington.*"

"I'm not Jimmy Stewart. I know how things work."

"You say you do, but I don't think you do. You want to work in homicide? Then understand this: the simplest explanation is usually the right one. Ernest Wheeler hated Jews. He hated them so much he actually had the balls to stalk a Jewish cop. Would it surprise anyone that he would kill an activist like Nathan Wald?"

"We still don't have enough on him."

"Right," Regan said. "But what difference does it make now?"

Beckman stood and fumed. He knew on some level that Regan was genuinely trying

298

to help him. Somehow that made it worse.

Beckman said, "Have you made a decision yet?"

After a moment, Regan said, "I don't know. I may want to do some thinking of my own. You say you don't go along with the Wheeler theory, but you can't articulate why. Well, if I believe it and I *can* articulate why, then that's going to be the end of it. It's still my case."

"And if I don't agree?"

Regan frowned, more in disappointment than in anger. He said, "Well, I sincerely hope it won't come to that. Because if it does, you'll be on your own."

CHAPTER THIRTY-SIX

Beckman went to lunch by himself. He wanted to be alone to think. He ordered a couple of hot dogs and a bag of chips and a strawberry soda. He ate standing at a counter while he read the *Chicago Tribune*. More stories about the snowstorm and the mayor and the threat of Jane Byrne. The man was running scared.

Beckman had been a policeman long enough to know the dangers of paranoia. He understood that many police officers suffered from the delusion that people were conspiring to get them, particularly the brass. When the truth was, the brass usually didn't much care about the rank-and-file cops. Beckman was a cop *and* he was Jewish. So maybe he should have been doubly paranoid. But for the most part, he wasn't. He believed that paranoia, at root, was a form of narcissism. He did not believe Lieutenant Greg or Chief of Detectives

Stumbaugh or the mayor was out to screw him. He didn't believe Regan was either. If anything, Regan was trying to help him. Beckman had come to not only respect Regan, but like him. He even forgot that Regan was Irish and he was reasonably sure that Regan no longer thought of him as a Jew. Forgetting was the biggest step to getting over prejudices.

But it pained him that Regan was trying to help him now. No question, Regan was pressuring him to go along with putting the murder of Nathan Wald and four others on Ernest Wheeler. Regan said he thought the theory made sense. But Beckman couldn't tell if Regan was sure. Regan could be very hard to read. This quality had no doubt helped him progress at homicide. Beckman hoped that Regan was sure because that would make things easier. Beckman wished he could be sure.

Beckman had killed men in Vietnam. He had only felt guilty about it near the end of his tour. But his guilt stemmed not so much from individual killing as it did from a growing realization that it was wrong for the Americans to be there in the first place. Until he had returned to the States, he had kept his reservations to himself. He later wondered if he had been a coward for not conscientiously objecting. He knew then that he did not want to be *associated* with the kids who protested the war. Maybe he didn't want to betray those he had fought alongside with. Or maybe he had just wanted to go along. Perhaps for fear that if he did air his disgust with the war, someone would say, "I knew it." As if they should have known better than to trust a Jew. Pinko, sympathizer, traitor, *other.*

Maybe he had killed Ernest Wheeler too. And though he believed he should not feel any guilt over it, he did feel guilt. Yeah, it had been Regan's idea to get the search warrant on Wheeler and Regan still implied that he thought Wheeler was the killer. But Beckman wasn't so sure. He wasn't sure about it all and he wished it could be.

He thought, *what difference does it make?* He had probably killed innocent men in Vietnam. Farmers and villagers who simply wanted to be left alone in a country that was theirs. Ernest Wheeler was a nasty, unrepentant hater. Put him in Berlin or Bavaria in the thirties and he would have gleefully murdered Beckman and Beckman's family. That, Beckman *was* sure of. And Beckman had been a cop long enough to develop that cynical rationalization that says, *if he wasn't guilty of this one, he was surely guilty of something else just as bad.*

But then he knew that really wasn't the point. Cops didn't arrest people because of what they were capable of or because of the hate consuming their thoughts. And in Vietnam, he was fighting a war, not enforcing the law.

Christ. Chicago. Less corrupt than South Vietnam, but maybe not by much. Mayor Daley was dead now two years, but his Machine was still running. Regan and Lieutenant Greg saw the prospect of an unsolved, high-profile murder stretching out before them and maybe threatening their careers. At least, Greg did. And now Ernest Wheeler had provided them an escape hatch. Regan had told Beckman that he was smart enough to one day become chief of detectives. But there was intelligence and there was political savvy. Beckman wasn't sure he wanted to join the ranks of the savvy, for there was a price to be paid for that too.

He walked back to the station, weary of it all, tempted to go to Regan and Greg and tell them to do whatever the fuck they wanted. And if they closed the case and hung it on Wheeler, maybe he'd put in for a transfer back to vice.

But then he got to his desk and saw Regan

look up at him.

"You were the one who interviewed Richie LaFevers, right?"

"Yeah. What about him?"

"He's been murdered."

"Oh, shit. How?"

"Shot three times. A girl was with him."

Beckman felt his heart race. *Mary-Beth* —His voice shook a little as he asked, "Who?"

"Let's see . . . Renee Aiken. You know her?"

Beckman sat down. He took a moment to come down from his fear. He said, "Yeah. She was with Richie when I interviewed him at his condominium."

"He got beat up, didn't he?"

"Yeah. I interviewed him at the hospital. He wouldn't tell me anything."

Regan looked at him for a moment. "You all right?"

"Yeah. I just . . . ah, I was worried about something else."

"It can shake you up a little when you know the victim. Even if all you did was meet him. Or her."

"Right," Beckman said. "Who got the squeal?"

"Let's see . . . Detectives Deegan and Os-ulnic."

"I don't know them."

"They're good. Talk to them, by all means. But I don't think it's related to our case."

"Maybe it is, though."

"How do you figure?"

"LaFevers knew one of the subway victims. Helen Futterer. Maybe he saw something or knew something and the killer wanted to eliminate him as a witness."

"Yeah, that's not unreasonable. But Wheeler was in county jail at the time of death. I know because I checked."

After a moment, Beckman said, "But you don't mind if I talk to Deegan and O'Sullivan, though?"

"Osulnic, not O'Sullivan. No, I don't mind. Maybe you can help them out." Regan didn't seem that bothered by it.

"Yeah, maybe," Beckman said.

Deegan said, "You worked vice?"

Beckman said he did.

Deegan said, "You work with Bill Cairn?"

"Not exactly. He was a supervisor by the time I got there."

"We were partners years ago. Good guy, Bill. I worked vice with him back in '63, on loan for about thirty days. Fag duty at Grant Park. Arrest all these sailors on leave from Great Lakes. Good times. Now they're

305

marching in the streets. But I tell you, overall, pinching whores and dopeheads wasn't for me."

Beckman said, "It's not for everyone." He was still trying to get past Deegan's nostalgia for sailors reaching for his crank at Grant Park. He was at their station, sitting at their homicide table. They ate Chinese takeout while they talked to him. Osulnic had a paper napkin tucked into the neck of his shirt.

Osulnic said, "You gotta be crazy to work vice. Crazy."

Deegan said, "And now you're with the elite."

Beckman gave him a thin smile and said, "Regan may have told you, I interviewed Richie LaFevers a few days ago in connection with the subway killings. He knew one of the victims, Helen Futterer. I interviewed him twice. After the first interview, he got beat up."

"Bad?" Osulnic said.

"Yeah, pretty bad. I questioned him about it at the hospital, but he wouldn't tell me anything."

Deegan said, "Did he seem scared?"

"Yeah," Beckman said. "But not scared, like he thought someone was going to kill him."

Osulnic said, "You think it had something to do with the subway murders?"

"I don't know. He wouldn't tell me anything."

"You say he knew one of the victims, a girl," Osulnic said. "But did he know the Jewish guy?"

"No, he didn't know Wald."

Osulnic said, "But Wald was the target, wasn't he?"

"Yeah, that's what we think," Beckman said. He hoped his reservations didn't show.

Deegan said, "You guys arrested a suspect a couple of days ago, didn't you?"

"Did Regan tell you that?" Beckman said, then realized he had spoken too quickly.

"Yeah," Deegan said. "Why shouldn't he?"

"No reason."

Deegan said, "Well, we want all the help we can get. But I don't think these two things are connected. What do you know about the girl?"

"Helen Futterer?"

"No, not her. Renee Aiken."

"Nothing. I never really questioned her."

Osulnic said, "Could be she was the target. Jealous boyfriend or pimp."

"Pimp?" Beckman said.

"Yeah," Osulnic said. "We've just made a few calls, but we've already found out she was a pretty dirty little tramp. Early indications are they both had cocaine in their bloodstream. So, when I see a pretty female victim with a coke addiction, I presume she's hooking."

Deegan said, "You met her. What did you think?"

Beckman said, "I guess I didn't give her much thought at all. She played with me a little."

Deegan's eyebrows lifted. "Make you an offer?"

"No, nothing like that. She was just trying to play me. She knew I was a cop. She was just trying to be a smart-ass, I think."

"Good-looking little hide, huh?"

Beckman kept his wince to himself. "Yeah, she was good-looking."

Osulnic said, "Do you think LaFevers got the beating because of her?"

"I don't know. I don't think so . . . I guess in hindsight, she seemed like trouble. But no, I don't think he got roughed up because of her."

"Why not?" Deegan asked.

"Because that wasn't the vibe. I think LaFevers was in trouble because of something he was involved in. Like he had a big gambling debt. Or, now that you bring up the coke, he was in trouble for that."

"Well," Deegan said, "he doesn't have any record. We got no information or reason to believe narcotics or DEA was leaning on him to give up a big-time dealer. Do you?"

"No," Beckman said.

"None of your friends in vice have anything on him?"

"No."

Osulnic was looking at him, his chopsticks pointed down. Osulnic said, "You wouldn't be holding out on us, would you?"

Beckman said, "Why would I do that?" His voice a little cooler than before.

"You guys at vice can be pretty protective of your CI's."

Beckman said, "If I knew something, I'd tell you. I'm not at vice anymore."

Osulnic backed off, some, and said, "Okay. He wasn't in trouble with the cops then."

Deegan said, "Anything else?"

Beckman realized Deegan was addressing him. He didn't know if he was asking if Beckman had any more questions or anything else to give them. Maybe both.

"No," Beckman said. "I think that's it. I'm sorry I didn't have much for you."

Deegan shook his head. "That's all right. We're grateful you came." He seemed to mean it.

Beckman said, "Oh. Have you got the ballistics report yet?"

"No," Deegan said. "You want a copy when we get it?"

"Yeah."

"It should be here soon. Call back in a couple of hours. Ask for me."

"I'll do that."

Beckman felt a little better when he left. Not because he felt the meeting with them had been productive. He didn't feel that it really had been. But because the older detectives had, for the most part, treated him as one of their own tribe. He was a homicide detective to them, not a recent transfer from vice who maybe didn't deserve to be there. Beckman wondered if he'd passed some sort of test in the last few days. Or maybe it was Regan who was responsible for the goodwill. A phone call from Regan telling Deegan and Osulnic that a young detective was coming to see them and then adding something like, "Beckman's a good guy. Treat him right." A little thing, but a good word from a veteran like Regan could go a long way at a place like the Chicago PD.

They seemed like good guys. But like Regan, they believed that the subway murders were not related to the murders of

Renee Aiken and Richie LaFevers. Beckman didn't see how they couldn't be related. But Beckman was going on instinct while the older detectives were going on fact. There was no evidence to tie the two sets of murders together.

Beckman thought back to his first meeting with Richie LaFevers and his only meeting with Renee Aiken. He had known they were snorting cocaine before he interviewed them. Yet he had not harassed either one of them over it. He did not regret that now. He had been there to investigate the subway murders, not make arrests for possession of narcotics. Had he arrested them for possession, Regan almost certainly would have been furious with him. Hot dog narcotics officer wanting to make a bust. *Get yer priorities straight, boyo,* or some such Irish shit.

Beckman had summed the two of them up fairly quickly. Richie, a yuppie asshole with a coke habit. Renee, a coldhearted little tramp who used her body to get what she wanted and probably usually succeeded. Beckman had not been flattered by the attention she paid to him. He knew she was just trying to work him. In fact, on some level, he had been insulted by the way she waved her ass in his face. Like he was simple and could be easily distracted. Now she was dead along with a guy who was also probably another lowlife.

Detectives aren't supposed to make distinctions between homicide victims. But they do all the time. Beckman felt a pity for the five victims of the subway shootings. He didn't feel much for Richie or Renee. But, then, he had met them. He thought it was probably for the best that Deegan and Osulnic were investigating their murders instead of him. As he signed out at the end of his shift, he told himself to let them handle it.

He was putting his coat on and walking down the hall when an administrative assistant stopped him and handed him a manila envelope.

Beckman said, "What's this?"

"The ballistics report from Detective Deegan. He had someone run it over. Do you want me to just put it on your desk?"

"No, I'll take it with me. Thanks."

CHAPTER THIRTY-SEVEN

He picked Mary-Beth up at the hospital. She waved to him from the exit and he felt better already. He unlocked the passenger door to let her in. She did not kiss him but did put her hand on his arm as a greeting. She wore a sweater under her coat, but had hospital scrubs on under. No makeup.

"I look horrible, don't I?"

"No," Beckman said. "You're beautiful."

He had not meant to embarrass her or even come onto her. It just came out. She might have blushed at that or her cheeks may have been ruddy from standing out in the cold.

She said, "I smell. I need to take a shower. Do you mind running me by my apartment?"

Beckman didn't mind.

On the way to her apartment, it started sleeting and by the time they got there it was snowing.

Mary-Beth said, "Not a great night to be going out to dinner. Would it be okay if we stopped someplace and got a pizza and brought it back to my place? I've got some beer."

"That sounds great."

She told him to go ahead and eat the pizza while she took a shower. But Beckman left the box closed on top of the coffee table. He sipped from the bottle of Lowenbrau beer and watched the evening news. There he saw a reporter standing near the gate of the old stockyards reporting on the murders of Renee Aiken and Richard LaFevers. The reporter said the victims' bodies had been "well preserved by the brutal cold temperatures."

"Christ," Beckman said. He turned the television off when he heard Mary-Beth coming out of the bathroom.

She was in jeans and a white T-shirt with a V-neck sweater over it. A different sweater than the one she had worn earlier. There was no antiseptic smell about her now. Her hair wet and smoothed back. She sat on the couch. Beckman wanted to kiss her.

She said, "You didn't have any pizza."

"I was waiting for you."

"Oh. Thank you. Do you want to listen to some music?"

"Sure."

She put the record on the turntable. Soon they heard Bob Welch singing "Sentimental Lady," here and warm.

Mary-Beth sat down on the couch next to him and sipped her beer.

She looked at him and said, "Is something wrong?"

"Sort of," he said. "Ah . . . Richie LaFevers was killed yesterday."

"Oh, God."

"Yeah. And Renee Aiken. They were shot."

"Oh Jesus. What happened?"

"We don't know yet."

"Are you investigating it?"

"No. It's someone else's."

"Do you think it has to do with him being beat up?"

"Probably."

"God." She put her bottle of beer on the coffee table. She sat very still.

Beckman reached over and took her hand.

"It's okay," he said. "You're not in any danger. You're not."

"I know that," she said. "I've seen people with gunshot wounds before. I've seen people die before. It's just that . . ."

"It's just that you knew this man?"

"I knew he was in danger," she said. "That's why I called you."

"And now he's dead," Beckman said. "And it has nothing to do with you. You had nothing to do with what happened to him."

"No. I told you something about him. And you came to see him and then later he was killed. I had something to do with it."

"Something good. Not something bad. You were trying to help me. You were trying to help Catherine-Anne."

"She's dead. And now Richie is dead, too. David, I'm scared."

"Don't be scared," Beckman said and he pulled her close to him. "It's probably not even related to the subway — to the subway thing."

"It's not?"

"Well, they don't think it is."

"Who doesn't?"

"The detectives investigating the LaFevers case. My boss doesn't think so either."

She looked up at him. "But what do you think?"

". . . I don't know."

"You don't agree, do you?"

"No, not necessarily. But it doesn't matter what I think —"

"What do you mean, it doesn't matter —"

"These guys are *senior* to me," he said. "It's Tom's case. I'm just assisting him. He wants to close it, he can. I don't have any say."

She sat up and looked at him more directly.

"Senior to you . . . what are you talking about? Are they smarter than you?"

"They're more experienced."

"That's not the same thing."

Beckman sighed. "At Chicago homicide, it amounts to the same thing."

Mary-Beth Hanley said, "I'm not sure I understand what you're talking about. Do you want to tell me more?"

"Not really."

"Why not? Don't you trust me?"

"Of course I trust you." Beckman sipped his beer and popped open the top of the pizza box. He looked inside and let the top drop.

"Yes, I trust you. Look, there are people at homicide who think the subway thing has been solved. I'm not so sure they're right. I wish I was sure, but I'm not. And it's not . . . it's not an ego thing. I hope they *are* right and that I'm wrong."

"But what if you're right and they're wrong? Have you thought about that?"

"I've thought about nothing but that."

She looked at him for a long moment. And then she smiled.

"What?" Beckman said.

She said, "You've just confessed your feelings to me. You *are* a modern man."

"Yeah, Alan Alda and I subscribe to the same magazines."

She laughed. Beckman didn't understand why, though he thought her laugh was pleasant and not derisive.

"What?" he said again. He felt he had lost control of this conversation. A few minutes ago she had been frightened. She didn't seem frightened anymore.

"I knew it," she said. "I knew it the first time I saw you. I thought, there's a guy who's *very* sure of himself. No, don't take it the wrong way. I like a confident man."

"I don't feel so confident right now."

"Oh, but you do. You know you're right and you know these other detectives are wrong. You *do* have an ego. But that's a good thing."

"How is that good?"

"Because you're not going to go along with something that's wrong. You're a very proud man, Detective Beckman. You're not going to allow them to talk you into it."

"Into what?"

"Lying, hiding things, keeping your mouth shut . . . whatever it is people at the top want you to do."

318

After a moment, Beckman said, "I think you're presuming things that maybe you shouldn't presume."

"Whatever," she said. She leaned forward. Smiling, and then her mouth parting . . .

She said, "Are you going to kiss me or not?"

"Kiss you?" Beckman said. Then he kissed her. Her mouth was soft and wet. She put her arms around his neck. He drew back a little and said, "I don't understand you."

"You will," she said, her voice almost a whisper, and she kissed him again. She moved around the couch to straddle him.

Mary-Beth said, "Do you think about what would happen if it didn't stop snowing? If we had another snowstorm like last month? We could be stuck here together for days and days."

"Two relative strangers," Beckman said.

"Strangers who just finished making love. Am I still a stranger to you?"

"Not exactly."

"Something tells me we'd find a way to fill the time. And how."

"Yeah," Beckman said. "But what would we talk about?"

"You know how to talk," she said. "You think about everything you say before you say it. You'd make a good lawyer."

Beckman smiled. "You sound like my mother."

"Oh God. Let's not get icky."

They were quiet for a while.

Beckman said, "We got something here, I think."

"I think so too." She turned to him. "Not that it's any of your business, but I don't do this a lot. I mean, not with anyone."

"You're right," he said. "It's not my business."

She said, "Did you see that movie *Looking for Mr. Goodbar*?"

"Yeah, I saw it."

"Did you like it?"

"Not really. A little too sordid for my tastes."

"That's good to hear," she said. "I have to say, I didn't get it. This schoolteacher decides she's going to be promiscuous and in the end she gets murdered. I mean, aren't the seventies supposed to be about celebrating free love?"

"That was my understanding."

"Yet that movie and movies like *Carnal Knowledge,* they're saying it's all empty and gross."

"Was that the one with Ann-Margret?"

"Yes. You liked seeing her naked, I bet."

"Better her than Art Garfunkel. Yeah, I think they were about the abuse of sex. Pretty conservative messages, really. Jack Nicholson at the end, telling the prostitute to say dirty things to him. But . . . I kind of missed the sexual revolution."

"You did?"

"Well, I was no saint. But I married my high school girlfriend. And outside of when I was in the Army, I was faithful to her."

"Were you married when you — when you were in the Army?"

"No. We married after."

Mary-Beth said, "You didn't miss much." She moved closer to him. "Richie, Renee, Helen . . . that wasn't my scene, you know."

"You don't have to explain anything to me."

"I know. But I just don't want this to be . . . it."

"It isn't."

"Not that I asked you to make any promises."

"You didn't."

"But you're a bachelor now. A free man. And there are a lot of beautiful women out there."

"Are there now."

She laughed. "Your voice. The way you said that just now, you sound like an Irishman. *Are there now.*"

Christ, Beckman thought. She was imitating him, making him smile inside. An Irish-American girl with golden hair that got in her face when she made love and who said, "I like you" in a husky, honest tone as he kissed her neck after she had an orgasm. He was forgetting that she was Irish and that he was Jewish and he was wondering why it should have mattered in the first place. He did feel free. But not in the way she had suggested.

He said, "Would you like me to be a lawyer?"

"What? Where did that come from?"

"You said I'd make a good lawyer."

"I was just talking. I don't care what you are."

"Don't you?"

"Why would I? I think you're wonderfully sexy with or without your gun belt."

"Do you like cops?"

"You're the first cop I've known."

"Oh. Well —"

"Wait a minute, you don't think I'm one of those cop groupies, do you?"

"No."

"Give me some credit, will you?"

"Stop it. I don't think that." He kissed her cheek.

She smiled and said, "Okay. I believe you."

He said, "It would make my mother happy, me being a lawyer. This guy I work with, the guy I told you about before, he thinks he's lucky being a sergeant in homicide. And I think he's right to feel that way. But where I come from, my people, it's looked down on."

"Being a police officer?"

"Yeah."

"Why would they look down on that?"

"I don't know."

"Do you look down on it?"

"Not at all. I never have."

"I didn't think you did. Like I said earlier, you're a proud man."

Beckman still didn't understand what she meant by that. But he liked the way she said it. Elyse may have said the same thing to him a time or two. But when she said it, it seemed to mean stubborn more than proud. It was nice to be with someone who didn't think he was misguided or some sort of failure.

Beckman said, "What you said earlier, about me not having missed anything. I understand that."

"Missed — do you mean career or are we back to sex?"

"We're back to sex," he said. "I understand

what you mean by that. Maybe because of my work. The pickup scene, the singles bars, the skates, it's all pretty cold."

"Skates?"

"That's a term for orgies. You never heard that?"

"Apparently I don't move in the same circles as you."

"Well, neither do I. But I did once go to one of those key parties, though."

"Key parties? You mean, where the married couples put their car keys in the bowl and the wife picks out a set and goes off with someone else's husband?"

"Yeah."

"You did that?"

"No, I didn't do that."

"But you said —"

"I said I *went* to a party where that went on. But we didn't go through with it. They were Elyse's friends. She didn't know that was going to happen."

"What did she do? Your wife, I mean."

"She pretty much freaked out. This was about six years ago. She pulled me into the bathroom and told me we had to get the hell out of there. God, she was so upset." Beckman laughed at the memory of it. He had laughed then too. He said, "Elyse wasn't exactly cut out for that."

"And you?"

"I don't know. It might have been fun."

"That's gross . . . Did you see anything?"

"You mean a lot of naked bodies on the floor?"

She snickered. "Was that what it was like?"

"No. The couples went into separate rooms. We left when no one was looking."

"But you were tempted?"

"Curious, yeah. Tempted, I don't know."

"I think you were curious *and* tempted. Well, maybe you'll get another chance someday."

"I doubt it. The seventies are coming to an end. And people have figured out that our parents didn't switch partners mainly because they had too much sense."

"All that work in vice," she said, "did it put you off sex?"

"What do you think?"

"I think you've demonstrated that you're healthy. Will you stay with me tonight?"

Beckman turned to her, took in the smooth tan of her neck.

"Healthy?" he said.

CHAPTER THIRTY-EIGHT

It was around six a.m. when he heard her in the shower. He got out of bed and dressed and went into her kitchen to make a cup of coffee.

She came out of the bathroom in a bathrobe and slippers. She saw that he was in a coat.

"You in a hurry?"

"No," Beckman said. "I was just cold, I guess."

They looked at each other for a moment, both of them wondering if there was something between them or if this was a first and last encounter, both of them vulnerable.

Beckman said, "I'd like to drive you to work. If that's all right."

Mary-Beth Hanley smiled. "I'd like that. There's bread over there, if you want some toast. I'm afraid that's all I have."

He looked at her in her bathrobe and saw that her hair was wet again. Wet the first time he met her. It seemed like quite a while ago. Asking her about her roommate. They had not discussed her last night.

". . . David?"

He was staring at her, seemingly blank. Fading out on her.

"Are you all right?"

Beckman said, "I need to go out to my car for a minute. I have to get something."

"Is everything okay?"

"Yes. I'll be right back."

"If you don't have time to —"

"I'll be right back."

He ran down the stairs, cursing himself for leaving the report in the car. Someone could have broken into the car and stolen it. Stolen a report? Well, maybe not. But he shouldn't have left it out there overnight. Dumb, dumb, dumb.

He unlocked the car and saw that it was still there. He read it as soon as he got back in the foyer. He read it on the first floor and went immediately to the cartridges.

An old woman opened the door to retrieve her newspaper. She too wore her bathrobe and slippers. She bent over to get the paper as Beckman said, "Oh, shit."

She looked up at the young man standing by her door. Beckman looked back at her and said, "Excuse me."

"Yeah," she said, offended, and slammed her door.

An indignant reaction at about six in the morning. Beckman suspected it would not be the only one of the day.

Beckman said, "It couldn't have been Wheeler."

"Hold on," Regan said. "I just got here. When did you get here?"

"About an hour ago. I got an early start."

"Well, good for you." Regan still had his coat on. They had the homicide desks more or less to themselves. This pleased Beckman.

Beckman said, "The ballistics report on the subway murders showed the victims were killed by a nine millimeter round. All of them. But they were nine by nineteen rounds. A Makarov shoots a nine by *eighteen* round. Wheeler did not kill those people. Now. Look at the ballistics report for Richie LaFevers and Renee Aiken."

Regan sat down and looked at it. A few moments later, he said, "Nine by nineteen."

"Right. The subway victims, Aiken, LaFevers all killed by nine by nineteen rounds. Likely a Browning. I should have seen it before."

"Yeah," Regan said. "I suppose I should have too."

After a moment, Beckman said, "Well, Tom, what do you say? Are you going to suggest that Wheeler had another nine millimeter that he used and threw away after the murders?"

Regan glared at him. "Don't accuse me of that."

"I was just asking."

"No you weren't. No, I'm not going to suggest that. This is exculpatory evidence. I'm not going to hide it."

Beckman said, "I haven't written my report yet."

"You write your report and report your findings."

"Even if it annoys —"

"Yes, even if it annoys Greg. Tell the truth, son, and then you never have to worry about keeping your lies straight. But a word of advice: don't give the impression that you're all too happy about this finding. Not in front of Greg or anyone else for that matter. Tempers may rise."

"I hear you."

"I hope you do." Regan leaned back and processed it. Beckman watched him go through a range of emotions. Disappointment, frustration, anger, maybe even resignation. Then Regan shrugged in a way that made Beckman think he was actually relieved. Not because Wheeler had likely been exonerated. But because now there was solid evidence to back Regan against the brass. Regan was not a man who liked to gamble, particularly with his own career.

"All right," Regan said. "You said you had another lead?"

"Yes. Lester Wayne. The John Doe."

"Okay. Check that out right away. If Greg asks, I'll tell him we have to tie up a few loose ends first. If he gets more specific, I'm going to tell him that *I'm* having difficulty with the cartridge size and that *I* have to investigate it further. Now hold on. I'm not trying to take the credit from you. Greg's not going to like hearing about the cartridge, but he'll take it a lot easier from me than he will you."

Beckman said, "So you can tell him he's wrong, but I can't?"

"Yeah. Greg will defer to me. He may not like it, but he'll do it. But he won't defer to you. You just haven't been here long enough."

Beckman studied Regan for a moment.

And Regan said, "You're going to have to trust me on this. Okay?"

"All right," Beckman said, not sounding all too sure.

"You got an address for Wayne?"

"Yes."
"Better get going then."

CHAPTER THIRTY-NINE

The hotel manager was a tall Ukrainian guy with thick gray hair and horn-rimmed glasses. He wore a brown cardigan over a yellow polyester shirt. He gave Beckman the same quiet hostility he gave to all non-Ukrainians. Beckman followed him up a couple of shabby flights of stairs. Narrow halls, peeling paint, the smell of dried urine.

The Ukrainian said, "I not see this bum for two weeks."

"That's because he's dead," Beckman said. "He was one of the victims in the subway shooting. Did you know about it?"

The Ukrainian did not turn around to answer him. He only waved his hand behind him, showing contempt for the dead and maybe the police too. It had nothing to do with him.

The Ukrainian unlocked the door to a room on the third floor. Beckman stepped in and was hit by another wave of stench.

The Ukrainian was unfazed.

The Ukrainian said, "What I want to know is, who's going to clean this?"

Beckman turned to him and said, "We'll deal with that later. Who came to see this guy? Who did he associate with?"

"I don't want to get involved. It's not my business."

"Look old man. You can answer me here or you can answer me downtown. Which will it be?"

"No one come to see him. He's a bum. Drinking and the drugs. No one come to see him except this nigger who was no good. I talk to Wayne about that. I tell him I don't want no nigger criminals in my place. No drug dealings here."

"A black guy? What did he look like?"

"They all look same to me."

"About how old?"

"I don't know. Thirty, forty. I don't know. He wears these glasses like he's smart or something."

"Know his name?"

The Ukrainian looked around the filthy little room to see if there was anything he could steal. He wished he'd known earlier that Lester Wayne was dead. It would have given him the chance to go through his room before the policeman came here.

"Do you know his name?"

The Ukrainian said, "He come here once, I tell him to get out. He look at me like he was going to do something. Maybe shoot me, I don't know. Lester says, 'Leon, don't.' I remember him saying 'Leon.' "

"Leon what?"

"I don't know." The old man stood up a little taller, puffing his chest. "He not come back here after that."

"He didn't?"

"I tell Lester I see that nigger again, I throw him out. Have to find another place to live."

"You told Lester you'd throw Lester out?"

"Yes."

"You didn't tell the black guy that?"

"I tell him too! He don't scare me."

Beckman suppressed a smile. "All right. Leave me alone for a minute. I need to go through this room."

"What you look for?"

"Get *out.*"

There wasn't much in the room. A cot with a couple of blankets tossed on it. No sheets. A dresser with a few articles of clothing. A heating plate on top of the dresser next to two cans of chili and two empty bottles of Old Style beer. He didn't find any hypodermic needles in the room, but there were traces of cocaine on the nightstand next to the bed. Beckman looked in the trashcan and found a discarded razor blade, its side lined with white powder. He looked back to the nightstand and examined the ashtray, which was still filled with cigarette butts. He dropped down to the floor and looked under the bed. He found a couple of spank magazines under there, which he pulled out. Then he reached back and pulled out a discarded matchbook. The matchbook said, "The Orchid."

Beckman used the pay phone in the bodega across the street.

Fortunately, Ray Wilson was still at home in bed.

Ray said, "The fuck you calling me so early for?"

Beckman said, "You shouldn't be sleeping this late anyway, you lazy shit."

"I'm in vice," Ray said. "We work doper's hours. Remember?"

"I remember. That's why I thought I'd find you at home. Hey, I need your help on something."

"Again?"

"A massage parlor called the Orchid. Do you know it?"

"The Orchid . . . oh, yeah. I know it. You

know it too. It was called Fifty-One up until about a year ago."

"Oh Jesus Christ, really?" Beckman's voice raised now. "Are you shitting me?"

"No. It used to be the Fifty-One. You remember it."

"Fuck yes, I remember it. That was Leon Murray's place, wasn't it?"

"Yeah."

"Is it still?"

"I guess. We haven't hounded him for a while. We never could get him on anything. He's getting older, I guess. Or smarter."

"I'd say smarter," Beckman said. "I'm coming by."

"Ah shit, Deke, come on. I was up till four last night."

"Stop whining, pussy. I'll buy your breakfast."

CHAPTER FORTY

Regan cleaned his spoon with his napkin before he stirred the milk into his coffee. As he stirred he looked across the table at the vice cop with the long hair and sideburns. The vice cop dipped both his bread and his bacon into his egg yolks and did not use his napkin between bites.

Beckman was both amused and agitated by the contrast between these two men. Both of them Chicago police officers, both of them graduates from the same police academy. But all cops are snobs and all cops seek out sub-tribes within the cop tribe itself. Homicide detectives, of course, were the biggest snobs of all. It was up to Beckman to mediate whatever breach or distrust existed between the partner he had now and the one he had had at vice. He hoped that Ray did not ken to the distaste that so clearly registered on Regan's face. He wished that Regan had spent at least a month or two working vice so he could understand they weren't all degenerates.

Regan said, "This Ukrainian, has he identified Murray?"

Beckman said, "Not in a lineup, no. I think we should hold on that for now."

Regan said, "And what if he did? What would it prove? That Lester Wayne was associated with a known pimp and drug dealer? It's not much."

Ray Wilson said, "I don't think you understand. Leon Murray is a killer. We think he's responsible for about a dozen murders over the last seven years."

"Why didn't you tell us, then?" Regan said.

"We tried to," Ray said. "More than once. But even we knew there was no evidence against him. He's a slippery guy."

Regan looked at Beckman. "You're familiar with this fella?"

"Yes," Beckman said. "A couple of years ago, we were close to getting him on a major drug bust. Then our snitch disappeared. And not just the snitch, the snitch's girlfriend too. And that was the end of our case. We know he killed them and he knew we knew, but we had nothing to prove it."

"And now you want to pin this on him," Regan said.

"I didn't say that," Beckman said. "I'm just saying it's a lead."

"Well," Regan said, "I see a gleam in your eye that tells me you'd like to see this man go down. But what would be his motive for killing five people at a train stop?"

"I don't know," Beckman said. "I don't know yet. We know he's a dealer and we know he knew Lester Wayne well enough to visit his apartment. And we also know that Richie LaFevers was using coke. And all of the victims were killed by a nine millimeter pistol."

Regan said, "So under your theory, Nathan Wald was not the target, but this fella Lester was."

Ray Wilson said, "I know what you're saying. Too much coincidence. But you don't understand Leon. He's got his fingers in a lot of pies. He started out as your run of the mill gangster and small-time pimp. But one thing leads to another. Nightclubs, pussy, bars, you want to be a big man in that life, you want to stay in business, you have to have cocaine. That's how it is now."

Regan reared back his head, offended at the suggestion that he was old and unaware of how things were "now."

Ray Wilson did not seem to notice it. He said, "But just because he's a success at girls and drugs, doesn't mean he's retired from killing. He's still doing that. Sometimes to protect himself, sometimes for pay."

"A contract killer, too, huh?" Regan said. "Does he need the money?"

"He likes money, yeah," Ray said. "But he likes killing too. He's good at it."

Regan said, "It still doesn't hold water. Why would this Renaissance man you speak of bother with killing a nobody like Lester Wayne? And in so public a place?"

After a moment, Beckman said, "I don't know. Maybe Wald *was* the target. Maybe Leon used Lester to help set it up. Had Lester follow Wald and then call him or something to let him know where he would be."

"David," Regan said, "you are about as far out on the limb as you can be. Five people were killed, Lester Wayne included. A professional hit man does not do that."

"Something went wrong," Beckman said. "Maybe Lester panicked. Or maybe it was Leon's plan to kill Lester all along."

Ray said, "I'm sure that was the plan. He wouldn't leave a guy like Lester around to talk about it."

Beckman looked at Regan and said, "It wasn't Wheeler, Tom. You know that. Here's a suspect we *know*. This is a legitimate lead.

Please don't dismiss it."

Regan shook his head and smiled. "All right, David. I'll back you. But I hope you like Oak Park, because that's where we'll both be walking a beat if this falls through."

CHAPTER FORTY-ONE

Regan was the one who said they shouldn't try to talk to Leon Murray right away. Beckman disagreed.

Beckman said, "He's a suspect, isn't he?"

"You've established that he's a person of interest," Regan said. "Not the same thing as a suspect. You haven't told Deegan or Osulnic about this, have you?"

"No. Just you."

"Good. Keep it under your hat for a while."

"If you say so," Beckman said. "But if we — if I think that Leon's a person of interest, I think Deegan and Osulnic should know. After all, I think he probably killed Renee Aiken and LaFevers too."

"You tell Deegan and company that and they're liable to bring Leon to the station and start beating him on the head with a phonebook to get a confession out of him." Regan turned to Beckman. "Much as this may surprise you, that is not a method I approve of."

"That's good to know," Beckman said. "I thought you were going to tell me they'd tell me to go fuck myself."

"They might do that as well. Does this Leon know you?"

"We've met. Friend of a friend, not so much man to man. I was undercover at the time. If he remembers me at all, it would be as Deke Waters."

"Back when you had the long hair and beard?"

"Yeah. But I don't look like that now."

"He'll remember you, though. That kind tends to remember."

Beckman smiled. "That kind?"

"The smart kind," Regan said. "What did you think I meant?"

Beckman didn't answer him. He remembered Regan telling him he didn't like his kids using the word "nigger." Maybe because it was wrong. Or maybe because Regan wanted his kids to become something more than cops or construction workers.

Regan said, "For now, we're going to keep our heads down and spend some time tracking Mr. Murray. I want to get a feel for him."

■ ■ ■ ■

They picked up Leon Murray coming out of the Orchid. Saw him get into a Lincoln Continental. They followed him, Regan driving the Chevy Nova, keeping cars between them and the Lincoln. Soon they were on Lake Shore Drive headed south, Regan's eyes like a hunter's.

Beckman said, "They'd do that?"

"Do what?"

"Transfer us to Oak Park. You were joking about that, right?"

Regan shook his head.

"And yet you defend Lieutenant Greg," Beckman said.

"Why wouldn't I?" Regan said. "We lose our shields, it wouldn't be his fault. Wouldn't be his decision. Greg is one of about twenty-five thousand city employees. Don't put it on him."

"All right."

"You fought in Vietnam, didn't you?"

"Yes."

"And came back filled with distrust and bitterness about the establishment, eh?"

"You make it sound like a cliché. There was some pretty dirty shit going on there."

"Nothing new under the sun, David.

Young people like you think it's all corrupt and dirty. Like you think no one saw it until your generation came along. What you don't realize is things are much cleaner now than they were twenty years ago. In the fifties, you could count honest cops in Chicago on a couple of hands. It was part of the natural order. Like cold weather and polluted rivers. Things are better now and maybe they'll be even better now that the Boss is dead."

"The Boss . . . you mean Daley?"

"You didn't hear me say his name," Regan said. "Like him, I'm a Bridgeport boy. It's where I was born and where I'll die. Daley built this city and he never stole a dime. But he didn't rat on people who did. He knew the time he lived in."

"But you're suggesting it's better that he's gone?"

"I'm suggesting that some changes are for the better. The police department isn't squeaky clean now — no police department is — but it's a lot better than it used to be, trust me. It's certainly cleaner than New York. So I'm not complaining and you shouldn't either."

Beckman said, "I didn't think I'd hear that from you."

"You didn't."

■ ■ ■ ■

Leon Murray parked outside the Taft Gardens and went inside. Regan parked nearby.

Regan said, "Let me see the file."

Beckman handed him the Leon Murray file. A moment later, Regan said, "The Gangster Disciples?"

"Yeah," Beckman said. "Though he quit wearing the six-point star years ago. Went on to better things, I guess."

"Cocaine dealing."

"It was a smart play," Beckman said. "Every pimp's got to have cocaine. He figured out it'd be better to supply his own clubs than to buy it himself. He sells to other pimps too. One of them, a rival pimp, went into dealing too and made the mistake of trying to sell to Leon's customers. We found his body near the Fullerton station."

"But couldn't pin it on him?"

"No witnesses."

"None here either," Regan said. "I vaguely remember this guy. The Disciples were formed about ten years ago by McCoy . . ."

"Ike McCoy and Jimmy Coolidge. Jimmy Cool. Leon was a protégé of Cool's. They had what could be called an amicable split. Ray said the Taft Gardens has been claimed by Leon's crew."

Regan said, "We had so many murders at this place. All of the victims black. We hardly solved any of them. Nobody ever sees anything. Not that I blame them for keeping quiet. They know if they talk, they'll be killed next. One woman I interviewed said to me, 'You tell me, Sergeant, where am I supposed to go?' A good lady too. They built these places for the working poor and now they're just imprisoned here. It breaks your heart."

Beckman looked at his partner. Expressing what some would foolishly call liberal sentimentality. Beckman thought of what he had told Mary-Beth. A cop can't believe that everyone and everything is shit because eventually it'll destroy him. Regan was strong.

Regan said, "But then a few years ago, the murder rate here dropped to almost nothing."

"About the time Leon took it over," Beckman said.

"Ah," Regan said. "A peacekeeping strongman. Like Tito in Yugoslavia keeping all them Slavs from killing each other. And now you want to put him in jail."

After a moment, Beckman said, "Yeah, I do."

■ ■ ■ ■

It was dark later. Beckman asked if they could turn on the engine so they could get the heater going. Regan said no, smoke would come out of the exhaust and Leon might see it when he came out to his car. Beckman got a wool stocking cap out of his coat pocket and pulled it down over his ears.

Regan said, "Having second thoughts?"

"About this? No."

"Just checking."

Beckman saw the Irishman smile in the dark. Christ, enjoying himself. Probably savoring the moment when the younger man would start whining about being cold and tired. They'd been there about two hours, looking at an empty car in front of a massive, ugly apartment complex. Even if Leon Murray had gone in there and shot a dozen people, they wouldn't be able to hear it.

Regan didn't talk much after making comments about Daley and the bad old days. Beckman wondered if he'd hear more from Regan. His childhood, how he became a cop, what his wife nagged him about, which one of his kids drove him crazy, and so forth. The usual things partners talk about and become intimate over. But Regan hardly said anything. He was comfortable being silent, which is actually unusual for a cop. Beckman did the math and saw that Regan had long since gotten his twenty in and could retire with a full pension. He asked Regan why he hadn't.

Regan seemed not to hear him at first. Then he said, "And do what?"

"I don't know," Beckman said. "Loaf. Spend more time with your kids."

"My kids are in school during the day."

Beckman said, "I don't think you're the type that would —" Beckman almost said, *eat his gun.* "I don't think you're the type of cop who would fall apart when he retired."

Regan grunted. A few more moments passed and Regan said, "And what about you?"

"I've got another ten or so years before I got my twenty in."

"No, that's not what I'm talking about. You're young. You're going to law school, aren't you?"

"Yeah."

"Why don't you finish? Practice law and double, maybe even triple your income. Get out of this business."

Beckman said, "You asking or suggesting?"

"Ah, take the chip off your shoulder, lad. I'm only asking."

"I don't know, exactly. You asked me before if I became a cop to prevent the rise of the Fourth Reich. Maybe you were curious or maybe you were just trying to give me shit. But it doesn't matter. I don't really know. Everyone who's close to me . . . almost everyone . . . wonders what I'm doing here. My mother, my brother. My ex-wife, she never understood it. Like I was too smart or something to be doing this. I think they give me credit I don't deserve." Beckman laughed. "More likely, they're just embarrassed by me."

Beckman saw the older cop shake his head in the dark. He was offended at the notion than anyone should be embarrassed to have a cop in the family, but he didn't want Beckman to know it. In some way, Beckman was almost touched by this restraint.

Beckman said, "When I was in high school, I played basketball. I was pretty good, actually. Made All State. Was the team's leading scorer. Got my name in the papers. Before I got drafted by the Army, I had these dreams of playing for the Knicks. Be the next Bill Bradley. Dreams . . . more like delusions. I had completely overestimated my abilities, of course, but I didn't know that then. But when I was about seventeen, my father told me that our people didn't *play* for teams, we *owned* them. I really hated him for telling me that."

"Maybe he was trying to be kind."

"Being kind wasn't his style," Beckman said, staring out the window at the black night. "He was expressing contempt. Maybe for me, maybe for my teammates, very few of whom were Jewish. He knew full well I'd never own a professional team. Or play for one."

Regan said, "Your father's dead, isn't he?"

"Yeah."

"If I were you," Regan said, "I'd let that go."

"What do you mean?"

"You know what I mean. Your old man is dead. Being angry at him isn't going to make life any better or more purposeful."

Beckman smiled. "Okay. But I hope you don't think I do this to get back at him in some way."

"I never thought that," Regan said. "No, the truth is, you do this because you're like the rest of us. You like the hunt, you like the rush. God help you, you might even like the fraternity. No nobler than the next detective, no worse."

"So then we're both trapped," Beckman said.

"Pretty much."

"Listen, Tom —"

"Ssshh." Regan lifted a hand to silence him.

In the distance, they saw a shadow approach. The outline became Leon Murray as he walked to the Lincoln Continental and got inside. They heard the engine kick and saw the brake lights come on. Then go off.

The Lincoln remained where it was. Smoke came out of the tailpipe.

Regan took his hand off the key ignition. He remained still.

Beckman said, "Christ, you think he's made us?"

"I don't know."

Regan unbuttoned his coat. Then he reached inside and took his snubnose .38 revolver out and set it on the seat. Beckman watched him and took out his own revolver and held it in his right hand.

Regan said, "Keep your hand off the trigger. We don't want any accidents."

Six long minutes passed. And then they saw the beams of approaching headlights. Flinched at first but then saw the lights weren't coming to them.

A Cadillac pulled up next to the Lincoln. Leon Murray got out of the Lincoln and got into the Cadillac.

Beckman took a pair of binoculars out of the back seat. Lifted them to his eyes.

"Can't see the tag from here," Beckman said. "We need to get behind him."

Regan said, "It's a new one."

Beckman said, "With our luck, it'll be an alderman."

Another twelve minutes ticked by. The Cadillac and Lincoln parked next to each other, both of them running in the hard, cold night. Two men sitting in plush seats with the heater on, another two sitting in a Chevy Nova trying not to let their teeth chatter. Then Murray was back in his Continental and driving away even as they saw the brake lights flash red and then the Cadillac pulled away and came toward them. They dropped down beneath the dash. The beam of lights filled the top of the car, then passed.

Beckman came up. He put the binoculars on his eyes and looked out the back window. It was too dark and too far to read the license plate.

Regan said, "You get it?"

"No."

Regan turned the key in the ignition.

Started the car and put hand over hand to turn the steering wheel. Then they were going after the Caddy.

Beckman said, "What about Murray?"

"He'll keep," Regan said. "I want to know who this other fella is."

CHAPTER FORTY-TWO

Mandel had wanted to think things were the same between him and Leon. He paid him his usual sum tonight for maintaining order at the Taft Gardens and they had their usual chat about events. Only it wasn't the usual. Leon was guarded and almost defensive. It was as if Leon had gone back to being black, back to remembering that Mandel was white. Mandel was not entirely surprised. He had long since grown used to people reverting to tribe in times of stress. The Pole summoning up his ancient hatred for the Jew, the black his resentment of the white man.

Mandel thought this was unfair because he believed he had always been kind to blacks. He had not treated his black tenants as other white landlords had. He had not carved four units into sixteen and jacked up the rent. And he had not joined other whites who lobbed rocks or eggs at the blacks when

Dick Gregory and Martin Luther King had come to town and persuaded them to march through the white neighborhoods to demand equal access to housing. Mandel's thought then was, why? Why be hateful to the blacks? They needed homes like everyone else. It was just a question of where to put them. Mandel had learned from experience that every upheaval — societal or otherwise — presented a business opportunity for a smart man who knew how to exploit it.

Mandel agreed with most whites in power that the blacks should remain tenants, not owners. He kept this belief to himself because he was smart enough to know that people like Leon would accuse him of being a paternalistic bigot. The sort who is personally kind to blacks, but is none too comfortable with them being up. But Mandel knew how to play the Urban Renewal game. He too supported the clearing out of slums, only to replace them with apartment complexes with rents far too expensive to house the blacks.

Yet in spite of these attitudes, he had always felt that he and Leon had understood each other. If he looked down on blacks as helpless little children, he believed that Leon didn't give them any more consideration. Indeed, Mandel believed that Leon exploited the blacks far more than he did. Mandel gave them places to live. Leon sold them dope and killed them when they got out of line.

Maybe LaFevers had gotten out of line with Leon too. But Mandel suspected it was Renee who had probably provoked Leon. Renee always did have a sharp tongue. Now Mandel realized he missed her.

It was time for a change. Time to sell the Taft Gardens and break himself away from Leon Murray. He had thought about it before. But Renee's death had been a sign. Mandel had seen such signs before. Like when the Germans invaded and he over- heard a Pole telling a friend not to bother paying the Jewish doctor his bill. The Pole knowing the Jewish doctor wouldn't be in business much longer.

Now Mandel pulled his Caddy up to a stoplight. Waiting, he looked in the rearview mirror and saw a car behind him. There were two men in the car. There was enough light to see that the men were white. Two white men in a plain wrapper Chevy in a very black neighborhood. His heart rate increased and he felt his temperature rise. The light turned green. He hesitated for a moment, then he drove forward.

■ ■ ■ ■

"Shit," Beckman said. "I think he made us."

Regan said, "Yeah. Damn. I should have stayed back, but there are no other cars out here."

"Well, he saw us," Beckman said. "I wrote the tag down."

Regan surprised Beckman then. He said, "What do you think we should do?"

It took Beckman a second to realize that Regan was serious. No rhetorical question. Christ, was Regan admitting he'd made a mistake?

Beckman said, "Get up on him, pull him over."

"For what? He's not speeding."

"I'll handle it," Beckman said.

Regan accelerated and brought the Nova up to the Caddy. He put the red light on the dash and flicked it on. The Caddy went another block and then pulled over to the side.

Beckman put his revolver into his coat pocket. He took his stocking cap off and put it on the seat. He stepped out of the car and held his gold shield up in the glare of the Nova's headlight.

"Police officer, sir! I just want to talk to you."

Beckman approached the Caddy. The driver's side window rolled down.

Mandel said, "Can I help you?"

Beckman said, "Good evening, sir." Beckman showed him his shield up close. "Sorry to bother you."

"Was I speeding?" Mandel said. "I don't believe I was."

"No, sir, you weren't. My partner and I are on patrol. We were afraid you were lost."

"Why would you think that?"

"Well, sir, this is not exactly a . . . a safe neighborhood. I presume you don't live around here."

"I don't."

"Are you from out of town?"

"No. I live in Chicago."

"May I see your driver's license?"

"I suppose."

Mandel took his wallet out. He debated putting a folded twenty dollar bill next to the driver's license and handing it to the policeman. He had done it before. But something told him it wouldn't be a good idea this time.

Beckman examined the license.

Beckman said, "Mr. Mandel?"

"Yes."

"You're okay, aren't you?"

"Yes."

"You haven't been drinking?"

"Oh, no. I don't drink."

"Just asking. What are you doing down here?"

Beckman looked steadily at him.

And Mandel said, "I own some properties down here. Just checking up on them."

"Not meeting with anyone, are you?"

"No, officer."

"Oh. Well, like I said, my partner and I were afraid you were lost and this being a rough neighborhood, we had some concerns for your safety."

"I see."

"A word of advice, sir, if you're checking on properties in this part of town, you might want to bring someone with you. It's really not a safe area."

"I know the area," Mandel said.

"Okay. Well, just to play it safe, we'll follow behind until you're out of it."

"Thank you, but it really isn't necessary." His voice a little sharper now.

"We'd feel better doing it," Beckman said, and handed him back the license. "You know how to get out of here?"

Mandel sighed, no longer trying to hide his irritation. "Yes."

"Okay. Well just to be clear, you go up this road for about five blocks and then you make a right on Hoover. That'll take you to Lake Shore. Okay?"

"I know that."

"All right. Have a safe evening, Mr. Mandel."

Regan rolled his window back up when Beckman got back in the car. Regan smiling now.

Regan said, "You're a smooth one, aren't you?"

"I have moments," Beckman said. "We're going to follow him for the next couple of miles. Escort him out of this dangerous area."

"I heard."

CHAPTER FORTY-THREE

Regan said, "Is he a Jewish fella?"

"I think so," Beckman said. "He has an accent. Polish, I believe. His license said he was born in 1919. Ugly guy. Wears these thick, tinted glasses like Onassis. But he's fat faced. Looks like a bug."

"And you say he lied to you?"

"Well, I would say he did. I asked him if he was meeting anyone and he said no. So he lied about meeting with Leon."

They sat at a diner near the station. Regan breaking crackers over a bowl of soup. Beckman eating an egg sandwich.

Regan said, "You're taking a chance, sonny."

"How's that?" Beckman asked.

"Eating an egg salad sandwich. Never order egg salad, tuna fish, or meatloaf at a restaurant. They're positively swimming in bacteria."

"More pearls of wisdom from the man on

the mountain," Beckman said. "How do you know someone didn't sneeze in your soup?"

"Anything's possible," Regan said. "But, yeah, I was talking about Mandel too."

"I figured. You think looking into Mandel is risky?"

Regan said, "He may be nobody. But I doubt it. A rich old man with a Cadillac and a Polish accent. Meeting with a known criminal, a killer."

"And lying about it."

"Well, who wouldn't lie about something like that? Doesn't make him a murderer."

"What if he knew Wald?"

"Yeah, I'm thinking about that too. But something else. I've heard that name before."

"Has he got a record?"

"Not that I know of," Regan said. "No, I think I saw his name in the newspaper."

He had. The next morning, he confirmed it by calling a reporter he knew at the *Sun-Times*. He discussed it with Beckman at their desks.

Regan said, "He's a slumlord. *The Sun-Times* did a feature on him three years ago. The title of the story was 'Portrait of a Slumlord.' He let Royko interview him. Apparently, he enjoyed it."

"Being a slumlord?"

"No. The interview. He even liked the Royko column, even though Royko went after him pretty hard. My friend said he was charming, liked being a celebrity. He said he wasn't a slumlord, that he liked negroes and he was simply supplying a demand for clean, affordable housing."

"Does he own the Taft Gardens?"

"As a matter of fact, he does. And odds are, he has some arrangement with Mr. Murray to maintain order."

"What else?"

"He is Jewish. And he is Polish, like you thought. He came to Chicago after the war. The Nazis wiped out his entire family. He's never married and has no children. He likes nice cars and young women."

"Christ," Beckman said. "He's a Holocaust survivor."

"Yep. He came from a town called Love?"

"Lvov," Beckman said. "It's also pronounced Lviv. It's not in Poland anymore."

"Pardon me?"

"The town became part of the Soviet Union after the Second World War. We gave it to them."

"We . . . ?"

"The Allies. The Americans, the British. We let the Soviets take that part of Poland.

What it means is, after the war, the man had no home to go back to."

"And no family either."

"No."

Regan studied Beckman for a moment. "So now you feel guilty?"

"What do you mean?"

"Last night, you harassed the man and had a Cheshire grin afterwards. Now you want to leave him alone because he lost everything?"

"I didn't say that, Tom."

"Good. Now you met this Renee Aiken, didn't you?"

"Yeah."

"Pretty young girl, liked nice shiny things?"

"Yeah. A hustler."

"Do you think it's possible that Mr. Mandel knew her?"

"Anything's possible, I guess. We can talk to friends of Renee's, see if they know him. Or we can go to Deegan and Osulnic, see what they know."

Regan lifted a hand. "Not yet. We need to talk to someone else first."

Beckman was relieved. He didn't want to talk to Deegan and Osulnic either. Not yet, as Regan said. But he knew that if he'd suggested avoiding them, Regan would have scolded him for hoarding leads. Which was exactly was Regan doing. His eyes lit now with anticipation.

On the way there, Beckman said, "Is this guy Mafia?"

Regan said, "Come now. This is 1979." And didn't say anything else.

Beckman said, "Is that a yes or a no?"

The guy they were going to see was Curly Quinn, boss of the ward in which the Taft Gardens was located. Officially, the ward was supposed to be under the authority of the elected alderman, a black guy named Simmons. But in old Chicago and new, the alderman took his marching orders from the ward boss. An Irishman named Quinn who may or may not have been a front man for the mob. The things Regan kept from him. 1979, his ass.

Curly Quinn had a real-estate office with a view of the Chicago River and the Wrigley Building. He was a few years older than Regan and he had a healthy mane of white hair. He embraced Regan like a cousin and asked him how his family was. They talked about Curly's little brother, who Beckman later learned had grown up with Regan. Then Regan introduced him to the young detective who was now his partner.

Quinn eyed him a little too long and said, "Beckman?"

"Yes," Beckman said. Thinking how quickly people could put you outside.

"Breakin' him in," Regan said. "This fella's going places."

Beckman looked at Regan, surprised. Thinking he was joking, but seeing Regan's delivery was directed at Quinn. He wanted Quinn to believe it.

Quinn said, "I've been to the Policeman's Ball for the last ten years. I don't think we've met before."

Beckman looked back at the silver-haired Irishman with the suspicious gaze and thought, *what*? Tell him Elyse refused to go? Elyse looking down on policeman's balls and Irish ward bosses who clapped Irish cops on the shoulders and talked about the old neighborhood.

Regan said, "That's the problem with this young man. He's always burying his head in work. We need to talk, Curly."

Quinn released Beckman from his stare and led them into his office. It was a nice, sumptuous affair with a big oak desk and golden shag carpet. A picture of Quinn with his arm around the late Mayor Daley.

They took their seats and Curly Quinn

said, "Christ Jesus, Tom, can you believe it? It looks like Janey Byrne is actually going to win this thing. A woman mayor."

Regan smiled and said, "All because of a little snow and ice."

"Ah shit," Quinn said. "That could have happened to anyone. But I should have seen it coming after Dick died. It's all chaos. The man at City Hall, he's a nice guy, but you gotta have a bastard there. Otherwise, things don't get done. The expressways, the airport, the towers. It's Daley's Chicago and it's all slipping away."

Beckman saw Quinn glance at him at the end of his sentence. He wondered if Quinn held him partly responsible.

Regan said, "I know you're busy, Curly. So I'll come to the point. Peter Mandel. What do you know about him?"

The old Irishman looked at Regan for a moment. Beckman could see that he was thinking it over. Quinn knew that Regan knew that Mandel could not do business in his ward without kicking something over to Quinn. It may have been a small sum, perhaps five hundred a month. Maybe a lesser sum to the alderman. Enough to keep the building inspectors from sticking their noses in. Quinn knew that Regan did not judge for accepting gratuities. He was the ward boss after all, and this was still Chicago.

Quinn said, "Can I ask what this is about, Tom?"

Regan said, "It's nothing to do with you. I promise."

And there it was. Regan was letting him know he wouldn't be touched. But also letting him know he needed to be a good citizen and offer them some guidance.

"What do you want to know?" Quinn said.

"Just enough to get a feel for the man. Who his friends are. His tastes."

"Peter's good people," Quinn said. "A Jew, but I like him. Likes a good laugh, likes the girls. Doesn't touch alcohol."

Regan put a photograph of Renee Aiken on the big oak desk.

"Did you ever see Mandel with her?"

Quinn looked at the photo. His eyes snapped back up at Regan.

"Yeah, I've seen him with her. Not recently, but a year or two ago. But I've seen him with a lot of young girls. He likes them young."

Regan took the photo back.

Quinn sighed and said, "You're still homicide, aren't you Tom?"

"Yeah."

"Has that girl been murdered?"

"Yeah."

"Ah, Jesus. You don't suspect Mandel, do you?"

"Oh, no. No, we're just checking out all the possibilities."

"Well, I don't think Peter would harm anyone. He's a gentle person."

Beckman said, "He owns a lot of apartment buildings in some pretty rough areas. I imagine he'd have to be pretty tough to do that."

Quinn seemed to acknowledge Beckman for the first time. "Yes, he would. And he is tough in his way. Yeah, he runs with a few rough types and the girls he gets involved with are not the sort you'd bring to the family reunion. But he's not a bad man. I read that dirty piece the paper wrote about him a few years ago. They made him out to be some sort of ogre. But those people don't appreciate anything."

Beckman said, "You mean black people?"

Quinn grinned. "Ah, a bleeding heart. Yes, black people. Daley gave them all those swimming pools and they *still* complained. But Mandel likes the blacks. He treats them better than most. Better than they treat each other."

Regan said, "What about Leon Murray? How does Mandel treat him?"

370

The bonhomie vanished. Quinn frowned and said, "I don't know anything about him."

Regan said, "Does Leon work for him?"

"I haven't the slightest idea. As I said, I barely know the man."

Beckman said, "That's not what you —"

Regan silenced him with a gesture. "Okay," Regan said. "Well, I guess that's all I wanted to know."

Quinn led them out with a forced smile.

In the elevator, Beckman said, "He was lying. He knew something about Murray."

Regan smiled and said, "Picked that up, did you?"

"What?"

"Of course he knew. He all but told us. Did you notice the way he looked at me after I brought up Leon? Like a sort of plea for sympathy. That was his way of confirming it for us."

"I saw him look at you, but . . ."

"You expect a politician to tell you the straight truth, you may as well turn in your badge right now. You take what the defense gives you."

"He said he barely knew Mandel."

"Ah, he didn't expect us to believe that. What he was saying was that he'd told us enough. If Mandel is involved in this, then he'll say he met him only once or twice and it was in a crowd. See, Curly's no fool. He doesn't know anything, but he senses that Mandel may be in very big trouble. And when that happens, political friends tend to vanish."

Beckman said, "So what do we know now? We know that Peter Mandel was involved with Renee Aiken, a sometime call girl, and that Mandel works with Leon Murray, maybe pays him to keep order at the Taft Gardens. Maybe something worse. But that doesn't connect him to Nathan Wald."

The elevator doors opened and they walked out into the lobby.

Regan said, "Curly may start some gossip. Some people do that when they get scared."

Beckman said, "So Mandel's going to hear we're interested in him."

"Right," Regan said. "Let's pay him a visit before that happens."

CHAPTER FORTY-FOUR

Mandel had tea with an alderman representing a ward on the West Side.

Mandel was considering building public housing there, but construction of public housing could not begin without the consent of the alderman. The alderman was greedy and, worse, loud. He set the price of his consent at eighty thousand dollars and Mandel had to tell him that he had committed to nothing as of yet, not even the financing. If the terms were too unreasonable, he would simply walk away from the project. The alderman got louder. Mandel never raised his voice. He just said, "This is unfortunate" and got up to leave. The alderman settled down and within twenty minutes agreed to take twenty-five thousand.

Mandel felt better when he left. If the West Side project came together, he would be in a better position to sell the Taft Gardens and ease Leon Murray out of his life.

He drove to his office. When he got there he would call Sally and see if she would be free to meet him for lunch at the Berghoff. Maybe he would buy her a present after. It was almost warm enough today to walk down Michigan Avenue.

He opened the door to his office and saw two detectives sitting on the couch in his waiting room. The older one holding his hat and chatting with his secretary. The younger one he remembered from the night before.

Mandel managed to put a smile on his face. He'd survived Nazis and Soviets. He could handle a couple of American cops.

Mandel looked directly at Beckman and said, "We meet again."

The detectives stood up. The younger one said, "Right. I apologize for not introducing myself last night. I'm Detective Beckman. This is Sergeant Regan."

Mandel's heart skipped a beat. Standing before him was the Jewish detective Renee had told him about. His bête noire. A young man with thick dark hair, handsome and confident as Mandel himself had once been. *You've survived worse.*

Mandel made a gesture. "Still concerned about my safety?"

Beckman said, "In a way, yes."

Regan said, "We'd just like a moment of

your time, sir."

Mandel was conscious of his secretary watching him. Two homicide detectives in the reception area, not building inspectors holding out their hands. Mandel had hired the secretary for her looks, not for her discretion.

Mandel said, "Well, I do have a lunch appointment."

"We'll be brief," Regan said.

Mandel made a point of not looking at his secretary. He must not appear weak or frightened before her. He sighed and motioned the detectives into his office.

Mandel sat behind his desk. He put his hat on the desk, but left his coat on. The key was to look annoyed, but not worried. He would not worry.

"Well?" Mandel said.

Regan said, "Renee Aiken was murdered. You know that?"

"Yes. I know about it. A horrible thing."

"She was a friend?"

"She was a very close friend. About a year and a half ago. We spent some time together."

"Romantically involved?"

"Yes. We lived together for a while."

"When was the last time you saw her?"

"Well, I saw her . . . good heavens, you

don't suspect me, do you?"

"Oh no," Regan said. "We're just trying to get some background. When was the last time you saw her?"

"Oh, it was a couple of weeks ago."

"Where?"

Mandel leaned back in his chair a bit. "Let's see . . . it was at a restaurant. I was with my girlfriend, Sally."

"Sally who?"

Christ. Would they talk to Sally too?

"Sally Ryan."

"Could you give us her address and telephone number?"

"Why do you need that?"

Regan frowned at him, disappointed. "It's a homicide investigation, sir. We have to be thorough."

Beckman said, "We have to check every lead."

Mandel said, "You say I'm not a suspect?"

"That's correct," Regan said.

"Then why were you following me last night?"

Beckman said, "Well, I'm afraid we can't tell you that at this time. But I will tell you that it wasn't you we were following."

The detectives let it hang there. It was up to Mandel if he wanted to admit he was meeting with Leon Murray. They had just told him they were tracking Leon.

Mandel decided not to admit it. He just said, "I see."

"Mr. Mandel?" Regan said.

"Yes." Mandel was afraid they were going to ask him what he was doing on the South Side last night. He had already told the Jewish detective he was checking on his properties. Nothing about Leon. Christ, what did they know?

"Ms. Ryan's address?"

Mandel relaxed, relieved that they weren't going to press him about Leon. He gave them Sally's address and number.

Regan said, "Did you know Mr. LaFevers as well?"

"Yes, I knew him."

"Do you know of anyone who would want to harm Mr. LaFevers?"

"No, I can't think of anyone."

"What about Ms. Aiken?"

"No one would want to hurt Renee. All she did was give people pleasure."

Regan said, "You feel bad that she was killed, don't you?"

"Well of course I do. I was very fond of her."

"She was a little wild, perhaps?"

"She liked to have fun, yes, but —"

"But she didn't deserve to be killed, did she?"

Mandel found himself looking to the young Jewish detective. Looking for . . . what? An appeal for sympathy? Help from a fellow Jew against the soft-steeled persistence of the Irish cop? The Jew was his enemy too. Maybe more so.

Mandel said, "No, she didn't."

Regan said, "But someone killed her."

"Yes."

Beckman said, "Before he died, Richie LaFevers got a pretty good beating. Bad enough to put him in the hospital. Did you know about that?"

"I — no, I did not know that."

"You sure?"

"Renee may have said something to me about it. Or maybe it was Sally."

"You don't remember which?"

"I think it was Sally."

"When did Sally tell you?"

"I don't know. A few days ago. Obviously, before Richie was killed."

"Did Richie use drugs?"

"I haven't the slightest idea."

"Did Renee?"

"I haven't the slightest idea."

Regan said, "Well, I can understand you not knowing if Mr. LaFevers used drugs.

But . . . you *lived* with Ms. Aiken. Surely you would know if she had a habit."

"I lived with her for a short time a long time ago. If she was on drugs then, I didn't know about it. I don't use them myself. I don't even drink."

Beckman said, "Who beat Richie up?"

"I don't know."

"Who do you think did it?"

"I have no idea. We were not friends."

"Did Renee have an opinion?"

"If she did, she didn't tell me."

Beckman said, "I'm going to tell you something, Mr. Mandel. I talked with Richie, before he was beaten up and after. He seemed like he was in a lot of trouble. Would you know why?"

"No."

"You sure?"

Mandel smiled again and Beckman saw that he actually did have a pleasant smile beneath the tinted glasses and the bug's face.

"Detective, you've twice asked me if I'm sure. As if I'm lying. But I have no reason to lie to you. I'm a businessman, not a gangster."

Regan said, "We understand that, Mr. Mandel. And Mr. Beckman certainly intends no offense. But in our business, we get lied to a lot. Usually by people who haven't committed any crimes. Even the best of us have something to hide." Regan smiled. "This is Chicago, after all."

Beckman said, "But good citizen or bad citizen, when questioned by the police, the best thing to do is just tell the truth."

"I have told you the truth."

"That's all we want," Beckman said. "Now —"

Regan said, "Mr. Mandel. Do you know Nathan Wald?"

Mandel stared at the Irish detective. Beckman stared at him too, for he hadn't expected the question either. At least not so soon.

Mandel said, "Excuse me?"

"Nathan Wald. Did you know him?"

"I've read about him. He was murdered, I know that."

"Yes," Regan said. "He was. Did you know him?"

"No, I didn't know him."

"Never met him?"

"No."

"But you knew who he was?"

Mandel said, "Yes, I knew he was. I read the papers for heaven's sake. He was in the news more than Jesse Jackson."

Beckman said, "What did you think about

that? What did you think about the fact that he was gunned down?"

Mandel turned to look at Beckman. His expression was one that Beckman hadn't seen before.

"I thought it was tragic," Mandel said. "All those people."

Beckman said, "You thought it was tragic that he was killed or that all those other people were killed?"

"Every death is tragic, Detective. I don't mourn for Mr. Wald any more because he was a Jew. Do you?"

Regan looked from Mandel to Beckman, then back to Mandel.

"Mr. Mandel," Regan said.

"It's all right," Beckman said. "No, Mr. Mandel, I don't mourn his passing any more than the others. I'm just investigating a series of murders."

Mandel said, "You came here to ask questions about Renee, not Nathan Wald. And I believe I've cooperated with you."

Beckman said, "But you do mourn the passing of Renee Aiken, don't you?"

"Very much."

"She was someone you were close to?"

"I've already told you she was."

"But not Nathan Wald."

"Not personally and not in spirit. Not by

381

any means."

Beckman regarded this man. He had survived the Nazis. Had survived persecution and the murder of his entire family. He was a survivor and Beckman realized the strength and endurance of this fat little man. They were a surviving people.

Mandel seemed to sense a hesitation and said, "Was there anything else?" Some iron in his tone then.

After a moment, Beckman gathered himself and said, "Yes. Leon Murray. Do you know him?"

Mandel continued to stare at him. Then he said, "Yes, I know who he is."

Beckman said, "How do you know him?"

"He's in charge of a tenants' organization at the Taft Gardens. He represents their interests. From time to time, I meet with him to discuss their concerns."

"Are you aware that he's a drug dealer?"

"What he does is his business. If what you say is true, he doesn't discuss it with me. He has always been a gentleman with me."

"What does he do for you?"

"I told you, he represents the concerns of the tenants. Much the same way a union president represents the interests of his union membership."

Regan turned his head and smiled.

382

Beckman said, "Wouldn't it be more accurate to say he's more like an enforcer?"

Mandel smiled again and Beckman realized he'd slipped up. Arguing with a witness. Which more often than not gives the witness more control.

Mandel said, "You can call it whatever you like, Detective. But my dealings with Leon are completely legitimate." Mandel stood. "Now if you'll excuse me, I have a date for lunch. I think I can get there by myself, but if you still have concerns about my safety, you're free to follow me. I'll be at the Berghoff."

CHAPTER FORTY-FIVE

In the car, Regan radioed headquarters. He was patched in to the administrative assistant. She told them that Lieutenant Greg wanted them to return to the station immediately. Regan rogered the call.

Beckman said, "We could say we didn't get the message."

"But we did," Regan said. "And I think I know what he's going to say."

"That he wants this wrapped up?"

"Yep."

"I thought you told him about the ballistics report clearing Wheeler."

"I did tell him. He said, 'What about all those other guns Wheeler had?' And I told him that none of them shot a nine by nineteen round."

"And what did he say to that?"

"He said he'd think about it. Now he's thought about it."

Beckman said, "And now he's going to

shut us down."

Regan nodded. "Probably."

"Christ," Beckman said. "It's just too fucking stupid. What difference would it make to City Hall if we cleared it now? The election's in two days. Even if we raised Wheeler from the dead and got him to confess to all the murders, it wouldn't save the mayor from losing to Byrne."

"David, you make the mistake of thinking too clearly. Politicians don't act out of reason, they act out of fear. Especially during an election. The Jewish donors are leaning on the mayor, he's leaning on the police commissioner, and somewhere down the line, someone's leaning on Greg. It's not about Renee Aiken or Richie LaFevers. No one cares about them. It's about Nathan Wald and four other victims killed in the sort of thing that makes national news. They want to say it's solved."

"Even when it's not. And what about Leon Murray? Mandel? We just let them go?"

"What do we have on them at the end of the day? Murray works for Mandel. Mandel used to bed down with Renee Aiken. Mandel may or may not have known Nathan Wald. What does that amount to?"

"Tom, did you see the man? He's up to

his ears in this. I can feel it."

"Your feelings don't constitute evidence. Mandel said he didn't know Wald."

"He knew Wald."

"How do you know that?"

"The way he spoke about him. Saying he didn't mourn his passing. He said something like 'not by any means.' That was too heartfelt. He was expressing contempt for Wald. It was like he couldn't help doing it. There is no way those two haven't met."

"Supposition."

"Instinct," Beckman said. "I don't think clearly all the time."

Regan said, "Say they have met. So what? Why would Mandel want to have him killed?"

"Mickey Shaivetz said Nathan had an eye for the girls."

"Over a girl, then? No, it doesn't wash."

"I don't think it was a girl," Beckman said. "Did you see the way he reacted to Renee Aiken's murder? Sad, but not that sad. He didn't love her. She was just a boost to his vanity. He showed more emotion for Wald. He felt something for Wald. An almost bloodlike hatred. There's something more there."

"You've got pieces, David, yes. Pieces that are certainly relevant. But they don't tie together."

"I know that. Goddammit, I know that. That's why we need time to put them together. If we could just — *fuck,* why is Greg so intent on wrapping this up?"

"I've told you why."

"It's not Wheeler. It was never Wheeler. Mandel is behind this, somehow."

They neared the police station. Regan said, "Where's your car?"

"Back that way."

Regan pulled the Nova over to the side of the street. The station was two blocks away.

Beckman said, "What are you doing?"

"I'm letting you out."

"I don't understand."

Regan said, "Mandel got tough with us there at the end. Telling us he would be having lunch with his girlfriend at the Berghoff. Go there. Only this time, don't let him see you. No more pulling him over and asking him if he's safe. No more showing off. See what the girl knows."

After a moment, Beckman said, "Are you sure you want to do this?"

"I'm not doing it. What I'm going to do is go upstairs and tell Greg you went to lunch. And if he says he wanted to see both of us, I'll tell him there must have been some misunderstanding."

Beckman started to smile but stopped. He didn't feel particularly cocky at this moment. Then he said, "Okay, Tom. But why?"

"Well . . . that business with Mandel telling us we could follow him, it wasn't just you he was defying. I'm a proud man, David. I can't take that sort of thing lying down."

"Okay."

"Stay off the police radio unless absolutely necessary. And don't answer it unless it's me calling. As far as I know, you're at lunch."

"Got it."

"Take the file with you." Regan looked at him for a few moments. Then he said, "It's your case now, Detective. Come back with something."

Beckman went into the Berghoff. He went into the bathroom, washed his hands, and walked out. He saw Mandel sitting with a pretty girl in her early twenties. Mandel handing a fork to a waiter, apparently unhappy with it for some reason.

Beckman went out to his Plymouth. About forty minutes passed and he saw Mandel and the girl come out. The girl was wearing some sort of leather coat with a fox wrap around the neck. She stood about four

388

inches higher than Mandel. She was very pretty.

Mandel hailed a cab. The cab stopped and Mandel opened the door. The girl bent down to kiss Mandel on the cheek and got in the cab. Mandel waved her off.

Beckman started the Plymouth and followed the cab.

Beckman kept the light on top of the Checker cab in his sights. He wondered what Mandel had told her at lunch. Had he told her how beautiful she looked today in her new coat and forty-dollar haircut or had he told her about the two cops coming by his office this morning? Had he flattered her or flattered himself or had he warned her? Maybe Mandel was on his way back to his office now to call his lawyer and tell him about it. Maybe he had saved it for his lawyer because he didn't want the beautiful young woman to see that he was nervous or rattled. Mandel had come a long way since being a penniless refugee from Poland. He had likely compartmentalized his life to become a success or maybe even survive.

The cab stopped at Marshall Field's. The girl got out and went into the department store. It was on Michigan Avenue and Beckman had to drive for a couple of blocks before he could find a place to park. Then he went inside and looked for her.

He saw her in the glass elevator going up. He saw her get off on the fourth floor. He took the elevator up and found her in the restaurant sitting at the bar. The bartender brought her a glass of wine.

Beckman sat near her — leaving one empty stool between them — and ordered a vodka tonic. He gave the girl a brief look and looked at his watch and sipped his drink. He saw the girl give him a not so brief look back. Not coming onto him, but certainly finding him appealing. Maybe even a welcome change.

Beckman realized he still had his gun on him, but it was under his sport coat and that was under his overcoat. She wouldn't be able to see the gun if he left his coat on. His hair was shorter now and his beard was gone, but he had worked undercover for years and surely his talent for role playing hadn't left him. Play the part, he thought. Pick out the character and *become* him. You've done it before.

Beckman looked at her and smiled. She smiled back and he said hello.

Beckman said, "You don't mind me sitting here, do you?"

"No," she said. "I'm not going to be here long."

Beckman said, "I'm David."

"Sally."

They shook hands.

Beckman said, "I think I've seen you before."

"Oh?"

"I think . . . Have you been to Faces?"

"Oh, yeah."

"I *have* seen you before. You're Renee's friend, aren't you?"

Sally Ryan frowned and her lower chin trembled.

"Oh, I'm sorry. Did I say something wrong?"

"No," she said. "You're right, I am a friend of hers. But Renee is dead."

"What? You're joking."

"No. She was killed a couple of days ago. Didn't you know?"

"No, no one told me. Jesus, I'm so sorry."

"It's all right."

"What happened?"

"She got shot. Her and a friend of hers."

"Who?"

"Richie LaFevers. Did you know him?"

"I might have met him. I don't remember." Beckman smiled. "If I did I was probably stoned."

Sally Ryan smiled back at him. "He probably was too. Shit, that's probably what got him killed."

"What? Dope?"

"If only. He was coking, the dumb-ass. Oh. Do you do that?"

"Ah, sometimes. If it's offered. A friend of mine told me, never buy your own and you'll be okay."

"That's smart. But Richie was buying a lot and giving a lot away. Wanted to be a big shot, I guess. Up to his ass in coke debt."

"Well . . . I mean you're just talking about rumors, aren't you."

"No. Renee told me."

"Who was supplying him?"

Sally Ryan looked at him.

"Hey," Beckman said, "not that I'm looking to buy. But if I ever did, I'd want to know who to stay away from."

"Well, you didn't hear it from me. But stay away from a spook named Leon."

"Leon who?"

"Leon Murray. He is bad fucking news."

"He kill Richie?"

"I didn't say that. I don't know *what* happened. But Richie knew him and he knew Richie."

Beckman looked ahead and smiled. He saw her watching him.

She said, "You think I'm shitting you?"

"I don't know," Beckman said, still smiling.

"What?"

Beckman said, "I met that guy you're talking about. Leon. I thought he was okay."

"Where did you meet him?"

"At a club. He sat at our table for a while. I thought he was interesting."

"Interesting? I met him too, briefly. He looked at Richie, that was it, just looked at him. And I'd never seen a guy look like that. Just fucking menace. Richie said, 'Hi, Leon.' And then walked off to talk to him."

"Wow. How incriminating."

"Shut up. They walked off together and I couldn't hear what they were saying, but I saw Leon just sort of tug on Richie's tie. You know, threatening him. Richie came back to the table and was all smiles, but you could see he was about to pee himself he was so scared."

"You saw this?"

"Fuck yeah."

"Why didn't you, you know, call the cops or something?"

She laughed. "Shit. And get my ass shot off? No fucking way."

"What about Renee? She was your friend."

"Renee should have fuckin' known better. Sleeping with black guys and all. I mean, don't get me wrong. I'm not prejudiced. But you lie down with dogs, you're gonna get fleas."

"I hear you," Beckman said and thought, did Mandel tell her about me? Did he tell her about the cops who came to his office? If he did, then he could be about to blow it. But she had the taps turned on now . . .

Beckman said, "Renee used to run around with this guy, older Jewish guy, didn't she?"

Sally looked at him. Her expression tighter now. "Yeah?" she said.

"Was she still seeing him?"

"No. He's with me now."

"Oh."

"His name's Peter and he's actually very sweet."

"Oh. Well, I didn't mean anything by it. You're his girlfriend now?"

"Not his girlfriend," she said. "Not really a girlfriend. He's a friend. A very good friend."

"So you can . . . hang out with other guys, then?"

Sally looked at him and said, "I can do whatever I want."

Sometimes the moment is there and you just have to take it. She was attracted to him, but then he always did get along well with prostitutes. When he was at vice, Wilson told him never to mistreat a whore and he never had. He spoke to them straight when he wanted something from them and treated them decently even when he didn't. He retained a sympathy for prostitutes, believing sometimes against even good reason that they were trapped in a lifestyle no woman would want to be a part of.

They took a cab to her apartment and when she let him in, Beckman said, "This guy's not going to come back here, is he?"

Sally took off her coat and threw it on a chair. "That's not his style," she said.

"He doesn't get jealous?"

"He gets jealous, yeah. But he doesn't ask questions. And we're not exclusive. I'm not the only one who's in Peter's stable. I know it and he knows I know it. But we don't talk about it. You want a drink?"

"Sure. Scotch, if you have it."

"I have it."

She went into the kitchen. Beckman walked around the living room. He saw a picture of Sally and Mandel on the mantelpiece. Somehow the disparity in their age was sharper in the photo than it was in the restaurant. A couple picture, too much in focus.

Sally came out of the kitchen with drinks.

"Peter says, ask me no questions and I'll tell you no lies."

Beckman took the scotch and said, "Very mature attitude."

He sipped the scotch. Lowered his glass as she put her arm around his neck and pulled him close and kissed him.

She leaned back and said, "Don't you want to take your coat off?"

"Maybe later."

She looked at him then, a vague, unwelcome sensation dawning on her now. Beckman's tone and demeanor changing.

"What is this?" she said.

Beckman took a photo out of his jacket pocket. The photo was of Nathan Wald.

"You ever see this guy?"

"What the — who are you? Are you a fucking cop?"

"Yeah."

"Private? Did Peter send you here?"

Christ, Beckman thought. "No. Peter didn't send me. I'm a detective with the Chicago Police Department."

"Oh *fuck.* How dare you! You son —"

"Calm down, Sally. I'm here to help you."

"Help me? How the fuck are you going to help me?"

"I can protect you. From Leon. Maybe from Peter too."

"Peter?" She laughed. "Peter wouldn't hurt anyone."

"Maybe not. But let's get back to this." He held the photo. "Have you seen this man before?"

"I'm not telling you shit."

"Have you? You have, I can tell. When did you see him?"

"I don't know. He came by Peter's office once."

"What was he doing there?"

"I don't know. He was wearing one of those Jew hats. I got the feeling he was hitting Peter up for money. 'Cause he was Jewish and Peter's Jewish. Only Peter doesn't talk about being Jewish much."

"Did Peter tell you Nathan was asking him for money?"

"No. He didn't say that. But after the guy left his office, Peter was . . . he was like I'd never seen him before."

"What do you mean? Upset? Scared?"

"No. Not scared. Excited. Maybe even hopeful. He was excited about something. He kissed me after he left and I saw tears in his eyes. I'd never seen Peter cry like that."

"He was happy?"

"Very."

"Why?"

"I don't know. Something the guy told

him or gave to him. I don't know what."

Beckman had her talking now. She stepped away from him and sipped her drink, relaxed now that she realized he wasn't going to take her downtown and ask her to pick Leon Murray out of a lineup.

Beckman said, "What did Wald give Peter or tell him?"

"He didn't tell me. He only said that something great might be happening. He said that he might have to go to Europe on a trip." Sally smiled. "I misunderstood him. I thought he meant he was going to take me to Europe. But he said, no, it would be business. Family business."

"He said that?"

"What?"

"Family business. He said family business."

"Yeah."

"Did he elaborate on that?"

"No. In fact, I asked him what he meant and he said he didn't want to talk about it anymore. You know, like he was afraid he was going to jinx it."

"Family. Did he have children? A child he left over there?"

"No. Peter couldn't have children. Never could. Something — something that they did to him over there. He never told me what they did."

"He never told you about the war? About the slave camps? The roundups, the massacres?"

"Never. I mean, I knew something about it. Because he was Polish and a Jew. I know they killed a bunch of Jews in Poland. But he never talked about it."

Beckman set the glass of scotch on the mantel.

"Did you see Wald again?"

"No. Only that one time he came to the office."

"Did Peter ever say anything about him again?"

"Not a thing. I know about a week after he came, Peter was real down. I mean, really down. Didn't speak to me or anyone for three or four days. And that's not like Peter at all. He's so social."

"Something was upsetting him?"

"Yeah. But he wouldn't tell me what. He didn't tell anyone."

"Did he make his trip to Europe?"

"No." Sally smiled and shook her head. "No, I asked him about that. And he said the trip was canceled. And when I asked him some more, he shut me down. Tried to pretend he'd never seriously thought of going. The feeling I got was that he didn't want me talking about Europe anymore."

"Did he threaten you?"

"No, he didn't threaten me. I keep telling you, Peter's not like that. It just made him sad to talk about it. So I dropped it."

"How did he react when he heard that Wald had been killed?"

The woman looked at him for a moment. "Killed? What are you talking about?"

Oh Jesus, Beckman thought. She genuinely didn't know. So he told her about the killings on the subway.

She said, "He was one of the people killed?"

"Yes."

"Well, I'll be damned. But you can't honestly believe Peter had anything to do with that."

CHAPTER FORTY-SIX

Beckman took a cab back to his car.

He played the scene at Sally Ryan's apartment back in his mind. Shook his head when he got to the part when Sally still wanted to fool around with him when he got done questioning her. He politely turned her down and left. So much for leaving her quaking in fear from the police. Being interrogated had turned her on. She was who she was. A superficial, pretty girl who liked money and told the truth even when it wasn't in her interest to do it. She was mercenary to be sure, yet strangely guileless at the same time. She would make a good witness in court.

She didn't love Mandel. Was not attracted to him, but was obviously fond of him. When she said he wasn't capable of hurting anyone, she believed it.

Beckman wanted to believe it too. He didn't really know why. Policemen don't generally feel sympathy for suspected killers. He didn't know why he should now. Was it because Mandel was a Jew? Because he had lost everything to the Nazis and the Soviets? Lost his family, his country, his ability to have children. They had taken everything from him but his life and what they had left of that wasn't much. The other cops would say that Beckman was protecting his own kind. "Sticking together" or some other ugly expression. But Beckman knew that wasn't it. Because even now he still felt a scorn for Nathan Wald that he couldn't quite put his finger on. Sympathy for the Jewish slumlord who associated with whores and drug-dealing gangsters, but none for the murdered Jewish rabbi who protested against anti-Semitism and on behalf of Soviet refugees.

It didn't make sense. But it had to make sense. Because if it didn't, it would mean he was losing his sanity. Letting the horrors of the Holocaust and Jewish extermination play with his head. Which would be funny, of course, as being Jewish was what got him assigned to the case in the first place.

And now you're here, he thought. Happy now?

Regan had told him he had been assigned for political reasons. And he had been disappointed to hear it, but he had not quit the case. Whatever principles he had were sacrificed to the gods of ambition and thirst for action. He wanted the case. He wanted to succeed as a homicide detective, wanted the glory of working the high profile murder. So they used him and he used them. A Jew's bargain, as his nasty old man would have said.

Something Nathan Wald would have understood.

FBI Agent Ken Gravley was pissed.

He had led Beckman out to the hallway of the downtown federal building so that people wouldn't hear what he had to say. Gravley made a pretense of getting a drink from the water fountain to show that he wasn't bothered by the Chicago detective. But Beckman could see that he was getting to him.

Gravley said, "You come down to my office without an appointment, you threaten me —"

"I did not threaten you," Beckman said.

"You said you'd go to the press. You'd call *The Washington Post.* That's not a threat?"

"Ah, that's just talk. Come on, we're on the same side."

"We are not on the same side. The FBI is

403

an intelligence gathering organization. You, you're just law enforcement."

Beckman smiled. And not for the first time, he was glad he hadn't sought a career with the federal government. Ken Gravley reminded him of a young Bob McNamara, someone Beckman had learned to despise years ago. The McNamaras of this world always suffered in the end.

Beckman said, "You were supposed to give us a file."

"I never promised that."

"Lieutenant Gregory and Sergeant Regan were there when you did."

"That's not what I said. I know what I said."

"Okay, never mind the file. We both know you didn't tell us everything you knew about Nathan Wald."

"I'm not obligated to tell you everything. These are issues of security, not local crime."

"Okay," Beckman said. "Just tell me: was Wald an FBI informant?"

"I'm not going to answer that."

"He implied he was. In an interview he gave to a magazine years ago. I read the article."

"He was lying."

"I don't think he was. I don't think he was

lying. I think he was boasting. He was working with you guys. That's why you never busted him when he blew up Soviet offices. He used you and you used him."

"That's purely speculative."

"Newspapers may not see it that way."

"You are *insolent.* These are issues that are way beyond your pay scale."

"Just confirm it for me. Yes or no. The only reason I want to know is for my investigation. Confirm it for me and keep it out of the papers."

"You're threatening me again."

"I am not threatening you. I'm making a proposal."

Beckman was threatening him, of course. But he knew Gravley needed to believe he wasn't being bullied. The FBI agent looked up and down the hallway.

"Okay," Gravley said. "Okay. Yeah, he did some work for us. Not that he was any great help."

"What did he do?"

"Wald was very politically conservative. He supported the Vietnam War. He was right on a lot of issues. So we . . . we asked him to go to a few John Birch meetings. Tell us what he heard."

"You had him spy on the John Birchers?"

"Yeah."

"What about the black militancy groups? Did you have him spy on them too?"

"No. He hated blacks and they hated him."

"Was there anything else you had him do?"

"No. That was it." Gravley looked at him. "Seriously."

Beckman said, "What about the Soviets? Was he working with you against the Soviets?"

Gravley stared at him for a few moments. Then he laughed. It took Beckman aback, because the laugh was genuine and not the typical forced civil service expression of scorn.

"Are you kidding?" Gravley said. "Nathan knew about as much about the KGB as my five-year-old daughter. Not that he didn't try to get into the international spy business. But we wouldn't let him go *near* it. When it came to the cloak and dagger stuff, he wasn't even a dilettante. No. It didn't take us long to figure out that Nathan Wald was just another small-time hustler."

Gravley walked back down to his office. Beckman watched him go, vaguely disappointed that the guy turned out to be smarter than he looked.

Beckman parked the Plymouth and walked

to a telephone booth. Closed himself in and got some protection against the downtown wind, but it was still miserably cold. He took his gloves off to dial the number and to drop in a dime. Put his gloves back on as heard the phone ring.

"Homicide."

"Sergeant Regan, please."

"Who's calling?"

"His son."

A few moments passed and he heard Regan say, "Hello?"

The concern in Regan's voice made Beckman feel guilty. The man had probably told his family to call only if there was an emergency.

Beckman said, "It's me."

Regan spoke in a lowered voice. "So now you're my son?"

Beckman said, "You told me I'd become Irish. And I thought it'd be a good idea not to identify myself. Am I being paranoid?"

"Not today," Regan said. "Greg wants you back here immediately. I told him I thought you were at lunch, but he didn't believe me."

"So he is shutting us down."

"Oh, yeah. He said he'd waited long enough."

"He can wait a little longer. Can you do something for me? Call Deegan and Osulnic and tell them Leon Murray's their guy. Sally Ryan fingered him . . . Sort of."

"Sort of?"

"She saw him threaten Richie LaFevers over a cocaine debt. It's certainly enough to bring him in for questioning."

"That's good work, David. For them. What about our case?"

"I see. You want to know what I'm going to do for you."

"I'm not the only one."

"I'm close, Tom. Very close. Give me a few hours."

"You don't need my permission," Regan said. "As to Leon Murray, I'm going to hold off on telling Deegan and company for now. They're liable to muck it up unless we're there to help them."

"I agree," Beckman said. "We're going to be ones that crack this motherfucker wide open."

"Don't stay out too late," Regan said and hung up.

Beckman put the phone in its cradle. He opened the doors of the phone booth and walked across the street to the offices of Illinois Bell.

CHAPTER FORTY-SEVEN

Esther Wald answered the door. She was in a ratty, plaid bathrobe and her hair was down. She had turned the television on after Beckman had knocked three times.

"What do you want?"

Beckman said, "I want to talk to Mickey."

"He's not here."

"Yes he is. His car's parked in your driveway."

Esther Wald looked at the driveway and frowned at the sight of the yellow Toyota. Her face fell.

"Go away," she said. "Please."

Beckman was saddened by it. A woman who was not broken but very tired. Her gray hair down around her shoulders, her face thin and withdrawn.

Beckman said, "Where are the children?"

"They're in Buffalo with their uncle. I don't know why you can't leave us alone."

"Let him in."

It was Mickey Shaivetz. He had come out of the kitchen or bedroom. Beckman didn't care which. It was a relief to see him fully dressed.

Esther opened the door and stepped back, the fight gone out of her. Perhaps too tired to hide things anymore.

Mickey said to Esther. "It's all right. We haven't done anything wrong."

Beckman looked from Shaivetz to Mrs. Wald. Two lonely people who needed each other. They had lived in the shadow of a selfish, greedy man who hadn't given them much of anything. Beckman had not liked either of them from the beginning, but now he felt a pity for the woman he had not really felt before.

Beckman said, "Mrs. Wald. Esther. I would appreciate it if you would give me and Mickey some privacy. Please."

Esther Wald looked at Mickey. He nodded to her and she went into the kitchen. Mickey seemed older than her at that moment.

Then she was gone and Beckman looked impassively at Mickey Shaivetz. Then he shook his head and said, "Mickey, you're in a lot of trouble."

CHAPTER FORTY-EIGHT

Sally finished her second vodka tonic while the cop was still in her apartment. She was feeling warm and cozy inside when she put a hand on his chest and let it drop down to his belt. But he took her hand off and said he couldn't. She said, "I thought we were friends now?" And he said, "We are." He didn't say anything else. He just told her to stay home tonight and that he would call later. Then he left. Fag. Fag cop, no less. Cops would fuck anything, but she had to draw one of the homos. The cops used to come into Torchy's when she was a dancer there and pay her to come over and put her tits in their face. Put a dollar bill down her panties as if that was supposed to impress her. They'd do that off duty. On duty, the cops would treat her like she was a street whore, berating her one moment, lecturing her about pimps the next. She had told them she never tricked, she was a dancer, for chrissakes. They didn't give her a break. Bunch of losers with sexual hang-ups, like her asshole dad. Cops made her tired. Well, fuck Detective Beckman and his black wavy hair and confident cop bullshit. She turned on the television and made another drink. Then another. After the fifth one, the television bored her so she put a Maxell cassette in her tape deck. Dave Mason singing there ain't no good guys, no bad guys, just you and me and we just disagree. She made another drink and lay down on the couch. She realized the television was still on. She turned it off. Then she heard someone pounding on the door. "Fuck!" she said. The cops were back! But then she figured out it was the neighbors telling her to turn down the music. She turned Dave Mason down and then pounded her fist on the wall and told the neighbors to get a fucking job.

She lay back on the couch and closed her eyes. Then she heard the door being opened and thought, now fucking what?

Peter stood by the couch. He was still in his hat and coat. He looked at her and frowned, disappointed and sad.

"You told me you were going to cut back."

"Oh, fuck Peter, give me a break, will you? Do you know how bored I get around here? I'm twenty-three years old and I don't have anything to do. Renee's gone. Richie's gone. I'm running out of friends."

"They weren't your friends."

"Yes, they were." She was talking like a teenager now. Pouting. "At least they knew how to party."

"Oh, why must you get drunk? Do you know how unattractive it makes you?"

"I'm lonely, Peter. Can't you see that I'm lonely?"

"I give you everything you want. You've got a good deal here."

"I don't want a good deal. I want to dance. I want to go out till the sun comes up. I want to go to New York. I want to go to Studio 54 and see Mick and Liza."

"I said I'd take you."

"Oh, don't you see? I want to go with people my own age."

Peter Mandel sighed. She could see that she had wounded him. She sat up and put her hand on his wrist.

"I didn't mean that."

Mandel said, "It's all right. I always told you that when you wanted to leave, I wouldn't try to stop you."

She softened. "I know you did. Peter, I'm sorry. I'm just drunk. Please don't listen to what I'm saying now. Please don't be mad at me."

"I'm not mad at you. Here, let me have that." He took the glass of vodka from her.

"No," Sally said. "Not about that. Something else."

"What?" Mandel said.

Sally bit her lip, an adolescent gesture he usually found endearing. "A policeman came here and asked me some questions about you and Leon."

Mandel worked his jaw open and shut. Sally had never seen him do that before. Mandel said, "What was his name?"

"Beckman. I think he was Jewish."

Mandel saw that was supposed to make him feel better. He was Jewish. Christ God, what a comedy.

Mandel said, "What did you tell him?"

"I only told him — I told him that Leon threatened Richie over some money Richie owed him. I didn't tell him anything else, I swear."

"Did he ask about anything else?"

"No. I swear on my mother that was it."

"Why did you tell him about Leon?"

"Because that's what I saw. I'm not protecting that nigger. I think he killed Renee. God, would you want me to protect him? She was your friend too."

After a few moments, Mandel said, "Yes, she was." Mandel looked at her again and

414

said, "Let's put you to bed, huh?"

He helped her undress and put her to bed. There was nothing sexual about it. He was as tender as a father.

When she was asleep, he cleaned the apartment and washed the glasses and the dishes in the sink. He thought about what Sally had told him. Probably it was the truth, but she had obviously left some things out. Beckman had not just questioned him about Renee. So there was little doubt his questions to Sally had been equally unlimited. And that was very bad.

Certainly there was a chance that Leon would leave town and never be caught. If he was warned. Or, even better, there was a chance that Leon would resist arrest and the police would kill him. But Mandel had never been that lucky in his life. He smiled at the irony of it all. The Russians or the Nazis would have just put a bullet in Leon Murray's head and been done with him and Mandel would have been eternally grateful for the deed. Grateful to the people he thought were the most barbaric on earth. But not even the Chicago police were that savage. They would capture Leon and Leon, no fool, would hire a lawyer and then he would talk. He would offer them what he had and what he had was substantial.

415

Mandel checked Sally's room to make sure she was still asleep. Then he went into the living room and picked up the telephone.

"Leon, it's Peter . . . No, it's not an emergency. But it is important . . . Yes. Come to my office . . . All right, I'll see you in a half hour."

CHAPTER FORTY-NINE

Mandel had kept the same office since he got into the real-estate business. It was a second floor walk-up with a big semicircle window off Milwaukee Avenue. It was urban, old, and unimpressive. In most other aspects of his life, he had worked hard to maintain fronts, but not here. He had never yearned for an office in the fashionable financial districts. He knew he wouldn't have fit. He never would.

But he was glad of that now. What respected security guard would let a man like Leon Murray into the building?

It was between seven and eight p.m. All the other tenants had gone home. Most of them had left at four because weather forecasts had said there was a forty percent chance of snow. It hadn't come, but Chicagoans didn't want to spend any more nights in their cars.

Now he sat at his desk, the only light com-

417

ing from his green shaded lamp. On his desk was the official book he kept on the Taft Gardens. Next to that his plans for the new housing project. To his left, his gray scarf. His little empire laid out in front of him. He would be sixty in a few months. Who would have thought he would ever reach sixty?

He heard steps from the stairwell. Then he heard the door to the reception area open. No one was there. Mandel saw a shadow through the opaque glass of his door. Then the door opened and Leon stepped in.

Leon said, "I presume this was important."

His tone was still hard. Maybe because he was still angry at him for questioning him about Renee, maybe because he didn't like being summoned.

"I'm afraid it is," Mandel said. "You know I wouldn't waste your time."

"I know you know better," Leon said. He took a seat in front of Mandel's desk. He spread his legs out in a gesture that may have been insolent. He kept his hands in his pockets. Letting Mandel know he needed to come to the point.

"I know better," Mandel said. "Well, here it is. I've decided to sell my interest in the

Taft Gardens."

Leon stared at him for a moment. Then he shook his head.

"I'm afraid I can't let you do that."

Mandel said, "It's not up to you."

Mandel pulled the pistol out from under his scarf and shot Leon Murray in the chest. He pulled the trigger three more times, putting more shots into Leon's chest and neck. Leon was knocked back, the chair tipping over and putting him on the floor.

Mandel came around the desk. Leon's right hand was still in his pocket. Mandel squatted next to him and checked the pulse on his neck. Leon was dead.

Mandel tugged on Leon's right hand. It came out of a coat pocket holding a gun. Mandel smiled.

"Put that gun down!"

Mandel looked up to see the detective pointing his service revolver at him. A two-handed stance.

"Put it down!" Beckman said. "Now!"

Mandel dropped his pistol and stood up.

Beckman moved closer to him. He motioned Mandel to step away from Leon. Mandel did so and Beckman checked Leon's pulse. Beckman frowned.

"It was self-defense," Mandel said. "He was going to kill me."

"Sit down," Beckman said. "That chair there. Put both your hands on the arms. Keep them there."

Mandel sat down and said, "Look at his hand. Look at it. He had a gun."

Beckman checked around the office. He used the telephone on Mandel's desk to call headquarters. Regan was still there. Beckman told him there had been a shooting and that Leon Murray was dead.

He hung up the phone and Mandel said, "It was self-defense. You know it was."

"I don't know anything of the kind," Beckman said. "I was coming up the stairs when I heard the shots."

"Coming to get Leon?"

"Coming to get you," Beckman said. "And you knew it."

"It was self-defense."

"No, it was murder. You did it because you were afraid he'd testify against you. You brought him here, didn't you?"

"You can't prove that."

"We'll see," Beckman said. He took the matching armchair across from Mandel. Beckman still held his revolver. He could have holstered it because Mandel was now unarmed. And even though Beckman knew Mandel had just murdered a man, it was still difficult to believe that Mandel could harm anyone.

Mandel said, "You're a very intelligent young man, aren't you? Very sure of yourself."

Beckman didn't answer him. He saw the man changing. No longer the smooth confident operator. Now he was restless. Breaking down, but Beckman didn't want to exploit it. The sound and smell of gunfire still hanging in the air, a dead man staining the floor with his blood.

"Right," Beckman said. He didn't want to converse.

But Mandel said, "It's easy, isn't it?"

Beckman sighed. He was very tired. "What do you mean?"

"It's easy to be sure of yourself, it's easy to be confident when nothing really bad has happened to you. When you haven't known real suffering."

"You know very little about me, Mr. Mandel."

"Oh, but I do. We're all part of the same family. The same tribe. You think you can just . . . quit, don't you?"

"Quit what?"

"Oh, come now," Mandel said. "You know what I'm talking about. I see who you are. You tell yourself you're not a Jew, that you're just another American. The way I

421

used to tell myself I was Polish, not Jewish. But they don't let you quit, you know?"

Beckman looked back at him and said, "This isn't Poland."

"You are confident about the time you live in. Yes? But did they ever come to your house and take your family away? Take away your home and your country? What would you do if they did? What would you do to survive?" Mandel smiled. "I was once young and handsome and strong. I was cocksure like you. You wouldn't believe it to look at me, but I was."

"You're strong enough," Beckman said. "You survived."

"Not really. When I was young, I had hope. But I lost that. Hope for all of the real goodness in life. A wife, children, a home. A daughter I could teach to play the piano. And now . . . loose women, cars, little gold trinkets . . . They don't really make up for the losses, for the emptiness. That's not something you can understand."

"The police will be here soon. I suggest you exercise your right to remain silent."

"But I don't want to. I know my rights. It troubles you, doesn't it? A man like me. You see something of yourself in me, perhaps? No, that's not it. But you feel pity for me and you don't feel any for that man on the floor. You don't want to feel pity, but you do. It's perfectly natural, you know. It's nothing to be ashamed of. Tribe is nothing more than an extension of family."

Beckman said, "I could never feel pity for the man who contracted for the murders of five innocent people."

"Oh, that. I didn't intend for that to happen."

"You intended it for Nathan Wald."

"Nathan Wald was the worst of us. Had he been in Poland when the evil descended, he would have turned on his closest neighbors and friends. He would have collaborated."

"You don't know that."

"I knew *him.* Better than you ever could have. He was a con man. And that's something I know plenty about."

Beckman said, "And yet he conned you. Someone who should have known better."

Mandel smiled. "Yes, I suppose I should have. What brought you here? What brought you back to me?"

"Mickey Shaivetz."

"Ohhhh. Him. I suppose you threatened to put him in jail?"

"I did. For conspiracy to commit murder."

"How did you get him to fold so easily?"

"He's the folding type. Besides, I had

phone records. Have phone records. Mickey called you a couple of days before Nathan was killed and told you that everything Nathan told you was a lie. That your brother was *not* alive and was *not* in the Soviet Union. That Nathan had no contacts with the CIA or FBI or the Israelis or anyone else who had information about your long-lost brother. That Nathan had made it all up and cheated you out of fifty thousand dollars."

Tears formed in Mandel's eyes. Beckman wanted to look away.

Mandel said, "Do you have a brother?"

". . . yes."

"When did you last see him?"

"A few days ago."

"I last saw mine about forty years ago. The Russians put him in a truck and took him away. My home is now part of the Soviet Union. The Allies decided just to *give* it to the Russians. Nathan Wald said he had information that Sam was alive. He said he could negotiate his release from the Soviet Union, but that he would need funds. Yes, I believed him. I figured that since I had survived, Sam could have too. Of course he had survived. Sam always was stronger. And Mr. Wald is quite a gifted speaker. He was very . . . persuasive."

"We believe what we want to believe."

Mandel seemed to want to change the subject. He said, "You know, I never asked Shaivetz why he told on Nathan."

"He didn't much like Nathan either," Beckman said. "May have been in love with his wife. Maybe it was something else. I don't think Mickey knew what you would do with that information. I don't think he expected you to have Nathan killed."

"But Nathan killed my brother. Nathan killed Sam. Brought him back from the dead and killed him all over again."

"The Nazis killed your brother," Beckman said. "Wald was just a hustler." Then regretted he had said it. Because it didn't make sense to talk rationally to this damaged man. A man who had lived through horrors in which nothing made sense.

Sirens approached.

Mandel looked up and said, "I'm not prone to jumping out of windows." He motioned to the pistol that lay next to the body of Leon Murray. "Would you consider leaving me alone for a minute?"

He wanted to kill himself. Because he knew it was all over for him now.

Beckman shook his head.

"Sorry," Beckman said. He was, too.

CHAPTER FIFTY

Regan stood with Beckman as two uniformed officers put Mandel into the back of a police car. Mandel without his hat, looking like a human frog in the cold. Nearby, Lieutenant Gregory talked with the chief of detectives. They did not seem unhappy.

Regan said, "He'll make an interesting figure for the sketch artist."

"Pardon?" Beckman said.

"At trial," Regan said. "They don't let news cameras into the courtroom. Mandel will make an interesting sketch."

"He won't live long enough for a trial," Beckman said.

Regan looked at the young detective. Then he reached up and put a hand on the back of his neck and gave it a mild squeeze. Something he'd done to his sons several times over the years.

"Come on, partner," Regan said. "Let's get something to eat."

ABOUT THE AUTHOR

James Patrick Hunt is the author of *Maitland, Maitland Under Siege, Maitland's Reply, Get Maitland, The Betrayers, Goodbye Sister Disco, The Assailant, The Silent Places, Bullet Beth, Reinhardt's Mark, Bridger,* and *Police and Thieves.* He lives in Tulsa, Oklahoma, where he writes and practices law.